Murder on Insel Poel

A THIRD-CULTURE KID MYSTERY

MURDER ON INSEL POEL

D-L NELSON

FIVE STAR
A part of Gale, Cengage Learning

GALE
CENGAGE Learning®

Detroit • New York • San Francisco • New Haven, Conn • Waterville, Maine • London

GALE
CENGAGE Learning·

LIBRARY OF CONGRESS CATALOGING-IN-PUBLICATION DATA

Nelson, D. L., 1942–
    Murder on Insel Poel / D-L Nelson. — First Edition.
        pages cm.
        ISBN 978-1-4328-2815-8 (hardcover) — ISBN 1-4328-2815-0 (hardcover)
        1. Excavations (Archaeology) —Fiction. 2. Paris (France) —Fiction. I. Title.
PS3614.E4455M89 2014
813'.6—dc23   2013041019

First Edition. First Printing: March 2014
Find us on Facebook– https://www.facebook.com/FiveStarCengage
Visit our website– http://www.gale.cengage.com/fivestar/
Contact Five Star™ Publishing at FiveStar@cengage.com

Printed in Mexico
1 2 3 4 5 6 7 18 17 16 15 14

To my wonderful nephew Rick. I don't know what I'd have done without you.

ACKNOWLEDGMENTS

As always to Julia of the twenty pages, but this time also for the two incredible car trips to Insel Poel and for her German that far exceeds my "shopping" German. She should be a professional interviewer with the information she gleaned. To Herr and Frau Lehmbecker and the wonderful women at the Museum of Insel Poel, thank you for a lovely day and for the introduction to the *Cap Arcona* catastrophe. The event should not be forgotten.

The oral histories of survivors at the Neuengamme Concentration Camp were painful to hear. Although I did not use anyone's experiences directly, they provided an overall view of what these strong people went through in a depth that the books in the museum did not. Facts do not match the horror as much as a quavering voice does in the retelling.

CHAPTER 1

Hamburg, Germany
November 1934

Hilke Fülmer often wondered if she had been born to the wrong family. If her mother hadn't given birth to her at home, she would have suspected that she was switched with a baby from another family, one that shared her interests and abilities.

She was not an intellectual like her professor father. Nor was she beautiful like her blonde, blue-eyed mother. It was not that she was ugly, just ordinary. Her brother, Joseph, took the best of both parents, but she could not hate him for it even though she had tried.

He was her protector: when their parents criticized her grades or her insistence on swimming every day, Joseph deflected their comments by drawing attention to himself. She had hated him doing it, until the night she hissed her dissatisfaction as they disappeared into their bedrooms. He'd come to her room that same night after everyone was asleep, including her. Shaking her awake, he whispered, "*Kleine Dumbkopf,* don't you see? They forget about you when I start talking about me, and then you're out of it."

She didn't need him to protect her from physical bullies, because she could fight her own battles. More than once she had pushed some older or bigger pupil, much to their astonishment. Physically, she also stopped the school bullies from picking on other *Kinder.*

Joseph protected her also by tutoring her in mathematics, her weakest subject at the *Lyzeum* schools for girls, where she was in the *Obersekunda*. She did okay, just a little above average in Latin, German, French and history. Her chemistry and physics grades were below average and her other courses were average.

She would present her report to their parents first and, before they could get too upset, Joseph would come in with his, which always had the highest marks possible. Her parents despaired of her ever getting the grades Joseph earned at his *Gymnasium*. He was destined to be an ancient-language scholar like their father.

Hilke walked through the corridor at Hamburg *Universität* until she reached her father's office. Her father had more space in his office since Herr Doktor Jacobson, with whom he had shared office space for fifteen years, had been informed his services were no longer needed. Her father had taken over some of Jacobson's classes, or at least they had been combined with his own.

Frau Ute Berchtold was sitting at her desk in front of the door with Hilke's father's name on it. "Hilke, how lovely to see you." His secretary was in her late thirties and unmarried, her fiancé having been killed in the war somewhere in France. She wore her hair in braids tied like a crown on her head and would have been pretty if she would only smile.

Hilke always wondered how real her welcomes were, because Frau Berchtold was the type of person who might smile with her mouth but the smile never reached her eyes. Or it could be she was still sad about her fiancé's death and her lack of a husband and children.

Before Hilke could say anything, Frau Berchtold said, "Your father is in class. Then he's going directly into a meeting."

"I'll see him at home, I guess. Sorry for disturbing you."

"Not at all. *Aufweidersehen.*"

Hilke, aware she'd been dismissed, backed out of the room

and headed down the stairs and into the night air. A few snowflakes were making their way to the ground, but none looked like they would stick. She pulled her hat down over her ears as she walked by the *Hauptbahnhoff*. Its clock tower read 17:42. She hoped that her mother wouldn't be angry that she was late.

Hilke turned the key in the door of their second-floor apartment. The building had been undamaged during the last war, although it had grown shabby from lack of care. The money just wasn't there to undertake any repairs. As soon as she opened the door into the large apartment entrance hall, she smelled onions cooking.

"Is that you Joseph?" Her mother came out of the kitchen wearing an apron and holding a wooden spoon. "Hilke. I'm glad you're home. Can you set the table please, and I think it would be a good idea if you take a quick run through Violin Concerto in D major, Op. 77 before we all play the first movement tonight after dinner."

Hilke made a face, which she thought her mother didn't see.

"The light is not that dim, Hilke. You haven't practiced all week, and you know how that upsets Papa."

There were strict rituals in the family, which upset Hilke. During the week everyone was busy with individual responsibilities, school or housework, but Friday night after dinner was music night. Saturday they all went shopping before the stores closed at noon. Then Sunday they might go for a walk along the river when the weather was good. Hilke always wanted to swim while her family walked, but that would not have been proper, she was told every time she broached the subject. Once or twice a year during the summer her mother would pack a picnic lunch and they would take the train to Bergedorf and find a place to eat in a field with a few cows looking on.

She would have preferred to do things as the mood came

upon her. Why not play cards on Friday night? Why not take a nap on a Sunday afternoon instead of the walk? She had proposed the ideas, only to be told that that wasn't what the family was going to do.

Because her father was a professor, the family had never been without an income, although inflation had taken its toll. But now with the *Reichs Mark* replacing the *Rentenmarks* things were improving, not that Hilke found talk about money all that interesting.

When her parents had other professors and their wives for dinner, financial issues were the subject of conversation, along with what Hitler was doing to help Germany. Hilke did not notice that her mother never said much about the new leader. In fact when his name came up, she found reasons to go into the kitchen, where Hilke and Joseph were eating their own meals so as not to interfere with the grown-up conversation. Her mother would rearrange the dishes, prepare a tray for the next course, or if everything had been eaten, go back into the dining room to clear the table—but never would she sit in on the political talk.

The flat was designed in such a way that all the rooms opened off the main entrance hall. Only the kitchen was attached sideways to the dining room.

Hilke's bedroom was large with a desk, a bookcase and a double bed. Her *Eiderdown* had been plumped by her mother and neatly folded and she was sure she would find the nightgown she had left on the floor neatly folded under the pillows.

She picked up the violin, opened her music to the correct piece and practiced until the call came for dinner. By the time she'd washed her hands, the family was waiting for her.

"Frau Berchtold said you came by today," Papa asked. "Anything special?"

"I had some good news."

Her mother passed the tureen around the table. The soup made the room smell homey. "You *are* passing maths, aren't you?"

"No *Mutti* . . . I mean I'm passing, but that wasn't the news. When I was at swimming practice, my coach said if I really work hard, I might be able to try out for the Olympics. I know I've a late start and . . ."

Her father served himself from the tureen. "I know you're a good swimmer, but no. No daughter of mine is going to be an athlete."

Hilke had just reached for a *Brötchen* but stopped midair. Her life for the past two years had centered around working on her swimming, trying to get everything possible from each stroke. Today, the coach told her after she'd clocked her best time ever that she had perfected her form. Her hips were in exactly the right position: her head came out of the water at exactly the right angle. He had her do it a second time, and she'd done it two seconds faster. "I beat my own time today. Twice."

"If you spent as much time on your studies as you do on your swimming, we wouldn't worry about your grades," her father said.

Hilke looked at Joseph for help.

"Tomorrow may I spend the afternoon at Gunther's? We need to go over our Latin verbs," Joseph said.

Hilke didn't dare smile at him, but she planned to thank him later.

Papa nodded, but *Mutti* put down the tureen. "I really think you should stop swimming, Hilke, until your grades come up."

The sixteen-year-old sat still for a minute. Give up swimming? Why didn't they ask her to give up her arm? Or her eyes? She felt Joseph's hand on her leg under the table. When she opened her mouth, he increased the pressure. So she said nothing. Later, after music night she would ask him for advice.

CHAPTER 2

Kirchdorf, Insel Poel, Germany

"Insel Poel, an island in the Baltic Sea, is bordered by the Bays of Wismar and Mecklenburg. When people look at a map of Insel Poel they see either a giant lobster claw or a gorilla walking on his hands. Insel Poel covers 35 square kilometres (22 square miles)."

The History of Insel Poel by Manfred Dederich

"I made it." Annie Young hit the send button and snapped her cell phone shut. Her parents, who'd loaned her their second car for the trip, would be relieved to read the message. She didn't drive all that much, and a trip from Geneva, Switzerland, to Northeast Germany, over 600 miles, had had her behind the wheel for more hours than she had spent driving in the past ten years altogether. Made it: but what a drive: two days of snowy roads from Geneva to Insel Poel.

She shut off the engine and peeked out the car window through the snow at the blinking hotel sign lighting the parking lot.

The trip had been wonderful despite the bad weather. What she'd loved most were the electric turbines on the hundreds of wind farms of various sizes. The first one she'd passed just as music from "Swan Lake" came on the radio. The white spires twirled as if under the choreography of Baryshnikov, Béjart or Balanchine.

Annie found herself so entranced at their grace and beauty that she'd pulled over to the side of the road, took out her phone and videoed it as tears ran down her cheeks. Okay, so she was a marshmallow who would cry at a commercial with babies, little animals or a touching story.

The dancing turbines' moment was one to share with her mother, whose artistic soul would understand. Her mother would want to see the video, would put a louder version of "Swan Lake" on her CD player as she watched, then say, "It's just as I imagined it from your description."

Her fiancé, Roger Perret, would only see the ecological benefits, which Annie could appreciate as well. Beauty and practicality. She supposed she was lucky that she would have understanding from two people that she loved—just not for both aspects at the same time. Expecting a person to be everything was unreasonable, although knowing that did not make her wish any less that Roger had a bit more imagination. Yet, as police chief of Argelès-sur-mer in Southern France, she couldn't really expect him to wax lyrical about the pattern of blood running from a shooting victim.

He did have a sense of humor, which for her was a necessity. Her first night on the road in Germany, she had stopped in Speyer and found a hotel. When she pulled her car into the hotel lot, she noticed that the parking area was full of green and white police cars and vans. The lobby was full of uniformed German police, too many for it to be a crime scene, never mind that they were laughing. Then she saw a sign welcoming them to a police training session.

"I'm sleeping with most of the German police 2nite" she'd texted to Roger, knowing that within minutes he would call her. He was not ordinarily jealous and she didn't play stupid games trying to make him so. When she explained, he'd laughed that at least he wouldn't worry about her safety that particular night.

He hadn't even complained about this assignment, two weeks to translate explanation cards in the local museum into French, Dutch and English. And then a locally written history book, albeit one she could take back home with her to do at her leisure.

That she spent so much of her time away from home to work as a translator and tech writer had, on occasion, almost destroyed their relationship. Maybe this time it was because he had become resigned to her regular disappearances, but more likely it was because of the shortness of the assignment.

As it was, Annie only worked about six months a year, accepting enough freelance assignments to pay for her studio-loft, her nest in a 400-year-old building in the center of a village that went back to the time of Charlemagne. After they were married, she expected to keep the flat as a bolt-hole as well as a place to do her translations and to indulge her other passion—historical research—something Roger neither shared nor understood.

What they did share was a fascination for each other and their differences. It had taken them many breakups to reach the stage they were at now, a unique closeness which meant that when she was away from Roger she missed him more than she felt relief to be out from under his smothering.

"I made it," Annie texted to Roger from her car. Her phone rang almost simultaneously with her hitting the send button; however, it wasn't Roger, but rather Gaëlle, Roger's teenage daughter who considered Annie not so much a mother substitute as an ally in her battle against an overprotective father.

"Papa had to go out, but forgot his cell," Gaëlle said. "How was the drive?"

"Don't tell your father, but horrible. Snowy roads all the way. I'm exhausted. Everything okay?" She didn't tell her how surprised she had been at how prosperous everything in the former East Germany looked or about the old border watchtowers she'd seen on the way. Her love of history had made her want to stop and investigate in several places, but she knew she was up against a deadline. Going back, maybe she might have time.

"Hannibal chased a rabbit out of the yard. I had an English test and got a nine. Guillaume wants me to go to a film, and I'm not sure how Papa will react to that."

Annie could picture the German shepherd chasing the rabbit through the pine trees that made up half of Roger's property. Gaëlle's grades were almost always nine out of ten. The boy in question lived on her street, the grandson of one of the *mammies*, the old women who would sit on the street in chairs, observing the world, knitting or snapping beans as they exchanged gossip.

Annie knew he was a good kid by the way he helped carry things for the old women, didn't smoke or hang out with the troublemakers and was always polite without being cloying. Although Gaëlle would often spend time at Annie's, her excuses to come over when Annie wasn't at Roger's had increased and it took her longer and longer to come up to the studio as she talked with Guillaume. "Here's what you do. Have him stop by the house when your father is home. He'll make a good impression and that will also give your father a chance to check him out. He'll know he's not one of the bad kids. Then say you want to go out with Guillaume."

"I'm not sure it will work. Papa still thinks of me as a baby."

"Most fathers are protective of their daughters. Ask your father to call me if he has doubts. However, I won't bring it up unless he does." There'd been enough times Roger had accused Annie and Gaëlle of plotting against him, at which point, they usually would put their arms around him and say, "*Bien sûr.* How could you doubt otherwise."

Her relationship responsibilities taken care of, it was time to get set up. She was due at the museum at nine thirty the next morning and she was tired.

She got out of the car. A two-story apartment/hotel building was next to the hotel. To her right between two matching bungalows, she could see an arm of the Baltic Sea, which looked dark and ugly in the fading afternoon light.

Pulling up her collar, she entered the hotel. The reception area had a fireplace with a fire that snapped and crackled.

The young woman behind the desk had her hair cut in a geometric bob, which could have been from the 1960s, but it looked good on her. Within minutes Annie had her key and the codes for the Wi-Fi.

For a two-week stay, Annie needed only one suitcase and her laptop. Long ago she'd learned to travel light, and they had promised her that the studio came with a washing machine and dryer.

The corridor leading to Number 0B flat was brightly lit once she hit the wall switch. Like many European buildings, hall lights were timed to save electricity. The walls were white and the floors were white tile, clean except for the boot prints stopping at 0A, the apartment before hers.

The front door opened and a drop-dead blond about Annie's age walked in. With Denmark only thirty-odd miles off the coast, he could have had Viking genes cruising through his DNA. He was tall, but then again Germans tended to be tall. One of Annie's short girlfriends said when she went to Germany that she was going to the land of elbows, because that was all she could see.

"*Grüss Gott.*" His voice was deep, almost caressing, but his accent sounded more like the *Schwäbisch* that was spoken in Stuttgart where Annie had spent three years. She couldn't identify all the German dialects, but she knew those from Stuttgart and Munich fairly well. As for the Swiss-German dialects, some of those she still found impossible to understand. Her

French and Dutch were much stronger than her German.

"*Kann ich Sie helfen?*" the Viking God said.

"*Ich habe alles, danke.*"

"Are you American? Your accent?" He switched to English.

Damn, Annie thought. I really have not lost a lot of my accent. But then again she didn't often have a chance to speak German. Translate from it yes, speak it, no. "*Ja.*"

"Will you be here long?"

"I don't know. Probably not." Annie didn't know why she lied. She just felt she couldn't share the information. "*Aufwiedersehen.*"

She let herself into the flat. It was twice the size of her studio in Argelès with a small kitchen area at one end, and a living room at the other. The furniture was modern and there was a huge red poppy painting behind the red leather couch.

Behind a screen decorated with a series of red flowers was a bed made up with a thick feather *Eiderdown* and pillows in matching rose covers. The furnishings certainly clash with my red hair, she thought, taking off her cap and letting her tangle of curls fall over her shoulders. When she took off her boots, she realized the floor was heated.

The bathroom had a large tub and next to it was a washer and dryer unit. A bidet was between the toilet and sink.

The kitchen had all the equipment she needed to make simple meals. Tomorrow after work, she would find a grocery store. She wasn't sure what the opening hours were, and she really was too tired to work it out.

Four doors down from the hotel she'd spied a *Gasthaus* sign flickering through the snow. It would do for dinner, she thought. Her taster was set for a *Würst,* hot potato salad and a beer.

The *Gasthaus* was warm with wooden panels decorated with framed sketches of what she guessed were local people. Along the wall were cushioned benches and their green checked coverings matched the tablecloths.

She was the only customer, and the waiter, who was only half as good-looking as her new neighbor, asked her where she was staying. She told him.

"We don't get many tourists in winter. In summer we're full up."

Annie was looking forward to exploring. However as she walked back to her place the snow had stopped and the moon had come out. She walked by the entrance of the apartment building and followed the small path that led through two houses to the sea. One house sported a deer skull and antlers over the doorway. The moon wasn't quite full but still threw enough light to make things out.

A ship or a boat, Annie never really knew or cared about the difference, bobbed up and down: music drifted from it over the water. As bad as she was at estimating size, she knew it could accommodate lots of people and she imagined some sort of party was taking place.

She shivered: much too cold to stand there.

She headed back to the flat and took a hot shower. As she crawled under the *Eiderdown*, she thought to check her cell for messages. Roger had texted her. "This time stay out of trouble I love u."

He was referring to how during her last trips to Geneva and Paris, she had gotten involved in murders. It wasn't her fault that her longtime friend in Geneva had killed her lover. Nor was she responsible for the fact that in Paris a former lover had been killed by his jealous wife. She debated writing him back saying, "I don't know anyone here, so jealous lovers shouldn't be a problem," but she was too tired.

As she shut off the lamp she was sure she heard someone crying in Flat 0A.

CHAPTER 3

Kirchdorf, Insel Poel, Germany
"Poel is a Polish word for flat land or field. Poel has had various spellings over the years: Poele, Pole, Pule, Pül. The co-ordinates for Insel Poel are 54°00'N 11°26'E. Today, the island is part of the state of Mecklenburg-Vorpommern. It rejoined West Germany after the fall of the Berlin Wall and the German Reunification October 3, 1990."

The History of Insel Poel by Manfred Dederich

Annie crossed the parking lot from her short-term rental to the hotel. Residents in either place could select the German breakfasts that Annie remembered from trips she'd taken with her family when her father worked in Stuttgart: eggs, a variety of cold cuts, sausages, cheeses, breads, yogurts, bacon, waffles, fruits. This spread also had a honey that was even better than the kind her friend Jean-Bernard brought her from the hives. She ate so much that she would have preferred to go back to bed, but today was her first day on the project.

Before walking down the street to the museum, she stopped at her flat to pick up her laptop. Again, she thought she'd heard crying from Flat 0A. When she knocked, the crying stopped, but no one came to the door. Pausing for a moment she debated whether to knock again, but then decided if the woman, it was probably a woman, since men don't cry all that often, wanted to answer she would. Had there been the sound of someone holding the woman back, she might have pursued it.

Before she could do anything, the handsome man from last night came in and gave her one of those smiles that had it been a movie a sparkle would have reflected off his teeth followed by a ping and probably the "Hallelujah Chorus." "*Grüss Gott,* my American neighbor."

"I know it's none of my business, but I thought I heard someone crying inside."

He held the key in his hand. "Probably my sister. She just left her husband. Another woman."

"I'm sorry."

He gave her another killer smile as he opened the door and slipped in. Annie noticed he did it in such a way that it would be impossible for her to peek in.

Once outside, she looked over her shoulder. She could see the window of 0A. A curtain moved. Annie spied a woman who disappeared as fast as she appeared. Maybe she'd realized her brother had come into the flat or more likely she just didn't want to be seen.

The houses between the complex and the sea were mostly one or two stories, reminding her a bit of New England Cape Cod homes, although these were brick, not wood. The sea, although almost smooth, was gray and she shivered.

The museum, which was a short walk down the deserted street, was in a small brick building with what looked like a playground to one side. Everything was snow-covered.

Before every new assignment, Annie felt a moment of stage fright. However, translating documents was much easier than trying to make software understandable in four languages. She opened the door.

Two women, one about Annie's age, one older, looked up at her.

"You must be Frau Annie Young. We've so been looking forward to your coming," the younger of the two said.

CHAPTER 4

Hamburg, Germany
May 1935

"A typewriter?" Hilke watched as her father took the large black machine out of the box and placed it on the table he used as his desk. The door of his study opened onto the kitchen and she could smell the soup her mother had simmering: onions and barley with very little meat. Meat was still much too expensive even with the more stable prices at the butcher shop.

Once it had been decided that Hilke and Joseph were too big to share a bedroom, the extra bedroom the professor used as his office was given over to Joseph. The only space left had been the pantry. Where Käthe Fülmer's preserves once filled shelves, textbooks had been arranged by subject, then author. Nights, Herr Doktor Professor Fülmer often shut himself up for hours preparing his next day's lecture or correcting papers.

However, there was nothing sacrosanct. Either of his children had the right to interrupt him if they felt there was something important to say or do, and do could be anything from helping with homework to playing a game of pick-up sticks before bedtime. It didn't matter that there was barely enough room for a second chair, the visitor used a less-space-containing stool.

The exception to the interrupt-me-anytime rule would be when a student that Herr Doktor Professor Fülmer was mentoring was in the office with him. Then the door would be closed and a red tie would be hung on the handle, as powerful a barrier as an iron bar and several locks.

Hilke hovered around the doorway of her father's study. She wasn't sure where this was going, and she felt she would be better off to wait and see what the situation was before speaking.

"A typewriter. I bought it used. This summer you will learn to type."

Hilke had been planning on spending as much of the summer as possible swimming, despite her parents' constant pressure not to continue. "But I don't want to learn to type."

"You will learn to type and Frau Berchtold has said she will teach you shorthand."

"Shorthand?"

Her father expelled air. "Look at your grades. You will never go to university like your brother, and although I firmly expect you to marry, what if something happens to your husband? You will need to earn a living, not just for yourself, but also for any children you may have."

Hilke, unlike many of her girlfriends, had not spent much time dreaming about marriage. She hadn't thought she wouldn't marry either. So many of the boys she knew just seemed stupid to her. A look at her father's face told her protest would be useless. Besides, what could it hurt? "When do I start?"

Her father reached back into the briefcase that he used to bring home papers and tests he planned to correct, to carry books and lecture notes to class and to hold the lunch his wife packed for him each day. He brought out a book with a drawing of a typewriter.

Hilke pulled the chair up in front of the machine. Her father opened the book. There were drawings of the keyboard and where fingers should be placed.

"Follow the drawings."

The first thing she needed to do was to use her forefingers to repeat *fg* with her left hand then *hj* with the right. She was to do it 100 times. Then she was to switch and do *jh* and *gf* another hundred times. She looked at that next page. Using the same fingers she was to tap the *tz* and the *ui* keys from the top line.

Her father rolled a sheet of paper into the machine. She covered the first two pages before her mother called her for dinner. Learning to type would not be that difficult.

Boring, maybe.

Difficult? No.

The next day when she presented herself to Frau Berchtold, she discovered shorthand would not be as easy. Typing was mechanical, like the way she held her hand to get the maximum force of her strokes through the water. Shorthand—well that involved the memorization of lots of little squiggles, much more like regular schoolwork.

Frau Berchtold, as always, was dressed in such a manner as to defy any stain to come near her clothing. Her hair was never out of place. After two weeks of daily lessons, Hilke realized that Frau Berchtold had only three outfits that she alternated wearing.

The lessons were in her father's office while he was in class or at the library and after Frau Berchtold's own work was over for the day. She would dictate to Hilke, who set her pencil to paper.

During the second class, when Hilke had broken three pencil points, Frau Berchtold went and made a cup of tea. "When you swim, there is a certain degree of force that works, but too much force destroys what you are trying to accomplish, is that not right?"

"How do you know?" Hilke looked beyond Frau Berchtold who was sitting by a window. Outside, there was a tree in full leaf. Their green was already getting darker from the first pale tones of the spring. She could hear, but not see, birds tweeting.

"My fiancé used to swim. I did too, but although he wanted

to be a champion, the war came . . . Don't bear down on the paper. It makes the *Einheitssystem* harder to read when you tear holes."

Hilke found the swimming part interesting and she opened her mouth to ask more, but Frau Berchtold picked up a book and began reading. Deciding that Frau Berchtold might be joking either about the swimming or reading through torn paper, she quickly put her pencil to paper and started taking down what was being said. She was missing some symbols so she left blanks as Frau Berchtold read, "Different swimming strokes change how a swimmer is propelled through the water. With a butterfly stroke, for example, you move your arms in a forward circle. With the breaststroke, your arms remain in the water . . . life has improved for all Germans since our great leader Adolf Hitler became our leader. Germans know . . ."

She put the book down and walked to the door where a man in a black Schutzstaffel uniform stood, seeming impatient. "May I help you *Untersturmführer?*"

Hilke was impressed because she couldn't tell one SS uniform from another.

"I'm looking for Goldstein."

Hilke noticed that he did not use the *Herr Doktor Professor* title for her father's colleague.

"I haven't seen him today," Frau Berchtold said.

"Yesterday?"

"He has no classes on Mondays, so he doesn't come to the university until Tuesday."

The *Untersturmführer* turned and walked away.

"Set the table," Käthe Fülmer called to her daughter. Hilke had not even had time to put her *Einheitssystem* book and her bag with her wet swimsuit into her room. Her mother came out of the kitchen. Her face glistened from the unseasonable heat

28

combined with the heat from the stove. Hilke could smell bacon for the first time since Christmas.

"One minute." She went to her room, and towel dried her hair. The distance from the pool to the house was too short and the humidity too high to have dried it. Maybe her mother wouldn't notice. Her parents hadn't forbidden her to swim, but the way they almost sniffed when she did, or asked if she had completed her other chores or studies, or shorthand or typing exercises, or, or, or . . . said "we disapprove" louder than any words.

Back in the dining room, she asked, "What are we eating?"

"I've made potatoes with eggs and bacon. Use the smaller plates and be careful."

Her mother always told her to be careful with the dishes, although it was Joseph who was the one more apt to break something. The dishes with the four soft-pink roses winding across the plate had belonged to Käthe's mother. On her death the set had gone to Käthe as the older daughter, causing a rift between Käthe and her younger sister. Hilke couldn't imagine herself and Joseph fighting over them when her mother died. He could have them; she didn't care. Dishes weren't important.

She shuddered.

Her mother might annoy her, but she didn't want her dead, not now, not ever, even though she knew that someday it would happen. She folded the linen napkins into a pocket and stuck the fork and knife in the indentation.

"Looks nice, the table. *Danke.*" Her mother put a vase in the middle with a rose from the bush that she had coaxed into flowering on their balcony.

"*Bitte.*"

"Call your brother to the table: I'll get your father."

Hilke knocked on Joseph's door and opened it before he invited her in. Sometimes it annoyed him, but mostly it didn't.

He was sitting on his bed reading. She couldn't see the title, but she was sure it was some boring book. He never read a novel, but was always immersed in something historical or scientific, which was even worse. "Dinner?"

She nodded.

At the table, her mother served the food as she had every day that Hilke could remember. Food and money were scarce, despite Papa's salary. They were better off than many families, both parents would remind Hilke and Joseph if either complained. Hilke didn't think it was fair that her father and Joseph had servings larger than she did. When she complained, her mother would remind her that Joseph was a growing boy. She'd been sent to her room when she'd said, "But, I'm a growing girl."

"And you get more than I do," her mother had said to Hilke's departing back. Although she didn't ever complain again, she still resented the unfairness. She needed her energy for swimming, but that would not work as an argument. In fact, she never said swimming, if she could avoid the word, in case her parents decided irrevocably to forbid her. Until now, she had been able to cajole them into letting her continue.

"How did the shorthand go today?" Papa asked.

"Quite well. You can test me if you want to dictate something to me later." Hilke cut a small piece of bacon and put it on her fork along with a similar size piece of potato and a bit of egg. She loved the flavors together. Joseph ate all his onions, all his potatoes then all his bacon, and made sure they didn't touch on his plate.

"Something funny happened, though," Hilke said.

Her father cocked his head.

"Frau Berchtold was dictating this story"—she almost said *about swimming*, but thought better of it—"and all of a sudden she changed in mid-sentence about how wonderful Hitler is. I was looking out the window, but she could see into the corridor and there was this SS man there."

Her mother and father exchanged looks.

"And," her father said.

"She asked him if she could help him and he said he was looking for *Herr Doktor Professor* Goldstein, only he didn't use the title. Just the last name."

Her father put down his fork and pushed back his chair. He walked over to the window and looked out. A light breeze moved the sheer curtains. Her mother had closed the *Rolladen* earlier in the day to keep the heat out then had drawn the damask drapes. Now there was a breeze. In the early evening light, the drapes were pulled back and the *Rolladen* were raised, allowing fresh air into the room.

Käthe got up and put her hand on her husband's shoulder. "You've known Reuben for a long time."

"We were at university together. We were in the same division in the war. We've cowritten papers."

"And ones that were really well accepted," she said.

Hilke knew that whatever her father did, her mother approved of.

"I thought when he asked me to take his class Friday that . . ."

Hilke looked at Joseph, who shrugged.

Käthe led her husband back to his place. For several minutes there was only the sound of cutlery on china. The food gone, Käthe started to clear the table, but Wolfgang Fülmer shook his head.

"Joseph, I've written a friend I met at a conference. His name is George Smythe and he teaches at Oxford. I think it would be a good idea if you went to England next year instead of the university here."

Joseph frowned. "But what about my education?"

31

"I'm sure Oxford will have excellent classes in your field. Dr. Smythe has said he will see if you can get enrolled."

"You've already written him?" Käthe asked. "I thought you said you were only thinking about writing him."

"Sometimes it's better not to postpone things."

"But my friends . . ." Joseph seldom contradicted his parents.

"You will make new friends."

"May I be excused?"

That was the way her brother dealt with disagreement. He ran from it. Although it was his turn to do the dishes, her mother indicated that Hilke should do them. Joseph could take the next two nights.

Then her parents went to their room where their voices drifted out. They never screamed at each other, but when they didn't agree, retired to their private area and muted conversations, too soft to be understood, were all that Joseph and Hilke could hear.

Hilke heated the water for the dishes. Hot water was produced by a small electrical heater hanging on the wall next to the sink. To save electricity, it was put on only during dinner so it would be ready in time to do the dishes.

Her mother was a neat cook: the pans that had cooked the bacon and eggs and boiled the potatoes were already washed and put away.

Hilke didn't mind washing dishes all that much. She loved the feeling of suds, although her mother always said she used too much soap. Hilke made the foam rise by stirring the water as hard as she could as she tried to imagine what the house would be like without Joseph. She had thought he would be going to Hamburg *Universität* and that life would be the same as when he was at the *Gymnasium*.

CHAPTER 5

Kirchdorf, Insel Poel, Germany

"Insel Poel receives an average of 535 millimeters (21 inches) of waterfall per year. A humidity of about 84 percent is normal, although naturally there are variations."

The History of Insel Poel by Manfred Dederich

Renate Klausson and Karine Schneider were the two museum employees. Their shared office was behind the reception area and they ushered Annie into it and invited her to sit at a round oak table. From there they could see the empty reception desk while they made coffee for Annie and themselves. "Almost no one comes in during the winter, and especially on a day as cold as this," Renate said as she took the coffeepot off the hot plate and poured the liquid into three demitasses. She was probably a little older than Annie with medium length black hair that fell into her black eyes.

Karine, on the other hand, was much older, with white hair but unlined skin, sharp cheekbones and blue, blue eyes. Annie thought she would make a great model for any ad for older women.

"We can't believe our good fortune in getting you up here to do this." Karine stirred two uneven cubes of brown sugar into her cup.

"It's Gunther's doing," Annie said. She hadn't heard from him since she had dated him when she went to a *Gymnasium* in

Stuttgart. He had found her on Facebook. Then they'd met up by accident when she had an assignment in Basel about a year ago. He'd worked for a drug company where she was on assignment to translate sales material. He was married with two little girls and found her life far more glamorous than she did.

Taking tech writing and translation assignments around European cities did sound great. However, often she worked so intensively that Paris, London, Vienna made little difference. She'd be at work at seven and often spent a good twelve hours before she headed back to whatever room she was renting.

The money was great. Because she could produce documents in Dutch, English, German and French, the companies saved on translators, but that upped her rate since they were saving: one person did the work of four.

Every now and then she took an assignment that represented fun, and doing the translations for a small museum on an island in the Baltic Sea was one of those. They had agreed to pay her hotel, food and travel expenses plus a tiny daily rate. What she got out of it was a chance to investigate a new part of Europe.

Gunther was also Renate's brother-in-law from her first marriage and something had clicked when, at a family get-together over the summer, Renate said how she would like to have all the information in the museum available in other languages for the tourists that came through, but unfortunately they had almost no budget. The museum was tiny, but it represented centuries of history.

"I can only give you two weeks," Annie said to the two women. After that she was scheduled to be in Geneva with her parents for Christmas. Roger Perret and Gaëlle would be there as well. Even Hannibal, Roger's German shepherd, was invited. During the day they would go cross-country skiing, or just sit around listening to music and relaxing.

"We know, and we've set some priorities," Karine said. "We

can give you a tour as soon as you finish your coffee."

Annie didn't think it would take too long to look at everything in the small two-story building. Renate had said that there were things in storage but that they wanted to concentrate on the permanent exhibits.

The museum was well laid out. One small room duplicated a post office. Old-fashioned telephones lined a shelf. The bicycle that a postman had used for deliveries rested on one wall. A weighing machine had a sample package on one scale and weights on another. "Why don't you start here?" Renate said.

Annie was fascinated by the stamps, old letters and equipment. Not everything had a write-up, but she was able to do an Internet search and get some information.

At noon Renate stuck her head into the post office room. "We're closing for lunch. Would you like to come home with me? It'll be nothing fancy."

Nothing fancy turned out to be a hearty beef soup with fresh *Brötchen*. Annie had always loved the hard rolls sold in every *Bäckerei*. They were to eat in Renate's kitchen, which had a small wooden table and wooden chairs with hearts carved out of the middle of the backs. The curtains were see-through, lacy-like doilies, typical of the houses she had visited when she lived in Stuttgart.

Renate fussed about putting out plates and tableware. "I can't believe we ever found you for so little money." She spooned the soup into a tureen. "Maybe I shouldn't have said that."

Annie put out napkins. "It's okay. These projects are labors of love for me. So much of my work is boring, but anything historical, well, I get all tingly."

"I think everyone needs some kind of passion in their life."

"History is mine. I would love to write biographies about real people, but I never really have time. No, that's not true; I haven't found the right person."

Renate was silent.

"One of our member's grandmother wrote about her experiences in the war; maybe I can find them in the archives, which badly need organizing."

A girl about the age of her fiancé's daughter, Gaëlle, burst in. The smell of cold rose off her woolen winter jacket.

"My daughter, Greta," Renate said. "Greta, Annie is the woman who is doing the translations." She ladled the soup into heavy ceramic bowls as Greta dropped her coat, scarf, hat and mittens on a chair. Her mother pointed to them and to the hook next to the door. Greta rolled her eyes.

"Are you a writer?" the girl asked.

"No, more a translator of other writers' works."

"I want to be a journalist." Greta took her place at the table.

"Let her be," Renate said to her daughter.

"Can I ask you questions in English? It will give me a chance to practice." Although Greta was speaking to Annie she was looking at her mother. "Speaking lots of languages is necessary if I want to work as a journalist. I don't want to be any old journalist, but an international correspondent." Only after the girl finished did she let out her breath.

Renate looked at Annie. "Do you mind?"

"Not at all."

Greta: "How come you speak so many languages?"

Annie: "My dad was transferred from the United States to Nijmegen, Holland, then Stuttgart and finally Geneva. Each place my parents put me in the local schools so I had to learn the language."

Greta: "Was it hard?"

Annie: "At first. Especially in Holland. But all of a sudden one day it made sense. In Germany, I took out a vowel and added a declension or two."

Greta: (laughing) "And French?"

Annie: "*Oh la, la.* Miserable language to pronounce and spell."

Greta: "I know, I take it."

"Let the poor woman eat now," Renate said.

"It's okay, Renate." Annie turned to Greta. "The problem wasn't so much the language as feeling like an outsider all the time. Only recently I learned I was a Third-Culture Kid."

Greta frowned. "What's that?"

"A person who doesn't grow up in his or her parent's culture but still is part of it. And they are also a part of the new culture, a *mélange* of cultures into a third."

Greta: "I've only lived here. Booooring."

"I know, you're deprived," Renate said. "Eat your soup. We need to get back to the museum."

CHAPTER 6

Kirchdorf, Insel Poel, Germany

"We know there were inhabitants on Insel Poel during the Bronze Age. Monuments and a burial ground were found in 1934 including a stone ring. However, we start having more information about our past in 804 when we learned the Obodrite tribe received the area as a reward for defeating the German Saxons."

The History of Insel Poel by Manfred Dederich

When Annie finished her first day at the museum, she didn't feel much like cooking. She felt even less like going to the grocery store, which would have meant having to go back to the flat, get the car and drive. Driving was something Annie was never a big fan of. She'd been twenty-six before she even considered getting her license.

Tomorrow, she'd go food shopping, but tonight she would go to the restaurant near where she ate last night. She knew if she stopped off at the flat, she would be tempted to stay. However, the tea and hot chocolate left by the hotel owners for guests would not tide her over until morning.

Her feet crunched against the snow, a sound she had always liked. But the wind off the water was so cold that she walked as fast as she could without risking a fall.

The heat in the restaurant was welcoming. Annie hung up her coat on the pegs.

As she walked toward a table a voice behind her said, "Ah, my new neighbor." She looked behind to see that she'd missed seeing her handsome neighbor seated at one of the tables. "Are you alone? I'd love to have you join me." He indicated a free chair.

Why not, she thought. Better than eating by herself as she would probably be doing for most of her stay. She couldn't depend on Renate inviting her to lunch every day. *"Danke."*

He had been looking at the menu but handed it to her. "I'm having the herring. It's good here."

She was really too tired to worry about what to eat. When the waitress came she duplicated his order including the beer. The only difference was the size. If she drank a big beer, she'd fall asleep at the table.

"My name is Gregor Theissen." He held out his hand.

"Annie." She took his hand. "Your sister didn't want to come out to eat?"

"She's gone back to her husband."

Annie wondered if his sister had been abused. Spousal abuse was not new to her. She'd befriended a young, abused bride when she visited her folks in Caleb's Landing in the United States, in a house they'd inherited from her father's aunt, two years ago.

"My sister is a drama queen," he said. "Rolf does something to annoy her and she storms out. Usually, he comes after her faster, but this time . . ." He shrugged.

"He didn't."

"She had to apologize to him. About time, too."

The waitress put down their salads.

"What are you doing here?"

"A project for the museum."

"Do you know, although I've lived here a couple of years, I've never been there?"

How would I know that, Annie wondered. What did it matter, anyway? "It's a cute little place. It seems to capture the history of the island, as far as I can tell after being here about twenty-four hours. And may I ask what you do?"

"Boat captain."

"Fishing?"

"Charter. This is a slow time of year."

As they ate, Annie stole glances at him. He was handsome, almost too handsome in a soap opera or Hollywood way. She guessed he must be in his late thirties. There were small laugh lines around his eyes, but that would be from exposure to the elements if he were a sea captain. He was not overly tanned as some people who spent a lot of time at sea.

"What kind of boat?" Not that she knew much about boats. She couldn't recognize a kayak from a canoe. She could tell a canoe from a big ship like the *Queen Elizabeth*.

"One that has twelve cabins, a lounge, a dining room. Rather nice really. It's not like having a real job at all, just being on perpetual holiday."

She didn't want to ask him if he owned it or worked for someone.

The waitress brought their herring. Annie felt grateful for her upbringing, one which had exposed her to so many different national cuisines. She could be plunked down almost anywhere and feel comfortable with the food.

Their conversation ranged from music to politics, history to art. He was well-educated, well-read and claimed he was eclectic in his interests, something she agreed with without voicing it. A man she might be interested in if Roger weren't in the picture. The idea that if something was too good to be true, it probably was, and Gregor was too beautiful, too . . . too . . . she wasn't sure, but too, nonetheless.

Neither wanted dessert or coffee.

Annie noted that he helped her on with her coat. Her mother had always told her to look to a man's manners: it was a clue as to how he was raised. But Susan Young would add that manners were just one criterion.

Snow was falling, light fluffy flakes where one could make out the pattern under a streetlamp. Enough had accumulated while they were eating to cover the dirty snow from the previous storm.

At the building, Gregor pushed the code. "Would you like to come in for a glass of *Glühwein*? I make a wonderful *Glühwein*. It will warm you up and help you sleep.".

Annie's keys were in her pocket where she could fish them out easily. She did. "Thanks, but I have a full day tomorrow."

He bent as if to kiss her, but she put her hands up.

"You don't kiss on a first date?"

"That wasn't a date. We met by accident, and I paid for my own meal."

"Tomorrow could be a date."

"You're lovely," she said. "But I'm engaged."

"You aren't wearing a ring."

Annie had given her ring back to Roger in a fit of anger, which she still thought was right. He'd used the word "forbid" and no one was going to forbid her anything. When they'd made up, he'd said she could have it back—when they were married. Since he hadn't used the word "forbid" since, she figured some greater understanding had been arrived at by some miracle.

"We've a June wedding date." She touched her fingers to his lips. "However, if I weren't engaged, a kiss would have been very, very nice."

Once inside, she smiled as she congratulated herself on giving such a great brush-off.

She showered and got into her pink pajamas with the tiny gray kittens. Before she climbed into bed, she heard a knock.

Opening it, Gregor stood there with a single cup. "*Heisse Glüh-wein*. No reason for you not to enjoy this just because you are engaged. And if you're lonely, it would be great to have another meal. Or I can show you around the island. As friends."

Annie took the hot cup. The smell of the wine and spices tickled her nose. "*Danke*. I'd like that."

Gregor nodded to her and went back to his apartment.

He was right. The *Glühwein* was wonderful. Her neighbor was a class act.

CHAPTER 7

Hamburg, Germany
September 1936

The grr-grr-grr of the pencil sharpener was part of Hilke's morning ritual at the legal office of Suchland *und* Suchland, where Hilke had worked since school closed in early summer. She found it strange not to be going back to school as the first few leaves changed color along the Elbe. Strange was the word, but she didn't miss classes at all, especially the homework.

What she had discovered about herself was that if she liked doing something, she wanted to do it as close to perfect as possible. And if she didn't like something, she didn't want to waste a minute of her time on it, which explained her bad marks in math and sciences. It had been a great surprise to her to find out how much she liked typing and shorthand. There was a precision, much like swimming required. Timing was important and when her typing tested at ninety-three words per minute, she felt she had accomplished something. Although she didn't time test herself, she suspected that she surpassed her speed often. Speed had to be accompanied with accuracy because most of the documents she typed had at least three copies, and it was even worse to waste paper by having to start over.

What she did miss since leaving school was swimming under a coach. During the Olympics she had cheered Martha Genenger winning the gold medal in the 200-meter breaststroke, her event. And her other heroines Gisela Arendt, Ruth Halbsguth, Leni Lohmar and Inge Schmitz had taken silvers and bronzes.

She should have been there. Her coach had been disappointed that she hadn't even tried to qualify once her father had threatened to stop her swimming altogether if she persisted in her "crazy idea" to participate in the Olympics. Her coach had gone to see her father, who said, "*Nein*—no chance of reconsidering, swimming was excellent exercise, but my daughter is not going to compete when her grades are only average. She needs to work on her studies more than her breaststroke."

Walter Suchland smiled when she placed the three sharp pencils and his demitasse of coffee with one brown sugar cube in front of him as she did each morning. "*Danke.*"

Suchland *und* Suchland handled wills and contracts mainly, things like a lease for the *Bäckerei* or the purchase of a house. She didn't find it fascinating, but it wasn't boring either.

She liked welcoming people into the waiting room, making them feel comfortable. Herr Suchland had said that his previous secretary had scared the clients off in her attempts to protect him. She liked guessing what they might be there for, and although what they told her boss was confidential, she could not type up his notes of the meeting without knowing what had happened behind the closed door. Some of the stories were as good as any radio program.

Her days passed quickly. If she had time at lunch she would slip out for a half-hour swim at the municipal pool, only two blocks from the office. If she didn't do it at lunch, she would do it after work, for only twice since she had started working for them had they asked her to stay beyond closing for what they called an "unusually important project."

The office suite had a small kitchen and a slightly enlarged closet with a toilet and a sink so small that two hands filled it. There were another three rooms: one for Herr Walter Suchland, one for his young son Herr Kurt Suchland and a conference room. They all opened off the reception area where Hilke's desk was placed directly in front of the door. The first thing the clients saw was her smiling face, and she made sure that when the door opened, a smile was ready.

The furniture, even the filing cabinets, was ebony as were the oversized desks with carved deer and boar. The carpets were red Persian. If it had not been for the light beige walls and the two floor-to-ceiling windows to the left of her desk, the place would have been dreary even on the sunniest day instead of just when it rained.

Frau Berchtold had taught her well. Hilke loved the precision of her work. Like swimming where she had to put her arms and body in the exact place, the transcription of the Suchlands' words, father's and son's, exactly as they spoke them was a challenge. Making sure that every letter she hit on the typewriter was correct and that the document looked clean and readable was a challenge. She prided herself on her spacing as well as her accuracy. Not often did either Suchland have to return something to her for a redo, and even then it was often because they changed their minds about a certain phrase. They did it with apologies for creating extra work for her.

Kurt Suchland, the younger Suchland son, had just turned thirty. He had not been old enough to fight in the war that had killed his older brother, Herr Walter Suchland's only other child. He was about to be married: Hilke had been invited to the wedding. "I have a friend for you to meet," he said. "Dieter Kälter. He's the younger brother of my best friend and he is a real athlete." When she looked doubtful, he added, "He's a nice chap, twenty-three, finishing up at the medical school soon."

Hilke had not dated much, although she and her girlfriends giggled over boys. Some of Joseph's friends were her buddies in a way, but buddies aren't boyfriends.

Maybe it was time to start thinking about men. A test would be how they felt about her swimming. Too many of her girlfriends, upon discovering that their boyfriends disapproved of some of their activities, had to make a choice, with the boy almost always winning out. Hilke didn't want that to happen to her. Don't prejudge, she told herself.

The senior Fülmers had guests for dinner and since Hilke was a working girl, she was allowed to join them if she wanted. She had told her mother only that morning that she would enjoy joining the party, partially because she knew her mother had been able to obtain a lamb roast and was making a *Schokoladenkuchen.*

Hilke liked her father's colleague, *Herr Doktor Professor* Fritz Welphal and his wife Lotte because the wife had a good sense of humor. Neither had ever talked down to her, even when she was a preteen, like many of her parents' friends did. The couple was younger than the Fülmers by ten years, but her father kept telling Hilke that age difference only mattered when one was a child. Life was more interesting when one had friends of several generations. Emotional or intellectual distance mattered much, much more.

No great intellectual differences existed between the *Herr Doktor Professors* Fritz Welphal and Wolfgang Fülmer. The wives liked each other as well, but the men dominated the dinner conversation.

As Käthe Fülmer was gathering up the salad plates before bringing out the main course, Herr Welphal said, "It's a mistake for us to fight in Spain."

Wolfgang Fülmer said nothing.

"You're quiet," Fritz said.

"I wonder if we are living in a time when we should have opinions," he said as his wife reentered and placed the roast in front of him and handed him a carving knife. The blade had a stag nibbling on a branch etched into the blade.

Lotte Westphal broke the silence. "That looks wonderful, Käthe. Tell me, what do you hear from Joseph? Did he come home this summer?"

"He stayed to do some research in a lab. He wants to be a chemist," Käthe said. She disappeared into the kitchen and came back with bowls of potatoes and green beans.

Hilke knew her parents had told her brother under no circumstances was he to return to Germany. Her father was convinced there would be another war, and he did not want his son to be a soldier, or that is what he told Hilke when she asked why Joseph had been sent away and not her.

CHAPTER 8

Kirchdorf, Insel Poel, Germany
"At one time there were two moors on the island. Today they are dry and used for growing hay."

The History of Insel Poel by Manfred Dederich

Annie pulled her car into the grocery store parking. Even with her bad sense of direction, she did not need a GPS to drive three blocks from the museum and take a right as Renate had directed.

The grocery was a stand-alone store, not a huge supermarket but respectable in size. Across the street were houses and a one-story tiny police station was on the other side of the street. How much crime could there be in this peaceful little village?

To get to the main part of the store, she had to walk through the bakery with a couple of stools for those wanting a coffee or a snack on the spot. Since it was her lunchtime, the pastries, many of which she remembered from her time in Germany, looked extra tantalizing. She'd buy the freshly baked bread on her way out. Never shop when you're hungry, she thought.

The fruits and vegetables were neither as fresh-looking nor as varied as in Argelès, where most of them were grown during the long season. She chose potatoes, onions, apples, grapes, and a squash. Annie described herself as shopping phobic. Every minute in a store was a minute stolen from her life.

Supermarkets were no better.

At least when she was shopping in Argelès, she could talk to the fishmonger who had bought the fish from the dock, or wait for freshly made mayonnaise in a quantity just for the meal at the *traiteur,* which made the experience bearable.

She knew she didn't want to eat out all the time, not just for budgetary reasons, but because going out at night in the cold wasn't as appealing as curling up by the fireplace in her studio. Better that she not run into Gregor again, either. His good looks and easy manner made him all too tempting. Maybe make some lentil soup, pasta or something. That would keep her for a couple of days.

As she turned down the canned goods aisle, she saw Gregor. *"Grüss Gott,"* she said and smiled.

He frowned and turned away from her. A pregnant woman waddled up to him and put bananas in his cart.

If it seems too good to be true, it probably is. The bastard was married. Maybe his wife had been away earlier. Maybe she'd been the woman crying. Anyway, it wasn't her problem.

She looked at her watch. Renate said not to come back until three. Some committee or other was meeting, and Renate wouldn't be available to show her the next part of her assignment. Annie was already a day ahead of schedule. She guessed the museum people had overestimated the project or underestimated how fast she worked. The translations were simple. She might even be able to get at least part of the history book about the island done before she left.

Instead of going back to the studio to unload she went in the opposite direction to check out the beach. A grove of trees and a parking lot were to her right. There was an almost one-story vertical stone monument that was built like a two-panel screen. Near the top was a bronze triangle. Obviously, some kind of memorial, she thought.

The waist-high fieldstone wall behind the monument had a

fresh layer of snow although in some places the wind had blown the latest deposit off, leaving a thin coating of ice.

When she was little she and her father would stop at every memorial, every historical site they passed. Love of history was in her DNA. She pulled into the parking lot. Even though the car had not had a chance to heat up during the short drive from the grocery, it had been sitting in the sun and was much warmer than the outdoor air.

She pulled her hat down over her ears. To the right of the memorial were four large—she suspected they were granite—triangles that were just about knee-height. Granted, she didn't know much about types of rocks.

One hundred twenty-eight people! This wasn't a memorial so much as a cemetery. A shudder, which was half cold and half reaction to standing on a mass grave, began at her shoulders and ran down her torso. She headed back to the car.

Looking at her watch, she still had time to kill before the committee meeting at the museum would be through and she could go back to work. She turned the car toward the beach. The houses gave way to a hotel, a restaurant. A souvenir and coffee shop was the only place open. She'd go for a hot chocolate or tea after a walk on the beach.

Annie had always loved water whether it was the Atlantic, North Sea, Mediterranean or even Lake Léman. The lake might not have as many moods as the sea, but it still could go from almost walk-on-top-of calm to surfable waves. In winter, an angry Lake Léman could throw water across the road encasing cars, benches and trees in ice for days.

Still, there was nothing like the sea, and she did not want to miss her advantages of being near one. Even before she stepped on the ash-gray, faded wooden plank walk leading to the water, she could see the whitecaps. The sea grass jumped and twisted in the wind.

Annie bent down. The sand was gray and very soft like the Good Harbor and Wingaersheek beaches of her childhood. Compared to New England, with most of the beaches she had visited, the sand here was coarse. In many places along the Mediterranean the beaches were tiny rocks. Annie had never understood how people could lay for hours with only a beach towel between them and the hard bumps, but then again she was too impatient to even lie on soft sand. She let a handful trickle through her fingers before the cold forced her to put her gloves back on.

Much of last night's snow had blown away. Annie set off along the shoreline at a brisk pace. Walking in boots on sand was different than walking on something solid, giving her a strange gait.

About halfway down the beach a sliver of red caught her eye where the sea grass almost touched the water. Annie walked over, looked down, then screamed.

The body of a woman with long black hair lay face-down. She wore a red bra and thong and nothing else. Some of her left hand and part of her right leg was missing. Annie didn't need to be a pathologist to guess that the body had washed up on shore nor that part of the damage was probably from sea creatures feeding on what she guessed was a young woman. The hair was too long and the skin too youthful, even with the water damage, to be old.

She did not need to be a pathologist either to recognize three bullet holes in the body.

Annie pulled out her cell then realized she didn't know the local emergency numbers.

"Slow down," the *Polizeiobermeister* said. He had his hand on the door of the green and white Panda car, parked outside the police station across from the grocery store, but since Annie had blocked him in he couldn't go anywhere.

"A body of a woman. On the beach." Annie pointed in the direction she'd come from. "She was murdered."

"How do you know?" He took off his hat and pushed his gray hair into place. His face was wrinkled.

"Bullet holes." Although Annie had had time to catch her breath in between the time she ran to her car until she'd pulled up by the police station, she still felt winded.

"We don't have murders here," the sergeant said.

Annie wanted to shake him and tell him there could be murders anywhere, anytime.

"I'm serious. The last murder on the island was back in fifty-seven or maybe even earlier. Something to do with the bird sanctuary. I don't remember all the details. It was before I was with the police."

"*Kommen Sie mit mir, bitte,*" Annie said. "I'll show you."

The *Polizeiobermeister* frowned as if he were considering not going. "Move your car and ride with me."

"I'd rather you followed me." She didn't want to be dependent on him on getting back to the police station. Although she could have walked it, the cold was getting to her.

He shrugged and headed toward the Panda.

The body was where she had left it, but the tide had come in just enough so that the outstretched arm was now in the water.

"I know we shouldn't disturb a crime scene, but if we don't move her she'll wash away," Annie said.

The sergeant shook his head. "If she washed ashore, this isn't a crime scene."

He took the body by its arm and dragged it about twenty feet deeper into the sea grass. Then he took out his cell. "I need to call Lübeck. They are equipped to handle this." As he waited for someone to answer he muttered, "Damn it, with only three more days until I retire, I have to run into this."

CHAPTER 9

Kirchdorf, Insel Poel, Germany
Polizeioberkommissar Hans-Peter Leiter stood by his car and dialed his soon-to-be ex-wife. He dreaded what she would say and she did say exactly what he expected her to—almost word for word.

"How can you disappoint the boys again? They were looking forward to it: their sleeping bags are all packed and waiting by the door . . . They were talking about the DVDs you promised to watch with them . . . That's just like you . . . work before all else."

He held the phone from his ear. He wore enough guilt between the divorce and the lack of time he had with his two sons. His working hours were one of the reasons for the divorce-to-come in the first place. His wife was justified in saying it would make no difference if she were a single mum or not considering how seldom Hans-Peter was home.

He couldn't help it if his caseload was sometimes overwhelming. As he rose through the ranks, it became heavier not lighter as he had promised her it would.

Polizeihauptmeister Fritz Gärtner, his partner despite being of a lower rank, came out of the Lübeck *Polizei* headquarters. "We've got Claudia Niemann as the medical examiner. She'll meet us there."

It was dark by the time they reached the Kirchdorf beach. Neither said much on the drive. It wasn't necessary. They had worked together long enough that they were two parts of a whole. If Fritz minded Leiter's two promotions while Fritz remained at the same P4 rank, he never said anything. He hadn't bothered to take the exams. Fritz was one of the few people that Hans-Peter knew who was truly happy with who he was and where he was.

Laziness wasn't his problem. He worked hard on all their cases, giving that extra when needed. Hans-Peter would be the first to admit that he never had, and probably never would, understand contentment.

Hans-Peter wondered sometimes if Fritz lacked ambition, but at the same time, his work was so insightful, so thorough, that Hans-Peter couldn't chalk it up to lack of caring. It was not a topic they discussed.

An old *Polizeirat* and a young woman with wild red hair flowing from under her knitted hat came out of the souvenir and coffee shop. "Much too cold to wait in the car," the *Polizeirat* said. "And why waste gas?"

Talk about lack of ambition, Hans-Peter thought: to be that old and still be in such an unimportant little burg. "Where's the body?"

"You'll need a flashlight or better even spots, if you have them," Annie said.

Hans-Peter turned to the woman. "And who are you?"

She stuck out her hand. "Annie Young. I found the body."

He frowned. He didn't need foreigners, even one who could speak good German, albeit with an accent that seemed *Schwäbisch* mixed with English. "Show me the body."

Fritz walked to the Panda to get three battery-run spotlights. As he held them in his arms, he could barely see over them and tripped, then strove to regain his balance, stopping himself from falling but not without looking like he was doing some strange dance.

The group traipsed down the boards and then walked along the water's edge. Although the moon was low on the horizon it was full, casting a little bit of light.

As they approached the body, Hans-Peter put his hand on the sergeant's shoulder to stop him.

"She was washed up. Not much of a crime scene to investigate."

Hans-Peter noticed that there were drag marks in the sand. "Someone moved the body."

"I did," the *Polizeirat* said.

"You should know better."

"If I hadn't it would have washed out to sea before you got here." He sounded truculent.

Annie decided she didn't like the Lübeck policeman. He hadn't bothered to introduce himself. He was treating the poor *Polizeirat* with almost no respect.

"Hans-Peter?" A woman called to them.

Annie could see she was dressed in a white plastic covering her clothes.

"Over here, Claudia."

When she came up to them, Annie guessed Claudia was about her own age. Her blonde hair was cut in bangs that peeked out from her blue cap along with a braid that went halfway down her white-plastic-covered back. Another man followed, also dressed in white plastic covering. "It'll be hard to get photos," he grumbled.

"Dieter, try your best."

The man following Claudia pulled a camera from his bag. "Can you shine the spotlight on the body, Hans-Peter. Fritz, step back and give some light to the area with the second lamp."

"I don't know your name," Dieter said to the old *Polizeirat*, "but go to the other side and do the same as Fritz with the third lamp."

"More to the right, Fritz, step back, Hans-Peter, just a bit." The camera clicked. Dieter encircled the body snapping photo after photo.

When he was back to his original stance, Claudia came up to him. Taking a flashlight, she angled it so she could see what he'd done.

"I don't think I can do better. We could wait until morning."

Claudia walked over to the body. The others stayed where they were. "I don't think so. She obviously has been in the water, but not overly long. A bit of damage. Looks like she was shot at least twice." She angled her flashlight. "Make that three times."

A wave came up almost to Hans-Peter's shoes. He jumped aside.

"No point in doing a body outline," Claudia said. "It'll be washed away. I hate cases where I can't do the normal procedure." She turned the body over. "She's Asian."

"We don't see many Asians around here," the *Polizeirat* said.

Hans-Peter found himself scowling. Idiot. "She could be from a passing ship."

"Is there a way you can measure the currents and determine from where she might have been dropped and check shipping records?" Annie asked.

He took a deep sigh. "Frau Young, leave this to the professionals."

"I'm sorry, I'm engaged to a French police chief, who used to be a top homicide detective in Paris, and he . . ."

"Insel Poel is not Paris. I'm quite capable of handling this without amateur comment."

"In that case, there's no reason for me to stay freezing my butt off. If you want me, I'm staying at the hotel/apartment complex two doors down from the museum. I'll be at the museum during the day."

Before he could say anything, she left. He turned his flashlight onto her departing back. Temper was the problem with natural redheads, and he was sure she was natural.

Yet she did have a point, although he was sure that if it were a small boat, there would be no record. He would have Fritz check with the harbormasters in the area. There might be a ship flying under an Asian flag.

Or maybe she'd been shot on Insel Poel, and the body taken out and dropped into the sea. He would also need to check on all the boats in the area. He'd get Fritz to ask the locals if any of them recognized the woman. Her being Asian was an advantage, because even without a photo of the corpse they would remember her if she'd been in Kirchdorf. But she might have been in another of the villages on the island as well.

Maybe she'd been summer help who didn't go home. Fritz interrupted his thinking.

"Since I can't mark anything here, we might as well get the body back to the morgue." Claudia said.

Glad to get out of the cold, he agreed. He still had to drive back to Lübeck. He glanced at his watch. It was too late to try and see his sons.

CHAPTER 10

Hamburg, Germany
March 1938

"What time is Dieter picking you up?" Käthe asked Hilke. The older woman was standing at the doorway of her daughter's bedroom.

Hilke was towel drying her hair. It was now down below her shoulders and she wore it loose, even though it was not the style for young people her age. It was thick and dark brown. She felt that her hair was her one good feature. "Seven thirty."

"And where are you going?"

"One of the other doctors is having a party at his flat." Hilke knew her mother was chatting, not being nosy. They liked Dieter: they liked that he was going to be a doctor. If anything they worried when he didn't call, not that they said anything to her, but her mother would ask when she was seeing Dieter again, and Hilke had to remind her that as he was a recent graduate from medical school his work at the hospital meant long hours and little sleep.

Tonight was the beginning of a three-day weekend for him. The party was tonight and tomorrow they planned to cycle along the river and have dinner at some *Stube* still to be discovered. They had no plans for Sunday. Dieter had very little money, but he would not allow Hilke to pay for anything, saying a man does not accept money from his girlfriend.

The doorbell gave its pitiful hiss. Käthe went to get it. Hilke could hear her mother say how her daughter was almost ready.

Once the young couple was outside, they decided to walk despite the wind. "It feels good not to be rushing from bed to bed," Dieter said. "Not to smell antiseptic, not to . . ." He stopped and pushed her into the doorway of a boarded up store that had a fading Star of David painted on the wood. He pulled her into his arms. "I know this isn't romantic, but will you marry me?"

You're right, she thought, this isn't romantic, but he wasn't romantic.

"Sunday, I told my parents I was bringing a young woman to lunch, and I'd like to tell them you are going to be my wife."

A light rain began to fall, but they were protected by the stone arch. Hilke couldn't remember what kind of store it had been and she thought when someone has just proposed she shouldn't be trying to remember about a store she had passed thousands of times, but never really saw. "Yes," she said.

"It may have to be a long engagement until I've finished my training period at the hospital."

That was fine. "It will give me time to start buying duvets and bed linens and dishes." *Gut Gott,* she was sounding as practical as Dieter. So much of her life had been spent thinking about swimming, although in the last few years, it was a dream that only came at night when she moved through the water at record speeds and perfect form to be greeted by cheering crowds.

Unlike other girls, she never dreamed about finding *Herr Right* or even *Herr Almost Right.* She never thought any man would really want her and no matter how much *Der Führer* talked about motherhood being the greatest thing women could do for the Fatherland, she never thought about fulfilling her national role.

"Does that *really* mean *ja?*"

"*Ja,* it really means *ja.*" Why else would she say it?

He picked her up and swung her around. The back of her legs felt the rain each time they emerged from the arch. Then he took her by the hand and they ran the last block to where the party was being held.

When the door opened to Horst's two-bedroom flat where he lived with his wife Regina, Hilke expected people to be swirling around, glasses of beer in their hands. They might be nibbling bits of cheese or sausage. Conversation would be a hum and words like gall bladder, embolism and thyroid would come from the men's corners, while the women would be talking about blue dresses, a new hairdresser that none could afford and nail polish.

Horst put his finger to his lips in way of greeting, and stood away from the door so Dieter and Hilke could enter. She saw the five couples that she knew from other parties, the men all colleagues of Dieter, the women their girlfriends or wives. All of them were sitting around a radio.

"What are you listening to?" Dieter whispered.

"The report of the *Anschluss.* Austria is now part of the Third Reich."

CHAPTER 11

Kirchdorf, Insel Poel, Germany

Renate Klausson was making Christmas decorations with her daughter Greta when the phone rang. The girl loved the ritual and Renate was grateful that she hadn't turned into an annoying teenager who wanted nothing to do with her mother. Thus, moments where they worked together with complicity were to be treasured.

She'd raised Greta alone since her first husband had died in a boating accident. Last year she'd married Karl Klausson, a Swedish businessman who had bought them this house, far nicer than the apartment where they'd been living. He had gone out of his way to win over Greta, who every now and then said that she had liked it better when she'd had her mother all to herself. For a little while, she had seemed to capitulate.

At least until lately, when Greta had started a personal vendetta against Karl. He would enter the room; her daughter would leave. She absolutely refused to be left alone with him and more and more she said that she wished they could go back to when there had been just the two of them.

Renate had responded that those were wonderful days, but asked the girl how she would feel if she went with her to university.

Greta had just stared at her.

"Well, if I hadn't built my own life for when you're gone, then you'd be stuck with me."

Greta had thought it over before saying, "I see your point."

Because Karl traveled more than he was there, Greta and she still had a great deal of quality time together.

"Are you going to answer the phone?" Greta asked. "Or should I?"

"It's probably one of your friends."

Greta pushed her chair back from the table. The phone was on the kitchen wall. "Karl." She turned the telephone over to her mother.

"How are you *Schatz*?" Renate asked. "And where are you?" Both were traditional questions whenever Karl called, which sometimes was daily, but when he got caught up in his business he might go a few days without calling her. As easygoing as he was, he made it clear to her that he didn't like being pressured. And he didn't like telling her where he was. She had his cell number and she could reach him if she had to.

"I'm at the Dubai Airport waiting for my plane."

Renate didn't want to ask when he would be home.

"I'll be back the day after tomorrow, and I don't have to leave until January third."

"That's wonderful."

"I was wondering if maybe you'd like to go skiing. We could go to Garmisch. A little skiing, a little hanky-panky, or a lot of hanky-panky."

"It might be late to get reservations, but I could try."

Greta mouthed, "Reservations?"

Renate tucked the phone under her chin and pantomimed skiing. Greta's eyes opened wide. She loved to ski.

"I can't leave the museum until we finish this project with the translator I told you about, but between Christmas and New Years—that would work."

"Perfect," Karl said. "I'd like a few days doing nothing around the house. They're calling my plane. I need to run."

"Ich liebe dich," Renate said to a dead line.

"Do I have to go with you?" Greta asked. "I could stay with the twins."

"We are building a family and that includes taking holidays together," Renate said.

CHAPTER 12

Kirchdorf, Insel Poel, Germany
"The island has two natural reserves that are bird sanctuaries. The *Insel Langen Weider*, begun in 1910, is the oldest bird sanctuary in Germany."

The History of Insel Poel by Manfred Dederich

"Don't get involved."

Annie paced around the studio as she listened to her fiancé Roger. His call had interrupted her plans to work on the translation of Dederich's book, and she had just made a mental note to visit the bird sanctuaries when her cell had croaked. She still was happy to be talking to him, half because it was Roger, half because the prose was turgid in places. Dederich jumped back and forth in time, unlike any German history book she'd ever had when she was at the *Gymnasium* in Stuttgart. Sometimes it was written more like a stream of consciousness. Maybe he wrote with an oh-I-better-put-this-in-now-so-I-won't-forget-it style. However, he was complete.

Outside the wind howled. She walked to the window and peeked into the black. An hour before she'd been out there then rushed home fantasizing a hot shower to warm her bones after standing out on the freezing beach with the detective and the poor dead girl. Instead, she decided to wait until right before she could crawl into bed.

Nor had she rolled down the *Rolladen,* which she had left up so she could watch the swirling snow whenever she glanced up from her translation. She deliberately let the silence hang, although she knew it was a bit bitchy.

"Annie, I mean it."

"I'm not going to get involved, other than I was the one to find the body. How could I?"

"You've a track record of involvement in things better left alone."

She ambled over to the kettle and ran water into it, cradling the phone between her cheek and shoulder. The heated floor felt wonderful on her cold feet.

"Do I hear water running?"

"I'm making tea. It's cold here."

"Then I won't tell you it was a beautiful sunny day, and I only needed my short-sleeved shirt."

"No, don't tell me that, but remember I find bad weather more interesting than good." She heard Roger sigh. "Listen, I've work to do here because I want to make sure I can get to Geneva for Christmas."

"Gaëlle and I have our train tickets. We arrive the twenty-third."

"I should be back there the day before."

"*Je t'aime, chérie.* But, stay out of it."

"Don't worry. The detective, or whatever his title is, is a real grouch. I love you too."

She clicked her phone shut.

Forget the translation for a while. Take a shower. The hot water beat out the cold. She found herself almost falling asleep leaning against the tile and lulled by the warmth. The room came with giant towels, in which she could wrap herself up. She padded out to the main room where she put on a jogging suit and was about to make herself some soup before crawling into bed. Granted it was early, but the day had been exhausting.

A knock on the door interrupted her as she was reaching for a pan. When she opened it, she found Gregor standing there. He was as handsome as ever.

"I heard you come in, and I thought you might like to join me for supper. I made some curry lamb. I'm quite a good cook."

"But not a polite one."

He looked confused.

"You blew me off in the supermarket earlier."

"That wasn't me."

Annie wondered if she'd been mistaken. The man in the supermarket had on pressed pants. Gregor was wearing jeans and a Nordic-type sweater. He would look wonderful by a ski lodge fireplace.

"It certainly looked like you."

"I've a common face. Come on. If you don't want to eat with me, at least let me give you a puppy bag."

"Doggy."

"Doggy?"

"Doggy bag, not puppy bag. "I'll come over to your place." That way she could leave whenever she wanted to.

His flat was almost identical to hers, except she could see through a door that there was a separate bedroom. He'd set the table for two, but without any romantic candles. The smell of cumin, turmeric and ginger hung in the air. She loved those smells.

He poured two glasses of wine. She watched carefully just in case he slipped a date rape drug into her glass, then felt a twinge of guilt about being so suspicious. But only a twinge. Annie was a well-traveled woman which made her suitably cautious.

The lamb and basmati rice were served from the same dish. The food was as good if not better than that served at Little India in Geneva and almost as good as that cooked by her Indian friends, who she thought should open a restaurant that would put all other Indian restaurants to shame.

Besides enjoying the food, she felt ashamed that she'd thought badly of him. "I'm sorry, that I was so . . . so . . ."

"Rude?"

"Short at least. I've had a horrible day."

"What happened? Museum work can't be all that terrible." He handed her the serving dish with the lamb.

She took a second serving. Until she started to eat she hadn't realized how hungry she'd been. Then she remembered she'd missed lunch. She'd left the groceries she'd bought in the car. The discovery of the body had wiped the earlier part of the day out of her mind.

"I found a body."

"You what?"

"Found a body. On the beach. Of a young Asian girl."

He jumped up so fast he knocked over the chair. A bit of an overreaction, she thought.

"Do you know her?"

"I doubt it."

Staccato-like, he asked her about the police, the condition of the body, where it was exactly, until she held up her hands.

"Enough. The police didn't ask me all that stuff."

He relaxed. "I'm sorry. I'm a real lover of detective stories and the idea of a murder in Kirchdorf, well it's a bit like fiction coming to life."

Annie hadn't mentioned the bullet holes in the girl. "I didn't say she was murdered."

"No you didn't." He drained his wineglass. "I guess I assumed it. My mother used to tell me I had an overactive imagination."

He began to clear the plates from the table. "I'd offer you coffee, but I'm all out." His body language told her he would just as soon have her leave. Not that he opened the door, but he didn't return to the table hovering at the divider rather than sitting at the table or suggesting that they move to the living room.

"No problem. I wouldn't sleep if I had some. And I'm more than ready to sleep. Do you read English?"

"*Ja.*"

"I've a detective story I've finished. I'll drop it off tomorrow." She walked to the door. "*Danke,* it was very good."

"*Bitte.*" He opened the door well before she headed for it.

Back in her flat she went behind the screen where the bed was. The *Eiderdown* was at least three inches thick. She turned on the electric sheet under the main sheet. When she was a child she hated to go to bed, but now it was a treat, sometimes the best moment of even a very good day. On the night table were the books she'd brought. Why not take the book to him now?

Out in the hall the smell of coffee was coming from Gregor's flat. Annie went back into hers, the book still in her hand.

CHAPTER 13

Hamburg, Germany
November 1941

Hilke stopped in front of her in-laws' and watched three Jews wearing the Star of David shuffle by. The house, dating back to the sixteenth century, included her father-in-law's office where he saw patients when he wasn't in the hospital wards. Her mother-in-law had managed to get through the rough years by selling off some of the antiques after the war, but they had kept enough together to create a worn elegance.

Hilke was late for their weekly dinner because there was a contract that had to be rewritten several times. Her boss kept apologizing, blaming the clients who kept wanting this or that sentence changed. Since the clients were sitting in his office, tapping their feet, Hilke knew she had no acceptable professional alternative. Her mother-in-law, often deserted for this or that medical emergency by her husband, would understand.

The wind blew off the Elbe and Hilke shivered in her woolen cape. She would have liked a new coat, but she was trying to save money for when the war was over and she and Dieter could set up their own apartment. It was planned he would go into practice with his father and brother, who was also serving as a doctor on the front. Only, she didn't know which front. Meanwhile, she still lived with her parents.

Frau Freja Kälter opened the door and swept her daughter-in-law in with a hug. At their wedding, their very small wedding at the *Rathaus,* her mother-in-law had whispered, "I promise to be the best mother-in-law possible."

She had lived up to her promise. For the first time in her life, Hilke did not feel like she was disappointing someone: she felt as if she really belonged to this family.

Her mother-in-law would go swimming with her, although she swum half the distance, then waited for Hilke to finish before they went off to a café for coffee and pastry. They kept the second part of their outings a secret, because Dr. Kälter was always saying his wife could afford to take off a few pounds. When he said it, he would give her a hug adding, *"Ich liebe dich."*

Frau Kälter would always tell Hilke that right after the last war, her husband was always wanting her to put on weight, would give up some of his food for her, which in turn she would give to Dieter when he wasn't looking and then she would roll her eyes and whisper "men" in that tone that said she really liked them but they had their strange ways and as good wives and mothers we still need to humor them.

Her father-in-law said that he knew, he just knew, that Hilke would make a good doctor's wife when the war was over and Dieter was home. Anyone who could devote themselves to swimming as she had done, who was a good secretary, would do whatever it was to support Dieter in his career.

"I've a letter." Both women said it at the same time then laughed.

Hilke reached into her pocketbook as her mother-in-law opened a drawer in the table at the entry next to the coatrack.

"It's all right if you want to just read me the less personal parts," Freja said, as she always did. Freja handed her letter to Hilke. "Mothers don't get the lovey-dovey parts."

Both letters were short of details and could have been copies of earlier ones. He was tired because he spent a good part of each day, and sometimes night, operating. A few parts were blacked out. They shouldn't get their hopes up, but he might be able to get home for a long weekend before the spring, but definitely not for Christmas.

"I hope he does, and I hope you make a baby," Freja said, then put her hand over her mouth. "I'm not telling you to, that's your decision."

Hilke moved into the living room, which was dark. The lamps with their thick-fringed shades did not throw much light. The room was dark even in the daylight when the heavy brown drapes were pulled aside. Yet, she didn't find it depressing, because of the laughter that was a regular part of any time that she spent there.

Her mother-in-law was one of those women who always voiced the good side of whatever happened. Dieter was a doctor so he was better off than the soldiers in the trenches, she would say, rather than let on how worried she was. If her husband missed dinner it was because he was helping someone. If it rained, the plants needed it.

Hilke sat down. "There's nothing wrong with wanting to be an *Oma*."

Her own mother had been shocked when they received a letter from Joseph announcing that his wife, an English girl called Mary, was expecting. "I'm too young to be a grandmother," Käthe had said.

"How are your mother and father?" Freja asked.

"My father is busy as always. My mother . . ." Hilke didn't want to be disloyal. "She still doesn't want to leave the house." For the past two years, Käthe had had Hilke do the shopping on her way home. She no longer went to see her friends, nor did she invite them to the house. The couple no longer went to dinner parties. When there was an event at the *Universität*, which could not be missed, her father went alone.

Sometimes Hilke would find her mother sitting by the window, the drapes drawn, but peeking through a small opening. Her father refused to talk about it. "Menopause," her best friend Else, had said when Hilke voiced her concern. "My mother acted weird for a few years then went back to normal."

"Since it's just the two of us, let's eat in the kitchen." Freja led her daughter-in-law through the glass-paneled door. The smell of hot cooking oil hung in the air. "I hope an omelet is fine."

CHAPTER 14

Lübeck, Germany

Hans-Peter Leiter's alarm startled him awake and jutted him into a bad mood. His studio had a bed, white walls and not much more. No coffee smells from the percolator started by his wife, no noises coming from his boys. Those noises once annoyed him: now he missed them.

The room was mostly dark. He stepped onto the cold floor and went to the window to raise the *Rolladen*. Outside there was a wannabe snow, the kind of tiny flakes that kept falling but never seemed to stick to the ground. He was sure they were falling to annoy him.

A shower did nothing to improve his mood. He was hungry, but he knew the refrigerator was empty. He'd get a *Brötchen* and coffee on the way at the little café near the station.

He'd made *Polizeioberkommissar,* the D2 rank, last year and was already angling for the next promotion. However, today, he didn't really care. He was tired, he had a new case on top of too many cases, and he needed to up his solve rate.

As he locked his studio door, his cell rang.

"Don't even try and see the boys this weekend. I won't have them disappointed again."

How could he once have thought his soon-to-be-ex-wife had such a lovely speaking voice? Who was he kidding? She did have a beautiful voice, speaking and singing. It was one of the things he fell in love with. But the nagging to spend more time at home, to spend more time with her, to spend more time with the boys, had put an edge into it that made him think of knives slicing into flesh.

Maybe his own guilt made him imagine the things he shouldn't be thinking.

Maybe if he had tried harder, he could have convinced her that he was not working just for his own advancement, but to better provide for his family, but he hadn't tried at all, thinking she should have known. His father had never worked all that hard before the Wall had come down. He hadn't worked that hard after the Wall had come down either. He'd been content to come home and read his paper, turn on the television and sit with a beer that he made last all evening.

"What if I come by when I can? If they're free I can spend time with them. Then they won't be disappointed if something comes up."

His wife did not respond.

"Are you there?"

"As long as you don't expect me to sit around and wait for you. I'm building a new Hans-Peter-free life, which really isn't all that much different than when you were here."

Hans-Peter started to say something, but thought better. Inflaming the situation would achieve nothing. *"Danke."*

"Aufwiederhören." The line went dead.

Last night, he'd arranged to meet Fritz at the *Leichenschauhaus* at nine. Claudia had promised them that she would do the autopsy first thing. Watching a body being cut up was his least favorite part of the job, but he'd learned long ago that often as he watched, he thought of questions. At least he didn't faint—in fact he'd never fainted, although when the knife began its Y cut on the chest, a wave of queasiness would ride from his stomach to his throat. Willpower made him force it down each time.

Lübeck was made up of ten zones and he lived as far away

from the *Leichenschauhaus* as was possible, not that it was a choice. His wife had found his studio, rented it and handed him the key after she'd moved his things into it without telling him.

Morning traffic was a bit lighter than usual and he had no idea why. It was still too long until Christmas for people to be taking holiday. Just thinking about the holidays made him unhappy. He pulled over in front of the *Kaffee*, put the *Polizei* sign on the dashboard and went in.

The woman behind the counter smiled as she always did, a quick smile, one that passed over her lips and disappeared. She was probably his age, attractive and with a wedding band on her right hand. Without being asked, she poured him a cup of coffee, wrapped up a *Brötchen* still warm from the oven and handed it to him. As a matter of principle, he paid her and stood at one of the round bolted-down tables, ignoring the high stools as he gulped down the roll and coffee before leaving the cup and dish for the waitstaff to clean up.

By the time he reached the *Leichenschauhaus*, Claudia, wearing her autopsy clothes, including a mask over her mouth, which he knew contained a few drops of mint to overcome the smells, already had the corpse on the table.

Fritz was seated above the floor. "At least, this will be a low-pressure case. No one cares about Asians."

His partner was right. In Lübeck a bit more than one percent of the population was Asian. He imagined they were even rarer in Kirchdorf, but he would need to check that out.

"Glad you could make it," Claudia looked up at the gallery.

There was a new *Diener* helping her. He had positioned the body on the table and now was taking photos from all angles while Claudia positioned three video cameras. Ever since she had had a problem with a murder case, she filmed everything, not being content with tapes and transcripts to substantiate in court what she had done.

"I doubt there is much point in doing this, but I'll check under the fingernails and toenails anyway."

Hans-Peter agreed, but he knew better than to say anything while she was working. Had the young woman fought back against the killer, everything would have been washed away by the sea.

Claudia collected skin scrapings. "I'm sure this will show salt and mineral content from the water as well as some sand. I've brought samples from the ocean in Kirchdorf as well as some sand for lab comparison.

"Damage, probably from sea life, to the little finger, right hand," she started and listed every bite that the "sea life" had taken along with its dimensions. "One of the critters lost a tooth." She pulled it out with tweezers and held it up to show Hans-Peter and Fritz.

"Does she think we're going to arrest a fish with a missing tooth?" Fritz muttered.

"Quiet." Hans-Peter did not want Claudia to get upset at any noise. He'd worked too hard on building a good working rapport with her to have Fritz's black humor disturb the medical examiner.

Hans-Peter had once driven Claudia home when her car had been in the garage. Her home was as pristine as the autopsy room and her office, where everything was always in place. If she took something out, she put it back.

As long as he did not have to live with someone that compulsive, he appreciated her accuracy, which made his job easier. When he lived with his wife, the confusion and lack of order in the house had annoyed him. Compulsively neat might not be as bad as he imagined. She was one attractive woman, and she would understand his need to work as many hours as he did.

Watching the autopsy meant that he did not have to wait for

the first reports. Some lab results would be delayed, but he could start working the case.

Working the case of an unknown victim made the task difficult if not impossible. Had the girl been German or even been living locally he might have had a slightly better chance. Along with his other hates, he decided to add unknown victims of Asian descent.

No, he told himself, don't be so negative. He was working for the victims. That was what his first boss, his mentor, had told him. They were speaking for those who could no longer speak for themselves. Only he didn't speak Chinese or Japanese or Korean or whatever language she spoke. He forced himself to concentrate on digesting what Claudia was saying.

Female.

Ninety-eight pounds.

Five foot nothing.

Asian, she guessed Filipino but couldn't guarantee it. Hans-Peter had faith that her guess might be close to reality.

The *Diener* put a body block under the woman's back, raising the chest to make the traditional Y-shaped initial cut from each shoulder down to the sternum easier. Hans-Peter swallowed hard several times. He hated seeing the exposed organs, which once functioned. They made him think of his own organs hidden under the tissue.

"Her lungs are clear, which means she was already dead when she went into the water," Claudia said. "There's some scar tissue which indicates she might have had TB."

Because Claudia had trained in the UK, she removed the organs in four blocks.

She bent over. "Damn. She was pregnant. Just."

By the end of the autopsy Hans-Peter knew that the young woman was just that, very young, in her late teens. Her vagina had been well used, and a .44 Magnum bullet had lodged in her heart.

By the time Hans-Peter and Fritz left the *Leichenschauhaus* it was almost lunchtime. Neither felt like eating. Instead, they headed back to headquarters. The wannabe snow was still falling and still not accumulating. The wind must be coming in from the Baltic, carrying with it a fishy smell.

Hans-Peter decided to write up his report so far then go meet his sons as they came out of school. Both boys rushed into his arms, fighting for hugs. He walked home with them where the babysitter waited. They were almost of an age where they could be left alone, but both he and his wife thought it better that they feel supervised. At least that was one thing upon which they agreed.

Just as he entered his old home, his cell rang.

"Don't answer it Papa, *bitte*," his older son said.

"*Polizeioberkommissar* Leiter."

"This is Annie Young. I went back to the beach to get some photos of the bad weather and sea grass. There's another body."

As he left, his older son looked at him. "*Mutti* is right. You care more about your job than you do about us."

CHAPTER 15

Kirchdorf, Insel Poel, Germany
"The Kirchdorf church, which is now Lutheran, has a 1450 triumphal cross and a 13th century Danish gravestone, re-affirming how closely the island had been tied to not only its Slavic roots, but its Scandinavian."

The History of Insel Poel by Manfred Dederich

"I'm a serial body finder, not a serial killer," Annie said to Hans-Peter Leiter and his assistant Fritz Gärtner as they sat around Annie's table. Even their coats, which they had not removed, smelled cold.

Annie waited for the percolator to stop gurgling. As much as she loved the smell of coffee, drinking it made her jumpy, but she knew it wasn't the caffeine. She could drink Coke or tea, both of which had caffeine, without the jumpiness. The kettle next to the percolator shut off and she poured the hot water over a teabag.

What she wanted to do most was to hold the hot cup between her hands. She'd waited in her car for a long time with the poor local policeman and when the police hadn't arrived, she told him where the Lübeck police could find her. They had arrived about fifteen minutes after she had come in her front door, not giving her time for the hot shower which would have warmed her bones.

"You shouldn't have left," Hans-Peter said from his seated

position. He accepted the mug of coffee she put in front of him.

"Was the body still there?" Annie asked.

"*Ja*. The medical examiner is doing her thing now. I should be there."

Annie didn't point out that what he'd done with the first body was stand around. With the filming, he could watch the videos from the warmth of his office.

She continued, "You saw the body was in a different place as if a different tide brought it in?"

"I saw." He tapped the smoked-gray-glass tabletop. "What were you doing at the beach?"

"I told you when I called; I wanted to get some photos of the beach grass for my blog." On her last two assignments, Annie had started a blog using photos and descriptions of where she was working. Somehow, it helped Roger feel more a part of what she was doing and reduced the tension that still existed whenever she was away from him. She handed Hans-Peter the camera. "Look."

He flipped through the photos. In one Annie had lain on the sand so the grass looked like trees. In another two ships, one probably an oil carrier and the other looking like a small cruise ship, were out in the water. Most of the other shots were of the room they were sitting in, the museum and things from the museum. He handed the camera back.

"This girl looked even younger and Asian. Are you going to check on the ships in the photo? I can e-mail them to you." Annie gave Fritz his coffee, and after getting her own cup of tea, sat at the table with the two men. Because hers was too hot to drink, she blew on it.

"Are you telling me my job?"

"Not at all." What she really wanted to do was tell the detective he was an asshole.

"And you shouldn't have left."

"The local policeman was there so you know the scene wasn't disturbed. The body was far enough up that it wasn't in any danger from the tides." She hated stating the obvious. That poor, old cop. He'd said that he was retiring in a week: he didn't need this at the end of his career. He'd told her that he and his wife were moving to the South of Spain after the holidays and all he'd wanted was his last week to be peaceful. "Do you think it could have been there yesterday and we didn't see it?"

Hans-Peter and Fritz looked at each other.

"Possible, not probable," Fritz said.

"She didn't look like she'd been in the water, just shot," Annie said.

"How do you figure?" Fritz's comment brought a glare from his boss.

"She was too far up on the beach to have been washed up. There was sand over her as if someone was trying to do a small cover-up. She was naked so her skin blended better with the sand." Maybe she shouldn't be telling the police how to do their job.

Hans-Peter finished his coffee and pushed the cup aside. "We need to get back to the crime scene."

Fritz gulped the last of his coffee.

Annie locked the door behind them and put the mugs in the dishwasher. Glancing in the fridge, she realized she wasn't hungry, even though she'd stocked it with healthy veggies.

Six in the evening was much too early to go to bed, but a hot shower would be relaxing.

Once in her pajamas she curled up on the couch and put on the television. There were about 300 channels from almost any country she could imagine. She settled on the Russian, which was broadcasting in English when her cell phone rang.

"Bonsoir ma chérie. Je t'aime."

"I love you too, Roger. You'll never guess what happened today."

"You know I hate guessing games."

She pulled the afghan up over legs. "I found another body."

"YOU WHAT?"

She knew he wouldn't appreciate the serial-body-finder line she'd used with the Lübeck police. Instead she talked about how she'd stumbled across the second body and how arrogant Hans-Peter was.

"He doesn't even respond to my suggestions."

Roger laughed then stopped. "I told you the other night, don't even think about doing anything yourself."

"Hmmm."

"Annie, I mean it."

CHAPTER 16

Hamburg, Germany
November 1942

Hilke was exhausted. Work had been hectic: then she'd stopped at Else's apartment to admire her new son after picking up potatoes, sausage and carrots for her mother. Although she tried not to be jealous, she was. Else's husband and hers had both been home on leave at the same time. That was fourteen months ago, the last time she'd seen Dieter.

Else had become pregnant. Hilke had had her period the entire three days she and Dieter were together. No amount of cuddling creates babies. Dieter had said it was all right, but it hadn't been. And he wasn't all right either. He awoke screaming the three nights they had shared her childhood bed. Her parents had come rushing in.

Her father had told her that he too had had nightmares when he first came home from the last war.

As she walked from her friend's house to her own, fog was rolling in from the river, leaving everything damp. Hilke pulled out her mittens, which her mother had just made for her using yarn from a sweater no longer worth saving. Käthe now spent most of her time knitting socks and scarves that Hilke took to the depository for contributions for the troops.

As she entered the building, she spied Frau Fritzler, who lived on the floor above the Fülmers' and was coming out, holding her grandson's hand. The five-year-old was known for the tantrums he threw. The other residents often heard him screaming. Tonight he seemed calm.

"*Guten Abend,* Frau Fritzler." Hilke held the door. The woman shrank away from Hilke. She acts as if I had leprosy, Hilke thought, the old cow. The neighbor had never been friendly. She never invited anyone in for coffee and always complained that the other tenants never properly cleaned the hallways as well as she did when it was her *Kehr Woche* to do so. About the only good thing one could say about Frau Fritzler was that she wasn't a gossip, but Hilke guessed that was because no one would share any gossip with her.

She stood looking after her neighbor just long enough for the hall light to go out. She pushed the button and the hall was bathed in a dim light again, casting its usual eerie shadows. As a child she had been afraid of the corridor and would only go through it with her mother, father or Joseph. The walls needed paint; the carpet was worn.

When Hilke arrived at her front door, key in hand, the door was ajar. The lights inside were out. Then the hall light went out.

"*Mutti?*" she called into the darkness.

Her mother didn't answer.

She walked toward the closest table, which held a lamp, and tripped on an overturned chair. "*Shei*β." If her mother had been in the flat she would have scolded Hilke for using an impolite word, but there was only silence. Picking herself up, she made it to the table.

She righted the lamp, which was lying on the table, and pushed the switch. At least the bulb hadn't broken and its dim light revealed the devastation.

Books from the shelves were scattered over the rug. A figurine of a shepherdess, which her father had given her mother years ago, was smashed. Family photos were taken from picture frames.

She shivered. There was no heat emanating from the living room ceramic stove that dominated one wall of the apartment and was used to warm most of the room. Probably the smaller stoves in the other rooms were not on either. Hilke could see her breath.

Hilke picked up the telephone receiver, but there was no dial tone. The wire had been ripped from the wall.

"Hilke, I'm so sorry."

She jumped at the soft voice of Frau Ratz, a neighbor who was as friendly as Frau Fritzler was nasty. Sometimes Hilke had wondered how the human species could produce such variations and have them all living on the same floor.

Frau Ratz went to put her arms around Hilke, the same way she had done when Hilke was a little girl and had stayed with her when her parents went out. She kept a toy box for both Hilke and Joseph until they were too old for the toys. Her nieces and nephews would also play with the toys when they visited. Hilke had wondered why a woman who so loved children never had any of her own, but then she was now in the same position: childless—although hopefully that would change when the war was over and she and Dieter could live a normal life.

Frau Ratz was thin, her still-blonde hair in a chignon. "I'm so, so sorry."

Hilke didn't understand what the woman was sorry about. "What happened?"

"About an hour ago, the SS came and took your mother away."

Hilke spent the next two hours putting books back on the shelf and sweeping up shards of picture glass and figurines, after refusing Frau Ratz's offer of help. Her mother, despite her refusals to go out or have people in, had kept the apartment spotless. Nothing was left out of place long. At least when her mother got back everything would be as normal as possible. If her mother came back, that is. When she checked her parents' bedroom, she saw that her mother had not taken any clothes.

She hadn't.

Hilke could not understand what the SS would want with her mother. It made no sense.

Where was her father? He didn't answer at the university when she'd called using Frau Ratz's telephone, but no one would be there that late. Nothing was said about him being late when they had drunk their ersatz coffee that morning. There was nothing on the calendar that her mother kept in the top drawer that marked his meetings or Hilke's plans to visit friends.

In her own room, Hilke slipped her shoes off and lay down under her *Eiderdown*. She didn't undress, but she wasn't sure why. She couldn't imagine the SS would come back for her, but she couldn't have imagined the SS taking her mother anywhere, a woman who'd barely left the building for the last three years. Sleep was impossible. Different things that she might do ran through her mind: go to SS headquarters, wait for her father, call her lawyer-boss—but she did none of them, because she had no idea what was the best thing to do.

At midnight, she heard the front door open. She threw off the warmth of the *Eiderdown* and tiptoed to her bedroom door, which she had left open slightly. Because she had left the light with the lowest wattage on, she could see her father stumble slightly over nothing. *Mein Gott*, she thought, he must be drunk.

He looked up and saw her. "Is it over? Your mother is gone?"

"Frau Ratz said that the SS took her."

He slumped into the olive brocade chair with the matching fringe and put his head in his hands. "I hated to do it."

"Do what?"

"Turn her in."

Hilke felt as if she were walking through the fog outside where nothing was visible and images she thought she recognized became something else. "Turn her in for what?"

"Being Jewish?"

"*Mutti* isn't Jewish." She might as well have been saying, "*Mutti* isn't a man, or an elephant." The smell of stale beer hit her as she walked over to her father and stood above him. She could see his bald spot in the middle of his head.

He didn't look at his daughter. "All her grandparents were. Her parents converted. That makes her Jewish."

Hilke sank to her knees. "Did you know?"

He still didn't look at her. "I knew. That is why we sent Joseph to England."

Why not me, she wondered.

"He was such a promising scholar. I couldn't let his brain . . ."

Hilke knew that her brother's intellect had been a major source of pride for her parents, and her ordinary mind was just that—ordinary. When they sent Joseph away, there was not that much talk of Jews, or if there was no one paid much attention. Then one of her father's Jewish friends and colleagues had been forced out of his job: and after that another and another.

"But they wouldn't have known, if you'd kept quiet?" Hilke asked.

Her father said nothing. He started to get up, but fell back into the chair.

Hilke felt the way she did when she woke in the middle of the night with cramps in her legs. The mental pain was excruciating. "Why, why did you tell them?" Her words came out a whisper.

This time he looked at her. "What else could I do? My work at the university . . ."

Hilke stood up and backed away from him all the way to the door. She grabbed her coat and ran from the flat.

Staying close to the buildings in the shadows where she wouldn't be spotted, she ran to her in-laws. Now her mother not going anywhere made sense, but why didn't either her mother or father tell her, and how could her father turn his wife, the mother of his two children, in to the SS. No bad film, no stupid novel would ever try and make sense of this.

At her in-laws' she rang the bell and her father-in-law opened the door. He wore flannel pajamas. Her mother-in-law was behind him. "Hilke, what is it?"

Sobbing, she told them what happened.

"You'll spend tonight in Dieter's room, but you can't stay here after that," her father-in-law said. "It would be too dangerous for us."

"But I'm not Jewish."

"We can't risk it," he said.

"Of course, we can," Freja said. "She's like our daughter. What would Dieter say to think we turned his wife out?"

"He would understand."

Freja led Hilke to Dieter's bedroom that was only a few steps long and not much wider. His medical books were on a shelf over his desk. That and a small oak *Schrank* for his civilian clothes and a single bed left almost no floor space.

Freja helped Hilke off with her coat and taking her by the shoulders had her sit on the bed. She left and was back in minutes with a flannel nightgown, washcloth, towel and toothbrush.

Hilke had not moved. "My father, my father . . . I can't believe he would . . ."

Freja said nothing: she simply started to help Hilke undress, but Hilke pushed her away. "I can do it." She didn't want to hurt her mother-in-law's feelings. "I'm sorry. I don't want to be rude."

"In these times, ordinary rules no longer apply."

"I'll leave in the morning."

"Don't worry, we'll find someplace for you to stay," Freja said. She put a lighted candle on the headboard. "So the dark won't be as frightening."

The door closed and Hilke lay in bed. Any hope her father or her in-laws would try and help her mother died as she blew out the candle. Light or dark made no difference. Terror for her mother as well as for herself battled with anger that her parents had kept such a secret from her all her life. She suspected Joseph did not know either, for he would have told her, although at that point she wasn't sure of anything as far as her family was concerned. At least he was safe, the beloved child. She wished she could find a way to get to England and join him.

Through the walls, she heard her in-laws talking. She couldn't make out all the words, but she was positive her father-in-law said something about the necessity of getting Dieter to divorce her.

CHAPTER 17

Colerne, Wiltshire, England
November 1942

"You won't forget the Ladies Flower Committee meeting on Tuesday, will you?" Vicar Harold Willson stood at the door of the vicarage with his hat in one hand, his coat over his arm, and his luggage in the other hand. A few red-colored leaves whirled on the brick walk leading to the gate and the main road.

"Mable Lafferty is trying to stage a coup and throw Janet Masters off the committee and wants to replace her with a friend who will guarantee that she has her way on all the arrangements."

"I have it in my calendar, not the political part, of course, in case someone sees it," Martha Willson, his daughter said. Stop letting in the cold, she thought. It will take forever to reheat the house. Leave for your diocese meeting. Reassure him and maybe he'll go. "Also I know about the carpenter coming to fix the floorboard, and to call John Steele if anyone dies. If anyone is sick, I will go around in your place." Go, go, go, she thought. St. John the Baptist Church has stood since the time of the Normans, it will last a few days without you.

"I should leave a chaperone with you."

No, you shouldn't, she thought. I'm twenty-four. She suspected her father was more worried about her virginity than he was about his own entrance into heaven. Keeping the vicarage and serving as his wife-in-absentia, since her mother died five years ago, left her little time to do anything much at all, never mind anything bad. Not that she wanted to be bad, she just wanted to have her own life, whatever that might be.

"And don't go near the air base. I hear some Yanks are coming in to fly with our boys, and you know what trouble that means."

"Father, you'll miss your train."

"I've enough time. And don't go filling the tub. I don't care if government says to use only five inches of water. You use four."

"Your train, Father."

"And don't forget to make sure the apples that Peter will deliver later are properly stored. And it is the time to make apple butter. Only use half. We'll eat the rest."

"Your train."

He left. No kisses good-bye. Kisses and physical touching were out. Martha never remembered her parents hugging or kissing. Nor did she remember them arguing. Life in this vicarage and the previous one had always been of quiet talk, tiptoeing to not disturb her father when he was working on his sermons.

Martha went to the kitchen and put on a kettle, planning to sit and read for an hour. At least she had been spared the "you can't be careful enough with your reputation" lecture by the wonderful train schedule.

She would fulfill all her church duties while her father was away for the week, but she was freed from providing meals, cleaning and all the other chores. Her plans included meeting Ruth for tea. Ruth was pregnant by one of those "flyboys" her father spoke of in the same way he spoke of the devil, but Ruth's flyboy had married her.

Martha went upstairs and put on an extra sweater against the cold wind that would hit her as she cycled into the village.

★ ★ ★ ★ ★

Ruth Ames was seated at the little round table closest to the door of the tearoom when Martha entered. They had been best friends from their first year of school. The table, one of four, was covered with an almost-white linen tablecloth that had a tea stain from an earlier customer. They wouldn't bother to show it to Sally, the owner, who had the attitude, if you didn't like something, go someplace else—only there was no place else to go.

As young women, they continued to meet every Tuesday afternoon despite Vicar Willson's disapproval of Ruth as a wanton woman. Even when they were still in school, he'd thought Ruth was much too fast for his daughter to be around. While his wife was alive, she would calm him down and say that Ruth was one of the most honest girls she knew. He would hem and haw and say, "Blurting out something without thinking doesn't necessarily make a person honest."

"I've already ordered tea," Ruth said as Martha took her seat. "Did your father get off without any problem this morning?"

"He left in a flurry of last-minute instructions and a fear I would debase myself . . ." Martha's hands flew to her mouth. "I'm sorry. I wasn't . . ."

"Making nasty remarks about me having to get married." Ruth rubbed her stomach, whose curve seemed to grow bigger each time the two women met up. "I know you weren't. It seems girls are either getting married before their boyfriends go to war in case they don't come back, or not marrying them in case they don't come back. And I'm sure more than one of us has been caught like I was and needed to go into hiding with whatever excuses their parents could come up with."

"But Alan married you."

"Still people will say for years how I had to get married."

Sally waddled over and plunked a pot of tea on the table

along with two slices of bread and honey. Rationing had put a small crimp in her offerings, but her pastries had never been wonderful anyway so it didn't much matter. The honey came from Francis Pull's hives. At least the local farmers were providing some of the things that locals needed.

When the owner had disappeared back into the small room behind the counter where she prepared her so-so concoctions, Ruth went on. "Besides, we won't live in Colerne after the war. We'll go up to Lancaster where his parents are from." Ruth reached into her bag and brought out a plain, thick white envelope. "You have to read this." She handed it to Martha.

Martha scanned the neatly printed two pages. "Amazing. Alan's mum is welcoming you to the family and she says that she's looking forward to a grandson or granddaughter."

"Not many mothers would do that. The only reason mine didn't throw me out was because, when I told her I was pregnant, I was already married."

Martha didn't want to think about what her father would do if she were in that situation. Burn her at the stake probably. Vicar Willson's God was not a forgiving one, but rather a God that would seek out sins and destroy the sinner, which was one of the reasons that Martha had given up on her father's version of the faith, while holding to a strong belief in a loving and forgiving God.

The two did not discuss religion because Martha's beliefs were an anathema to her father, who claimed his theological degree made his ideas the only right ones anywhere in the entire universe. Martha lived by the rule "Silence is Golden" when it came to her father. Let him think what he wanted: that kept his problems from becoming hers, or at least it did some of the time.

Martha did not want to think of Ruth's leaving Colerne. Her life ahead was going to be a series of chores for her father. She had no real training to enable her to get a job, and even if she had, she lacked the nerve to broach the subject. Like the Great War generation, she would be consigned to spinsterhood because too many men had been lost fighting for England.

Spinsterhood didn't really bother her as much as the idea of living a long life without anything of importance happening other than sorting out power struggles in the Ladies Flower Committee. She'd never been anywhere, not even out of Wiltshire, not even to Stonehenge. Her father had never taken a holiday at the seaside.

She didn't really fancy joining the Women's Land Army just to get away. Farming was not something at which she would be good. She had no medical training so being a nurse or even an ambulance driver was out of the question. In a way she felt that driving through a battlefield would be a little less daunting than telling her father that she was going to contribute to the war effort other than knitting endless socks and scarves. There was one thing, though, she had seriously been thinking about.

As Martha poured first milk then the tea into the two cups she said, "I've been thinking of joining the WAAFs. I've been out to the base a couple times on my bike, but then I've turned back."

Ruth clapped her hands together like a small child would do on being given a chocolate, a rarer and rarer treat with rationing. "That's a wonderful idea. What stopped you?" She looked at her friend. "You've got to break away from your father. How can he object to you serving your country . . . never mind . . . he would lose a household slave and church secretary all at the same time."

Martha wanted to say Ruth wasn't being fair, but she knew her friend was using information that Martha herself had given her.

"I've an idea. Alan's off tonight and I'll ask him to get all the information you need about joining up," Ruth said. "It will only take a moment out of the romantic evening I've planned."

"What about your mother?"

"Bridge night."

Before Martha could respond, the door of the tearoom opened, letting in a draft. The person entering wore an RAF pilot's uniform and carried himself as if on parade. He headed toward the table where the two women were sitting. "There you are, Ruth: your mum said I could find you here." He took off his hat and twirled it in his hands.

Ruth indicated he should sit down, which he did. "I can't stay. I'm bringing a message from Alan. He has to go on a mission tonight."

Ruth frowned. "Does that mean . . . who didn't come back?"

"Dickie Jones."

"Oh no." Ruth's face crumbled. "He was such a sweet kid, even for a Welshman."

"No one saw him ditch. Sometimes . . ."

"Sometimes they bail out and end up in prison camps."

"Don't forget Howard. He walked out and ended up getting a boat across the channel," Alan said.

"Howard spoke French better than the French." Ruth looked at Martha, who hadn't moved since the conversation between her friend and the airman had begun. "I'm being rude. Martha Willson, this is Gordon Tibbitts, one of Alan's best mates. Gordon, this is my best friend forever, Martha Willson."

The two shook hands. "Pleased to meet you," they said in unison then laughed.

"Tea?" Martha asked.

"I have to get back to base. I've desk duty starting in an hour." He stood up and looked at Martha. "I hope to see you again."

★ ★ ★ ★ ★

"Did Ruth believe you?" Alan tucked in his shirt and zipped up his civilian pants. He reached for his suit jacket.

Gordon was sitting on his bunk watching Alan get ready to go up to London for a "weekend of frolic" as he called it. "Of course, she did. Although I had to use poor Dickie as a reason you were on a mission." He lay down on his bunk, his hands behind his head. "You know if anyone sees you on the train, they'll tell her."

"I know you think I'm a real cad, but after the war, if I survive, I'll settle down and be a wonderful husband and father. In the meantime, I want to live life to the fullest."

Gordon had no answer for that. He wondered if he were jealous of Alan with his good looks and perfect teeth. No flower attracted as many bees. He had to smile at the image of Alan's face on a honeysuckle with a swarm of bees. It wasn't poetic. Bees sucked vital elements from flowers. He did not want to carry the image into honey making.

That was his problem: he thought too much. He turned off girls when he was younger and women now that he was in his early thirties. Granted it had earned him top grades at Balliol College at Oxford University, where he'd read economics, and an offer as a lecturer at the University of Glasgow before the war changed his life. He felt he was following in the steps of Adam Smith at both places, but at no time did he feel the equal of the great economist. He never regretted he had not followed his other love, astronomy, which he still practiced as a hobby.

The title of Doctor had given way to Flight Lieutenant. There was no need now to have theories of patterns of buying behavior. His goals now were places where he could drop a bomb that would reduce the time of the war. He closed his mind to the fact that innocent people might die because he released a lever above them. No calculation, no mathematical formula would be able to separate the people who were good from those that were bad that died in a war.

He brought his mind back to his room in the barracks at Colerne Field and his friend. "Alan, I'm not going to tell you what to do."

"And I wouldn't listen anyway."

"Which is why, I won't waste my breath. Ruth is lovely. I would hate to see her hurt."

Alan stuffed a change of underwear into his duffel bag. "I won't hurt her."

Making a fool of her is hurting her, even if she doesn't know it, Gordon thought. His parents, especially his mother, had always emphasized one must treat people fairly even if others didn't. She was a widow, having survived the Blitz that killed his father. When he'd been stationed at Colerne with RAF Squadron 184, she had rented a small cottage in Colerne, both for safety and to be nearer her only living relative. Some Sundays if she could get as good a joint from the butcher as rationing would allow, she would invite Alan, Dickie, Thomas and Gordon for a good home-cooked meal.

He still had to tell her about Dickie. He knew she'd be sad and glad at the same time. Sad, that this young man, who danced with her after lunch to music on the wireless, was gone, and glad that her son was still alive.

Whenever Gordon dropped a bomb, he tried to make himself believe that he was avenging his father, but good sense told him that the people targeted were not the same ones who had flown the plane over London the night his father died. The only justification he could come up with was that each of his actions might shorten the war, thus saving more lives long-term rather than short-term.

He would never share these thoughts with any of his other buddies in his unit. They were all for getting every Jerry they could and the more the Jerries suffered, the happier they were. Or maybe it was just like the bragging that men did about the number of women bedded. Only in his roommate Alan's case it was true: marriage might have slowed him down but it sure hadn't stopped him.

"I found Ruth in the tea shop. She was with a friend . . . pretty but not beautiful. Her name was Martha, Martha something."

"That must be Martha Willson. She's the vicar's daughter."

Gordon didn't say anything as he pictured Martha's smile and wavy brown hair worn short so it curled around her face, not long and up like most women wore theirs.

"Don't even think about her. Her father watches her like a hawk. Rapunzel locked in the tower had more freedom with men than that poor girl." Alan put on his jacket against the cool night air and picked up his duffel bag. "I'm off. Wish me happy hunting, if you can."

"Happy hunting." Gordon did mean it, sort of. He never felt he could decide things for others. They didn't want what he wanted and vice versa—he could want for them what they desired even if he disagreed.

Long after Alan left, Gordon stayed on his bunk thinking about Martha Willson. Even if he were an atheist maybe he should start going to church.

CHAPTER 18

Kirchdorf, Insel Poel, Germany
"The Treaty of Westphalia in 1648 granted two-thirds of Poel together with the large town of Wismar and the municipality of Neukloster to the King of Sweden."

The History of Insel Poel by Manfred Dederich

Annie settled in with the *The History of Insel Poel*. The more she got done on the Dutch, French and English translations here, the less she would have to do when she left. The last thing she wanted was to be tied to her computer during the holidays.

Before she left, she might have a chance to meet with Herr Manfred Dederich. Or she might not if he were having one of his off days. Renate Klausson had warned her that he was old, pedantic and more than a bit annoyed that they were not letting him do his own English translation, although he was satisfied that someone was doing the French and Dutch. "Frankly, we're hoping you can lighten it up a bit," Renate had said.

Making the text easier to read would not be difficult. Herr Dederich believed you never used one word if you could find ten to say the same thing. Fortunately, Renate had told her, he did not have editorial approval of the final English translation, the only other language that the writer knew. Something, she said, for which to be grateful.

When Annie'd sat down at her laptop, she thought work would get her mind off the dead bodies, especially the second one who'd seemed so young. A life not given a chance to live is stolen, she thought.

She wished she had more confidence in Hans-Peter Leiter. Granted, many people who were arrogant had reason to be. Personality and competence were not a necessary correlation.

Twenty minutes later, she'd translated one sentence. Her mind would not stay on topic. Had she promised Roger not to go investigating on her own?

No, she hadn't.

Besides, he couldn't object if she did a little nosing around the Internet. Moving out of her word processing program, she went to Dogpile.com, her favorite search engine for the cute little dog pictures on the home page. The first site she checked was useless unless she'd planned to take a cruise.

The second site wanted to sell her some equipment to trace any number of moving objects. Interesting, but unhelpful.

Then she hit upon a map with little red arrows, but had difficulty getting to the Baltic Sea. She found herself jumping around the Atlantic, the Channel and suddenly she was in the Indian Ocean. "Damn." She spotted the arrows, which took her directly to the Baltic and markers for each ship.

Could it be possible there were only three ships, two German, one Russian. All three were just off the coast. The information gave the country, the type of ship, its course, speed, track and more. And none of it meant much to Annie since she didn't know knots or that much about shipping. Her idea of boating was taking the steamer around Lake Léman, which at no point lost sight of the French or Swiss shorelines, sit on the deck and have a gourmet meal served to her.

She widened her search to distances that a ship might have reached in a reasonable time after throwing two bodies in the water. Even that wasn't terribly productive because she couldn't guess how long the bodies had been in the water. She wasn't even sure if the second body had been in the water. It was not impossible that everyone had missed it the first time.

Chances were good that two Asian girls would not have been on the two German military ships. She wouldn't rule out the Russian cargo ship. Maybe the sailors had picked up Asian girls in some port. Too much imagination, Roger would say.

A mistake she might be making was thinking that whatever ship had dumped the bodies was traceable. Maybe it was a smaller ship, a pleasure boat.

Tomorrow she would go talk to the harbormaster without mentioning it to Roger at all.

CHAPTER 19

Kirchdorf, Insel Poel, Germany
"It took approximately 140 years to build the church, which is in both Romanesque and Gothic style."

The History of Insel Poel by Manfred Dederich

"Do you want to come to lunch?" Renate asked. "You can meet my husband."

"I'd love to, but I've a couple of things I need to do. Any chance of a rain check?"

Renate searched through her purse for her agenda. "Tomorrow? Maybe dinner?" She delved into her purse and located her car key. That she found anything or could even lift the bag with all the things she toted around was a miracle.

Annie nodded as she went out the door and headed for the harbor. The noontime sun reflected off the clean snow. Thank goodness for her dark glasses, but even with them she had to squint.

The harbor was not all that big. On one side was a three-story, light-yellow stucco apartment building. To the left was a fish restaurant with two customers, both men sitting in the window. Annie decided to have lunch there when she finished. The yellow-brick building marked *Hafenmeister* was locked and had a telephone number.

Directly in front of the building was a bench made from a rough-hewn log. Annie sat on it to check out the scene, being careful not to hit her head on the statue of the fisherman that hovered over the back of the bench. Roger couldn't object to her just *looking*.

In the small parking area was a truck with writing that indicated it was used to carry polo ponies. Its back was open and empty. A faded blue truck, circa ancient, filled with ropes and fishing gear, was next to a Maserati and a Ferrari. Now that was an interesting social demographic comment, she thought. The island didn't seem to support that kind of wealth.

"You won't find anyone in there." A man in need of a shave and wearing rubber overalls tilted his head toward the *Hafenmeister Haus*.

"Will he be back soon?"

The man walked to the old truck and lifted some nets from the back. These he carried to a boat that looked as old as the truck. It had a cabin that Annie couldn't see into because of the angle. Fishing equipment, or what she guessed was fishing equipment, was tied tightly to the sides. The man jumped down.

"Only if you call the number on the door. He doesn't have much to do here."

"So what if someone is bringing stuff from Russia: where would they clear customs?"

"The main port, unless of course they were bringing in cocaine, heroin or anything else illegal. Then they would just wait until late in the day and unload the stuff."

"Does that happen very often?"

The man unlocked the door of the cabin and put the key in the pocket that ran across his chest. "Not really. Or at least not that I know about." He cocked his head. "You aren't from around here."

"I'm just here for a couple of weeks. I'm working on a project with the museum."

"Never been there."

"You going fishing?"

"Got a late start today, but thought I'd take a run. Sea trout are good at this time of year, but it is so cold, it's hard to stay out there long. Today . . . ?" He pointed toward the sun. Without the wind it wasn't uncomfortable.

After the boat pulled away from the dock, Annie headed for the restaurant. She chose a window seat behind the men she'd seen earlier.

"Bezahlen, bitte," one snapped his fingers. Annie was sure that the waitress had seen them and was pretending not to. Instead of rushing over with the check, she ambled up to Annie with the menu.

She chose the sea trout and French fries. What she was craving was salads and veggies. She'd make some tonight.

After the men paid and left, Annie gazed out the window at the dock and weather. She imagined it would be lovely in summer, but certainly not as deserted. In the distance, a boat approached. It was large. She wished she knew one boat from another. It looked as if it had interior cabins and there was a deck that ran around them.

When it docked, four people appeared on deck: two men and two young women. The women, both scantily dressed, kissed the men good-bye in anything but a wifely fashion.

The men wore overcoats that were finely cut. One had a haircut which looked like the barber had cut each hair individually using a ruler to get it just right. The other's hair curled over the scarf around his neck. Annie guessed the scarf was silk.

As soon as the men's feet touched the dock, the women scuttled inside the cabins.

The men chatted as they walked to the Maserati and Ferrari. The curly haired one leaned against the hood as they continued the conversation. From their body language, Annie gathered the topic could be sports, hunting, stock investments or which car might go faster on the *Autobahn.*

Then they drove off.

CHAPTER 20

Hamburg, Germany
November 1942

Hilke was the first one into the office that smelled of leather law books and pipe tobacco. Without taking her coat off, she looked around the darkened room. Only a small amount of light peeked through the slats of the *Rolladen*. They creaked as she opened them. The sun reflecting off the snow hurt her eyes. She thought she saw two *Polizisten* walking along the street, bathed in light, giving them the same glow as a painting of angels, which had hung in the youth hall of the Lutheran church where she and her friends had once gone to parties, but when her eyes adjusted to the brightness, she realized that they were SS.

She shuddered.

The way the taller put his head back and laughed as he opened the door of the café across the street made her want to take a gun and force them to tell her where her mother was, but she knew she lacked the courage with or without a gun.

Instead, she started the fire in the large ceramic stove, which was built into the wall between her office and that of Herr Walter Suchland. A smaller ceramic stove heated the conference room and the younger Suchland's space, but Kurt had gone to a client's for the day. No clients were scheduled to come in this week so the conference room would remain empty.

She would not light the second stove.

When the younger lawyer was in the office, they kept his office a little warmer. His bad leg, from a motorcycle accident during university, hurt him in the cold. Fuel was still too costly and too hard to come by to waste. Once Hilke and Herr Suchland's offices were warm, they would let the fire die down, shut the door to the empty rooms and let the sun provide heat. Besides, they all had thick sweaters. Hilke even had gloves with the fingertips removed for the coldest days so she could still type and take shorthand.

Her forest-green sweater was on the coatrack. The image of her mother knitting that sweater, having unraveled one of her own, made the girl choke. She'd heard too many rumors of what happened to people taken by the SS. She couldn't imagine that they would be looking for secrets, considering that her mother had barely left their flat during the last few years nor had anyone come in to visit, always giving the excuse she was unwell until friends had given up and stopped calling.

She vowed never to speak to her father again for turning her mother in. She supposed she would have to go home long enough to pick up some clothes to go . . . go where? Her mother-in-law would not disobey her husband and let her stay in their flat. Hilke had slipped out of Dieter's room before her in-laws rose. She'd left a note in the kitchen drawer for Freja, knowing that her mother-in-law would find it when she set the table for her husband's breakfast.

"Danke für mein Bett," she'd written. She had been grateful to sleep in her husband's childhood bed and amongst his possessions. However, she wouldn't put Freja in the middle.

Maybe her father-in-law was right: Dieter would divorce her when he discovered her mother was a Jewess. She hadn't looked Jewish. They had gone to the Lutheran *Kirche* at least once a month until her mother sentenced herself to being a prisoner in her own home.

An Army officer couldn't be married to the descendant of

Jews. All their plans for children when the war was over were gone. She couldn't afford to think of that now.

Taking the coffeepot, she measured out *Ersatzkaffee* into the metal pot and put it on the hot plate. Even that bitter brew was getting harder and harder to come by. No matter how bad it was Herr Suchland wanted the coffee poured into his squat blue porcelain pot, and served with the matching cup and saucer. All this was put on a silver tray with a spoon and a cloth napkin.

"Standards must be maintained," he would say two out of three times when Hilke brought him his morning coffee. How many times had he told her, how he would like to drink many cups, but even the *Ersatzkaffee* had to be saved for clients. No matter what memories he had of a good Kenyan brew from before World War I, he drank the coffee with only minimal complaints. And although coffee was in short supply, he always insisted that she have one cup.

The door opened and Herr Suchland came in with his usual smile and his battered leather briefcase with the carving of a stag in a forest embossed on it. "*Guten Morgen,* Hilke." His presence often sucked the air out of the room. Where his energy and exuberance came from she would never understand.

Hilke started to sob for the first time since she'd found her family's apartment door open and her mother gone. She was more surprised at her lack of control than Herr Suchland probably was, as he stood there in his coat and hat, clutching his briefcase, turning it into a wall against this unexpected emotion.

"Is it Dieter? Has your husband been killed?"

The waterfall of tears carried all her fears for her mother, for herself, for her marriage as she shook her head.

Herr Suchland fumbled for a handkerchief and handed it to her. He went into the office where she'd placed the tray with the *Ersatzkaffee* and brought back his cup and placed it before the woman who was now hiccupping.

"Tell me about it," he said.

She did.

"I wish I could help, but I think if I enquired it would cause more problems for your mother and your father with the SS if I tried to interfere. I speak from experience." He hovered over her.

She remembered how he had tried to intervene for a client when she first worked for him, but the client had disappeared.

"My dear, you realize you can't stay here. I will have to let you go."

Mein Gott, Hilke thought, not sure how to react, how to order her thoughts on the next step. She had no idea where to go. Friends: she ran through names of people she knew including Else and her old coach who might shelter her. However, even if they would, she was a pariah: she cared too much about them to put them in danger.

Herr Suchland went into his office and removed the painting of the small cottage next to a stream with a mountain behind it to reveal a safe. He whirled the lock and took out a month's pay. "I don't want you to think I'm heartless. I've an uncle out in the country. He is old and needs someone to help him on his farm."

"Where is it?"

"Bergedorf."

Hilke tried to take it all in. Bergedorf. Not that far from Hamburg, but a whole different environment filled with farms instead of buildings. Besides two picnics with her family, she had gone out there once with her father. He had something to do as part of his work that he'd never explained. She'd been very little that first trip and remembered how he made her hold his hand and had lifted her down from the train steps. She remembered seeing planted fields and horses.

"Don't go by train. Walk," Herr Suchland said. "No, it will be much better to bike. I'll give you a spare one that I have, which is in good condition."

CHAPTER 21

Kirchdorf, Insel Poel, Germany
"A chalky soil allows plants to flourish. The soil is also sandy with about approximately .5 meters (1.6 feet) of humus which aids the agricultural quality of the island."

The History of Insel Poel by Manfred Dederich

"Wilkommen." Renate opened the door. "In come quickly before the heat escapes."

Annie slipped from the dark night into the hallway. On the right was the living room with the fireplace flaming in full force and lit candles providing enough light to see comfortably and to create a muted effect.

Since Annie had been there last time, the house had been decorated for Christmas: a wooden angel and a nutcracker soldier on end tables on each side of the forest-green leather couch, a nativity scene in the center of the mantel surrounded by pine boughs. Annie guessed that they would not bring in the tree until Christmas Eve and that Greta probably had put her shoes outside the door for presents on December sixth for *St. Nikolastag.*

A blond man dressed in a blue, Nordic-design sweater and jeans finished poking the fire and turned toward her. "You must be Annie," he said in perfect English. "I'm Karl, Renate's lucky husband." He put his arm around his wife and kissed her forehead before she went into the kitchen.

Long ago Annie had given up the battle of speaking the language of the country she was in when people came back to her in English.

"Renate and I speak English together. She doesn't know Swedish, my German is okay, but we thought our marriage would have a better chance if we each communicated in our second language. And it helps Greta with hers as well." His smile was almost like another candle.

"I hadn't realized that Renate's English was so good." As Annie spoke, Renate came in with a tray of *Glühwein* in bright red mugs.

"That's because your German is excellent and the other women at the museum don't speak much English at all. Oh, and dinner will be in about fifteen minutes."

Annie took the mug. She chose *thank you* over *danke*. "Where's Greta?"

"In her room sulking, probably," Karl said. If he saw the frown flicker across Renate's face, Anne thought that he chose to ignore it.

Renate passed breadsticks. "I'm so lucky to have Karl home until after the holidays."

Annie was curious to ask what Karl did, but thought it might be rude.

As if he picked up on her curiosity, he said, "I'm an importer. I travel mostly to the Far East and sometimes to countries like Poland, Romania, Slovakia: the usual list of suspects from behind what you Americans called the Iron Curtain." His blue eyes held Annie. "But tell me what you do. From the little Renate has said, it sounds like a fascinating life."

Annie felt manipulated from asking what he imported, but she went on to explain how most of her work was tech writing in English and translating it into Dutch, German and French, or any combination thereof. "Every now and then I can get a really fun project working on something historical, or at least more interesting than talking about F7s or F9s."

"Are you good at it?"

"Probably better than the directions that come with putting toys together."

As Karl laughed, Renate announced dinner. She went to the bottom of the stairs and called to Greta, who galloped down. Annie felt a moment of longing to be with Roger and Gaëlle. She must call later to tell him that she missed him, but then realized if she did he would say it was her fault for leaving. Gaëlle, on the other hand, would laugh and make plans for them to do something when she came home.

The teenager ignored Karl and went straight to Annie and hugged her before taking her seat. "Annie, I'm so glad you're here. *Mutti* has made her special chicken that she only does when company comes." She picked up her fork. *"Guten Appetit."*

This time they were eating in the dining room rather than the kitchen. The furniture was heavy oak. The table had been set with holly motif placemats. A wooden candelabra held red candles.

"Guten Appetit, and I'm honored," Annie said. She cut into the oregano and parmesan crust on the chicken. "Renate, if you are one of those women who will share a recipe, I would love this one. If you aren't, I understand."

"Renate shares," Karl said. "She's almost too generous." Again, he either didn't see or decided to ignore the look that passed over his wife's face.

As Annie bit into the thin-sliced potatoes coated with the same parmesan and oregano, Greta said, "I can't wait another minute. Tell me about the bodies you found."

"Greta!" Karl barked.

"What? I want to know. It must have been frightening. Or

was it exciting in a strange sort of way?"

"Enough!" Karl put down his fork. "That is *not* table talk."

Greta looked at her mother as if pleading for support. "Why not?"

"It just isn't, that's all." Renate's comment was delivered far more softly than her husband's.

"You two talked about it last night when we ate."

"But Annie is company. It may have upset her. It's rude to bring it up," Karl said.

Before Annie could say it didn't upset her, Karl broke in. "Leave the table, Greta."

Renate opened and closed her mouth without saying anything.

Greta stood and picked up her plate.

"Leave your dinner here," Karl said.

"No! You can't bully me." The teenager stormed upstairs with her plate.

"Teenagers," Karl said.

"I've one at home. Not mine, but my fiancé's."

"Then you know how difficult the step relation is," Karl said.

"And for the biological parent too." Renate moved the potatoes around her plate with her fork.

Annie wanted to say that her case was a little different. She often ran interference for Gaëlle with Roger, telling him she had the inside track because he'd never been a teenage girl and Annie could understand how Gaëlle's beady little mind worked. But looking at the couple seated at opposite ends of the table, she thought they might not want to hear that.

"Maybe it's easier because I'm a woman and Roger and I are still not married. I'll get back to you after the wedding."

"When is that?" Renate asked.

Annie guessed she asked more in a desire to change the atmosphere than anything else, but Annie picked up on it to explain how she wanted merely to go to the *Mairie* and get the required civil ceremony over with and have a nice meal with her family and a few friends, but her mother was making "white dress and bridesmaids" sounds. She'd even tried a few on once when a friend almost forced her into a bridal shop. All that white froufrou wasn't for her.

At the end of the evening, Renate asked Annie if she wanted Karl to walk her home.

"No need for two of us to be out in the cold," Annie said. In reality, although he had been charming and funny after Greta disappeared, she just wanted to be on her own. "I'll see you in the morning and thank you."

CHAPTER 22

Lübeck, Germany

Hans-Peter Leiter sat at his desk studying the two autopsy reports. Both victims were Asian. Both had been killed by bullets from the same gun. Both had washed up on the same beach that had seen too many bodies wash up in the past. Fortunately, he had not had to investigate the deaths that happened so long before he'd been born. Everyone knew the cause of those.

The station was quiet. He knew the quiet should help him think. It didn't.

Both bodies were in about the same condition, which indicated that they had been in the water for about the same amount of time.

Hans-Peter did not believe in coincidence.

If he didn't believe in one coincidence, he definitely didn't believe in two. Both victims' last meal was the same. Had it been rice and oriental food, he might have not thought that much about it: but it had been veal, green beans and potatoes—good Germanic food.

Thus he assumed it was one killer.

The murder could have taken place somewhere on shore, the bodies put on a boat and taken out to sea for burial. The only problem with that theory, Asian women were not common in Insel Poel. Thus, they would have had to come from Lübeck or some other city. He needed to check out the local Asian community first to see if anyone was missing.

He had photos of the dead girls. That type of legwork he hated. Fritz had called in with the flu, something his partner almost never did. He'd taken the call, and Fritz had sounded like someone else. He looked around the room with all the empty desks: they were in the middle of a minor epidemic. He grabbed his coat, hat and keys.

Like in many places, ethnic groups tended to band together, and in Lübeck there was a cluster of oriental laundries, restaurants and small businesses. With only about 3,000 Asians, someone should know of two missing girls. It might have helped if he'd know whether the victims were Thai, Chinese, Japanese or from some other country. Claudia was trying to narrow it down, but it was a bit like guessing if a redheaded corpse were Irish, Scots, American, Australian, or even German for that matter.

Dentistry sometimes helped, because different countries used different techniques and materials. That had been another similarity: their teeth had been capped, but Claudia had said it looked like European work, which might help for identification later on. He needed a name to go with the reports he would give a dentist. And there were far too many dentists in the area to ask them all, but he could start with those that served the Asian community.

He would work with what he had. He wound his scarf around his neck, put on his coat and headed out.

For all the things he hated about police work, one of the worst for him was walking from place to place showing strangers photos of dead people. They would look at the photo, shudder and deny any knowledge. Hans-Peter believed them.

When people recoiled or teared up he knew he had a match, even if they denied any knowledge. He prided himself on sensing who was lying and who was not: his record was in the ninetieth percentile. He was wrong just enough to stay alert, which is what had earned him his last promotion and should be helpful with the next one.

Today was turning out to be useless, unless he wanted to establish that the girls might not be from the Lübeck Asian community. The wind had picked up from the harbor, carrying with it a salty smell. A few seagulls flew overhead complaining loudly.

A coffee shop was on the corner. He would have loved to be home with his wife and kids drinking a beer before dinner, a thing the divorce had made impossible, anyway. A coffee would have to do.

The shop was not the prosperous type with wonderful pastries and women with shopping bags consuming something highly caloric with hot chocolate and delaying going home to cook dinner. This was a plain drink-your-coffee-and-read-the-paper-type shop. The waiter came over and took his order.

When the coffee was brought to him, he showed the photos to the waiter, who was some type of Asian—he could never tell one type of Asian from another: Thai, Korean, Vietnamese were all the same to him.

"Arme Mädchen," the man said, and Hans-Peter had to agree, poor girls. Even if they were Asian, they did not deserve to end up like this. And he could never voice the phrase "even if they were Asian" without being labeled racist. He didn't like to think he was a racist, but he did prefer his own kind. However, under the law he treated everyone equally. Sometimes he even treated other nationalities better so as to not appear racist.

The coffee was too hot to drink. He looked out the window at the people, mostly Asians going by. He took out his phone. A little research on the Internet showed that Hamburg, another close-by city, had a six percent Asian population. He would go back to headquarters and put the photos out on the wires.

Tomorrow he would work the dentist angle. Although he hoped Fritz would be back to work, considering how his partner sounded that morning he doubted it.

Night had fallen by the time he got back to the station. Stupid phrase—night falling—it doesn't fall anywhere. No one ever said mornings falling.

The shifts were changing, although they were still obviously understaffed on both the day and night teams. He sat down at the computer and started looking for missing person reports for Asian girls, chiding himself that he hadn't done that before.

He hoped there would be a long list: anything to keep him from having to go back to his empty flat.

CHAPTER 23

Bergedorf, Germany
May 1943

"Personally, I don't understand how you stand the old bastard," the farmer's wife said to Hilke as she handed her *Reichsmarks* for the five eggs she had just bought from the Siegfried Suchland farm, which had a surplus of laying chickens. The woman wore an apron over a sweat-stained blouse and skirt and her hair was tied under a scarf knotted at the back of her head, but she kept making brushing-back movements as if a strand of hair had fallen in her eyes.

Hilke guessed that she was probably in her late twenties based on the ages of the two children who had come with her and looked so much like her that they had to be hers. They were no more than eight or nine. However, the woman looked much older, but farm life aged people, Hilke had noticed.

There were many answers she could have given to the woman's old-bastard question, such as, "I dream of smothering him in his bed," or "At least it's a job," or maybe, "I'm safer here than I am at home," but now she knew she had no home to go to. If she had to explain how she felt, it would be like when she was a little girl, and she would turn in a circle faster and faster until she was so dizzy she fell down and the room spun around her. Only this was worse. Her life had spun around her until she no longer recognized anything.

She'd received one letter from her former boss, or maybe it

was her current boss, because he was paying her a small amount to look after "the old bastard" or TOB as she christened him in her mind. That is how Hilke thought of Herr Siegfried Suchland, but she had never voiced it to anyone. How he could be so different from his great nephew, his only surviving relative, was something she didn't understand. Granted, the four members of her family were very different, but overall they did share the same value system, or at least they did until her father had turned traitor. At ninety-one, TOB partially proved that the good die young, or at least that the bad lived too long.

"Sometimes the old get crotchety," Hilke said to the farm wife.

"Crotchety?" The woman honked a laugh. "My father-in-law said Herr Suchland always was a bastard. When he was a boy, my father-in-law that is, Herr Suchland beat him for coming onto his property, just like this rotten little farm belonged to some noble." She leaned in as if the goats mulling around the barnyard would overhear her. "He buried three wives. Worked them to death. Make sure that doesn't happen to you."

Hilke would have loved to invite the woman in for a nice long chat. This was the only conversation that she'd had with another human outside of TOB in over two weeks. "I hope your hens start laying soon," she said to the woman.

"Maybe they just wanted a few days off." The woman picked up the willow-stick basket where Hilke had placed the eggs carefully. "And besides, I wanted to make sure you were all right. If you need help, my door will always be open."

Hilke shook the woman's hand. A feeling of sadness overwhelmed her as she looked at her hands, once soft, now calloused. Dirt traced the outlines of each cell of her skin and seemed permanently engrained under her nails. Not that she had ever spent a long time on nail care, but with the number of hours she had spent swimming daily, cleanliness was as much a part of her being as blood and tissue.

She had done the spring planting and then preserved the spinach, asparagus and strawberries when they were ready. TOB begrudged her every bite she ate, but since he spent most of his time sitting in the living room, issuing orders, he didn't see what she tasted as she prepared his meals.

"Get in here, you lazy bitch." The voice boomed from the farmhouse. The old man's vocal cords had not been weakened by age.

"*Es tut mir leid;* I'm sorry," the woman mouthed. Hilke shrugged then smiled to accept the woman's sympathy. In a subtle defiance, she walked in measured steps up the stone walk to the front door.

The house inside was dark and smelled of old man. The furniture, such as it was, must have been handed down for generations. Style and comfort seemed to be forbidden.

"The woman next door bought five eggs."

He held his hand out from his position in a faded chair.

She gave him the coins.

"Turn your pockets inside out." After she did, he said, "Now empty your shoes."

Hilke wanted to say, "Do you want me to strip naked? Open my body cavities?" She didn't. He had a cane that he would swing at her. Usually she could duck out of the way.

"Where's my lunch?"

"It will be ready in about twenty minutes." She left without being dismissed.

In the backyard a cup of water sat on a pump. Hilke primed the pump then worked the handle until enough water dribbled out to fill a leather bucket. Chickens pecked around at her feet. She wished for a bath with hot water and lots of soap and maybe even a bit of something that smelled flowery, but the house had no tub, and even if it had she would never risk a bath in a room where there was no lock on the door.

She didn't fear rape, for she was sure TOB was impotent, but she didn't want him seeing her naked. Her vulnerability was bad enough as it was: she didn't want to risk increasing it.

She had taken to swimming in the pond that marked the boundary between Herr Suchland's farm and the egg-buying woman's farm. After years of clear pools or the flowing river, sharing water with frogs, fish and algae was not that pleasant. As the spring continued the algae seemed to increase, but at least when she came out, she didn't feel as dirty as when she went into the water.

Back in the kitchen she opened a drawer of potatoes to the right of the table. She poured some of the water from the bucket into two bowls and washed the potatoes in one before peeling them. After they were all peeled, she washed them again in the second bowl. She thought of her mother doing that when before the war all they had to eat was potatoes. If only she could see her mother again.

Nights, before she went to sleep, she wished she had made more of an effort to understand her mother and worked harder to make her mother understand her. If she ever saw her mother again, after the war was over, she had so much she wanted to tell her.

If her mother came back, where would she go? Surely, she would not forgive her husband. Hilke was sure she would be able to get a post in another law office where she would make enough money to take care of her. Or maybe her mother would go to England and live with Joseph. Maybe Hilke would go to England, although her English was not nearly as good as her brother's was when he left and was probably perfect now. All her life now was "ifs" and "when the war is over."

And the biggest "if" was if she had someone to talk to, to share her fears. Her former employer had agreed not to tell her father or her in-laws where she went. She had never felt so isolated.

CHAPTER 24

Colerne, Wiltshire, England
May 1943

"I'm going to see, Ruth, Father," Martha said. She was halfway out the door as she threw her sweater on. Despite the calendar, there was still a cool breeze, especially when she was pedaling into the wind.

"Wait!" Her father's voice stopped her.

She turned around. "I've done everything. Your lunch is in the fridge."

"You're spending too much time with that girl."

"I'm helping her with her baby and her mother. Surely that's the Christian thing to do." The moment the words were out of her mouth she knew she shouldn't have said them.

"Young lady, you are being impudent."

Impudent was added to the seven deadly sins in the house.

"No, I'm not, Father. Since Eleanor's stroke, Ruth has had all she can do to take care of the baby and help her mother. Baby Walter is colicky and the poor girl hardly gets any sleep at all." She debated adding, "I'm watching everything while she naps," because that wasn't the reason she was going there. Martha hated lying, although long ago she had learned to be selective about the parts of the truth she told to her father.

She slipped out of the house before he could answer. As the lock fell into place she heard a small click. Her bicycle rested against the side of the house where she'd left it that morning after buying the food they needed and had on their ration cards, although a stop at William's farm gave her a chance to buy the first of the spinach. At Everett's she was able to fill the milk tin and buy six eggs. Everett would sell no more to any of his neighbors to make sure he had enough for each of his customers. The food question was solved for the next few days. She never stopped being grateful that they lived in the country and not the city.

As she pedaled down the lane leading to Ruth's she didn't dare look back in case her father was standing in the doorway. Hopefully, she wouldn't pay with what she called his icicle voice for the next few days, spoken to her as little as possible.

Ruth lived with her mother in the house where she had grown up. Her father had died in a Swansea bombing. No one knew what he was doing in Swansea leading to much speculation.

The cottage was well kept, with a vegetable garden in the front. Vicar Willson might think of Ruth as being too flighty, but Martha's friend had "risen to the situation," a favorite expression of her father's, even if he wasn't willing to admit that Ruth had done the rising he claimed he admired in others.

The lilacs were in full bloom as were the apple trees. Martha made a decision to concentrate on the beauty of the ride and not her annoyance at her father.

To the left of the stone step leading into the cottage was Baby Walter's pram, nicknamed "the coach" by Alan. "I could attach it to the train and people would they think it was another car," he'd said.

"It'll develop your muscles, Ruth," Gordon had teased.

Martha left her bicycle by the gate and made her way up the pebble walkway. Dandelions were between the stones and she spied a violet, her favorite flower, in a crack at the bottom of the stairs.

Ruth opened the door and motioned her in, one finger across

her lips. She pointed to the pram. Martha saw the baby asleep.

Inside were Alan and Gordon. Both stood, but Gordon came over and wrapped his arms around Martha. "You've escaped."

She nodded.

"We're off for a walk, then," Ruth said. "Mother's asleep." Eleanor slept most of the time these days, waking to give her guttural cry for a bedpan. Ruth needed to spoon-feed her, and even then she often choked. "We'll take the baby with us."

"And pray he doesn't wake."

"At least I have his feed with me."

"My son takes what is mine," Alan said. "I'll let him for another few months or so, then those breasts go back to their rightful owner."

"Which is me." Ruth pushed her husband out the door. "Let's give these two a chance to be alone."

Martha was home by late afternoon, in time to start the Saturday supper. Her father ate lightly on Saturday evenings, to be in "full fighting form" to deliver his sermon the next day. As she turned the corner she saw him peering out the window.

"You lied to me," he said as soon as she opened the door.

With precise movements she took off her sweater and hung it on the coatrack. "About what, Father?"

"Going to Ruth's. James Johnson came by and said he saw Ruth and Alan with the baby out walking." He folded his arms and tapped his foot.

"I stayed with Eleanor so Alan and Ruth could have an hour by themselves where Ruth didn't feel on call."

Vicar Willson stamped out of the room.

Martha went to the kitchen and took down the copper pans that had been in the vicarage probably since before it was built. They were well dented. She picked up a potato from the small supply left from the fall. It was full of eyes staring at her. If they'd been real eyes, she wondered if they would be accusing her, or sympathizing with her.

CHAPTER 25

Kirchdorf, Insel Poel, Germany
"Seagulls, sandpipers, ducks, geese and swans are just some of the birds that are on the island. During summer and fall birds use the island sanctuary as a resting place during their migrations."

The History of Insel Poel by Manfred Dederich

"I'm sorry you were caught up in our little family drama last night." Renate poured herself and Annie coffees. They were the only two in the break room. Karine and a volunteer worker were stringing holy and pine boughs around the reception area. "I really wanted it to be an enjoyable evening for us all."

Annie had debated with herself whether Renate wanted to forget about it, or talk about it. "No need to apologize at all. I understand . . . if you want to talk about it as one woman with a teenager daughter to a woman with a future teenage stepdaughter . . ."

Renate, who had been leaning against a flat-pack white cabinet filled with paper supplies as she drank her coffee, sat down. She cupped her hands around the mug and stared into it as if reading tea leaves.

"I'm a good listener, and the best part, when I go away your secrets stay secret."

Renate looked up with a half smile. Then she looked out toward the reception area. "On a small island, very few things stay secret."

"Which makes me the perfect set of ears." Annie reached out and put her hand over Renate's. "Is it that Greta resents not having you all to herself? Or she misses her father?"

"She doesn't really remember her father. He was killed in a car crash when she was two. And the man I dated before Karl, she liked. I think she was more upset when we broke up than we were."

"Why did you break up?"

"We wanted different things. I didn't want any more children, and he had the right to have one of his own. One would have made him happy."

Annie nodded. She'd learned long ago, silence often worked better than even the cleverest of open or closed questions.

"We started out as friends, and we stayed friends, which was the problem. There was never any spark." She blushed. "In bed or out."

Silence didn't work this time, although Annie gave it time to work. "And with Karl?"

Renate blushed again. "Fireworks that would make a Chinese ammunition factory beam with pride."

"How did you meet?"

Renate took a long drink of her coffee then blew on it. "Hot."

Annie hadn't drunk any coffee not wanting her movements to be a distraction. She wondered if "hot" was applied to the coffee or Karl or maybe both. Again she didn't say anything and waited.

"At the harbor fish restaurant. He'd come in on a boat with some of his friends. Greta was at the twins' house—her best mates—and I decided I'd rather eat out than cook. It was one of those beautiful, long summer nights when the sun is in no rush to set. I walked in and there was only one free place and that was at his table. As the saying goes, 'the rest was history.'

We were married three months later and that was two years ago."

"So how did Greta react to all this?"

"Mixed. At first she said, 'I suppose this means you and Werner won't get back together?' Werner was the man I just told you about. I pointed out to her that Werner had found someone else, and we were all friends with no hard feelings."

"But she still hoped about you and Werner?"

Renate nodded. "There are some biscuits, or as you would say cookies, somewhere." She opened the cabinet and among the reams of paper, ink cartridges, staples, pens, and empty file folders, she found a stash of chocolate cookies, which she brought to the table.

"Chocolate always makes conversations better," Annie said. "Go on."

"In the beginning, Greta was fine with Karl. He would bring her small gifts from his travels, nothing that would look like bribery and not every time. They both liked the same rock music—I'm a classical buff myself—and I thought that would be good to help them bond."

Annie was a cookie dunker only when she had coffee and chocolate cookies. She dunked and waited. She wondered about the change.

"How much does Karl travel?"

"He's gone about eighty percent of the time. When he's gone Greta is her lovely self, a bit overexuberant as you may have noticed at lunch the other day."

"I found her charming."

"She was always an easy *Kind*. I don't know if I'd have survived my husband's death without her. He was my first love. It started out as puppy love but it grew as we grew. Because of Greta I had to hold it together, get up every morning, go through every day whether I wanted to or not. It was almost as if she knew I couldn't handle a difficult child. But we genuinely had fun together, wrestling matches, making cakes together." Renate took a bite of her cookie before continuing. "I will admit some of the early childhood games were tiresome, but she never was."

Change, change, tell me about the change, Annie thought.

"Then about six months ago, shortly after her fourteenth birthday, whenever Karl was around, Greta would disappear. If he told her do something, she would give him a hard time."

"I noticed that you ask her to do things. Was it because he told her?"

"I don't think so. Because as you said, I tell her to do things as well with less than the normal teenage grumbling compared to what some of my friends say about their daughters of the same age."

Annie wasn't sure how to ask if the change happened after Karl and Greta had been alone. She might be raising an issue that could destroy Renate and Karl's marriage without any reason. But if her idea was right, Greta might need protection. Shit, *Scheiß*, *merde*. She hated these situations.

"Are you two ever going to get back to work?" Karine stood at the break room door. Today her white hair was in a bun at the back of her neck. If I could be that beautiful when I'm in my sixties, I'd be so lucky, Annie thought. Hell, if I were that beautiful now, I'd be lucky.

Annie was glad for the distraction. It would give her a chance to think about the conversation. Maybe she'd ask Roger when they talked that night.

CHAPTER 26

Kirchdorf, Insel Poel, Germany
"The Swedish King Albrecht 1547 and his son Albrecht II oversaw the island, but the Danes had the trading rights."

The History of Insel Poel by Manfred Dederich

Dressed in her double-layered pink flannel pajamas and bunny slippers, Annie settled on the couch, her feet on the coffee table with her laptop resting on her thighs. A battered copy of *The History of Insel Poel* by Manfred Dederich was next to her. The book had been privately printed some ten years ago for some celebration or the other. Renate had told her that the run was limited to 500 copies.

Manfred Dederich, a man in his eighties, had almost died last year, according to Renate. He had grown up in Kirchdorf, but had left the island to become a history professor at the University of Leipzig.

"Be careful when you meet him, if you meet him, which is less and less likely, that he doesn't rage on about how the university was founded in 1409 and their graduates include famous alumni like Goethe, Wagner, Nietzsche and Angela Merkel as well as multiple Nobel Prize winners. To listen to him you'd think he taught them all himself. But then again the last time we asked him about meeting you, he threw us out of the house yelling, he didn't want to know anyone that might ruin his work."

Regardless of his personality, Annie found the man's book interesting. His research throughout his academic career had been to delve into the past of small enclaves in Germany. Much of what he wrote was more about the lives of the people, what utensils they used, what crops they harvested, rather than the big events, but his history of Insel Poel was both. And his interest beyond rulers and wars was also what fascinated her about history.

He had written in his introduction, "I'm a historian with sociological leanings, but I'm also a child of Insel Poel. No matter how far I go, the memory of early mornings when I was called from my bed by my father to go milk the cows, the feel of the salt sea air as I walked to the barn, make me who I am. Next to my bed is a small jar with dirt from the family farm, which was taken over by the Communists after WWII. On a visit back, I visited the old farm and scooped up the dirt. That jar will be next to my future bed at the home my children have found for me in Lübeck." His style made her wish that she were the original author. So many subjects had interested her over the years, but why had she never set down and written about them?

Annie read and reread his introduction. She decided the best way to work on the translation was to do each section first in English, then French and lastly in Dutch. Her Dutch was the weakest at this point and she would be able to absorb the depth of his words by translating in the order of her own language levels. By doing small sections in all languages she would not lose the thread, which she feared would happen if she translated the whole book into one language then went onto the next.

"In this history," Dederich had written, "I want to capture both the big and little events. This is a tiny island but it acts as a seed of a giant tree that makes up the activities of mankind."

Annie was not sure she was looking forward to meeting Dederich. "He was better before his wife died two years ago," Renate had said and finally Annie had said, with her short time, it might be better if they didn't meet.

"You're probably right not to. It was as if he lost part of his essence. Hildegard had helped him in his research, even though she had never been to university. It was one of those marriages that all of us dream of having."

Marriage. There was that word that caused Annie to want to run away from it. Roger had once asked her why she was so afraid of it, especially since her parents were so well suited to one another.

Samen für einen riesigen Baum.

Graine pour un arbre géant.

Een gigantische boom zaad.

Seed for a giant tree.

Maybe she saw marriage as a seed that would grow into a giant tree imprisoning her within its boughs. An image of her sitting at the top of a redwood with sticky pitch all over her hands combined with a fear of falling to the ground bounced around in her head.

Like it not, Roger wanted them to be married before the summer. He had used the American phrase he'd picked up when he had done some police training in the States. "It's time to shit or get off the pot."

Whenever he came out with an Americanism, it made her laugh. Okay, she thought—June ninth. She switched to the calendar on her computer. Damn—that was a Saturday.

The pop-up window told her Roger was on Skype. She debated not answering, and claiming she'd been in the shower, but decided to be grown up and pushed the green telephone symbol.

"*Bonsoir, ma chérie. Je t'aime.*"

"I love you too." And she did. Despite all her reservations

about marriage, that she loved him was never in doubt. However, her ambivalence on how their relationship was to evolve was beginning to annoy not just her, but her parents and sometimes Roger as well.

They exchanged news of their days. Argelès was quiet. One of the men hanging Christmas decorations along *la rue de la République* had fallen, but only broke his arm. Gaëlle was still rattling on about that Guillaume boy, and he didn't like that one bit.

"Stop being overprotective. Let her be a normal teenager."

He sputtered a bit, and she let him before saying, "Be grateful that she's picked a nice boy. She could be attracted to the kids that hang out behind the church."

"And speaking of wrong people, are you behaving yourself and not looking for murderers?"

"There's another problem here." She explained her concerns about Greta.

"Probably just a teenager being a teenager," he said. "Minding your own business is never a bad idea."

Annie did not disagree with him verbally. She started talking about their Christmas plans when Roger got a call on his cell phone.

Damn. She'd forgotten to mention the possible date for the wedding so he could check with the *marie* to see if the mayor could work them into the marriage schedule. She'd just switched her screen to e-mail when the doorbell rang.

She'd heard noises in Gregor's flat next door when she came home. Maybe he wanted to invite her out to dinner or in for a drink: it was still early enough. She didn't feel like going anywhere, and the idea of having him around while she was in her pajamas, as unsexy as they were, was low on her list.

Opening the door, she was surprised to see Greta standing there.

"May I in come?" The girl's nose was red and running.

"Come in," Annie corrected the girl's English by example.

Greta pushed past Annie and unwound her scarf and opened her jacket, which had been buttoned unevenly.

"I'm having some hot chocolate. There's still some left. Would you like it?"

Greta nodded as she circled the table, touching each chair as she went by. "Don't tell my mother where I am."

Annie reached for a cup, keeping her back to Greta as she wondered what next step she should take with the girl, who obviously had something serious on her mind. So many people had told Annie that she was good with teenagers. She wished *they* were here in her place. As she poured the chocolate into the cup and put it in the microwave with her back still to the girl, she asked, "How long have you been out of the house?"

"As long as it took to come over here."

About ten minutes maximum, Annie thought as she turned to look at the girl gauging her body language before asking, "Does your mom know you're gone?"

"Oh, she knows all right. I could have broken the glass in the door if I'd slammed it any harder."

"Strong, huh?"

The girl let the beginning of a smile play across her mouth then made it disappear. "Strong, not strong enough."

Annie went to the coffee table, retrieved her own lukewarm chocolate to put it on the table opposite where Greta had stopped pacing. The microwave binged. "Sit, sit, sit."

Greta did as Annie retrieved the hot chocolate and placed it before the girl.

Greta cupped her hands around the cup, then blew on the liquid. Annie drank a bit of hers, which needed warming, but she certainly wasn't going to do anything that distracted the girl.

"I suppose your mom didn't know where you were going?"

"May I stay here tonight?" When Annie didn't answer, Greta added, "*Bitte,* please, *s'il vous plaît?* I can get down on my knees."

Go light? Go serious, Annie debated. Too light and the girl would feel patronized, too serious and she might put up barriers. "I'm not saying no, but I do need to know more. As you can see, there's only the couch."

"I can sleep on the floor. Move the coffee table. The rug will be soft enough."

"I'm still not saying no, but I need to know more. Did you tell your mom where you were going before you slammed out of the house?"

"Slammed?"

"That's what we say when someone bangs a door hard. Would you be happier if we spoke in German?"

Greta switched languages and a torrent of words and phrases came out, some of which Annie had trouble piecing together, not because she didn't understand the German, but because the thoughts were jumbled. "*Mutti* . . . Karl . . . bastard . . . wouldn't believe me . . . jealous . . . lies . . . fine before he came . . . can't say more . . . no one would believe . . . not my fault."

"What isn't your fault?"

"If you won't help, I'm going." Greta upset the cup when she stood. The unfinished chocolate spilled over the table. Greta began to cry.

"Sit down!"

The tone was so harsh that Greta did.

"Don't worry about the chocolate." Annie didn't want to say what she thought because if she were wrong she could plant the idea in Greta's head. Ninety-nine percent of her was sure she was right and the girl was probably in danger.

Greta sat back down. The chocolate dripped off the table onto the floor tiles. Annie was glad they weren't in the living area with the carpet, but spots weren't her main concern at this point. "Why don't you tell me about it?"

"Are your parents still alive?"

Annie nodded.

"Together?"

"Yes."

"I don't remember my real father."

"Your mom told me."

"Sometimes it was just the two of us, sometimes, not often, she had boyfriends." Greta slipped off her coat, giving Annie hope that the girl wouldn't run out the door.

"Did you mind that?"

"Not too much. Some of them were nice, some of them were nice to me to get to her, but I never minded the chocolate or the dolls given to me." What was almost a smile crossed her lips.

"I guess that makes you a normal kid. What child would turn down chocolate or a pretty doll?"

"I wasn't into dolls that much. I never played house. My dolls did things."

Annie cocked her head.

"They were architects, or Greek and Roman goddesses. Sometimes they were cowgirls rounding up my cows. I had a collection of cow statues."

Annie laughed before she could stop herself. "I'm sorry, it's not funny, but I love your imagination." The imagination could also set up a situation, which could cause real problems for Greta's mother and stepfather.

"Do you? Then I can stay? I'll be safe."

"Safe?"

Greta started to say something then stopped. Annie left the silence alone. She could even hear the wall clock ticking behind her.

"Er . . . from freezing to death sleeping on the bench at the harbormaster's house."

"Greta, you aren't going to do that and you know it. If I say no, you'll either go home or go to a house where one of your friends lives."

"I prefer being here."

"Then tell me what you'll be safe from."

Greta got up and went to the window. Because the shutters were down and the drapes drawn she looked out only on cloth.

The maxim, "a problem shared is a problem halved," ran through Annie's mind, but she decided it was too, too . . . maybe too glib. Instead she waited.

Greta's cheeks were wet and her eyes were red. She was not a teenager that cried prettily. "Will you promise you won't tell my mom? It would kill her."

"Maybe if it is that serious, she should know. Moms are a lot stronger than kids think."

"Not with this."

"You told me you wanted to be a journalist." Annie figured if she changed tactics she would be able to get Greta to relax a bit before she tackled it again. The girl's shoulders relaxed a bit and she let out a breath of air. "Yes, I have for a while. I love seeing the women on the TV who are out in the middle of the action."

"You need courage for that."

"You're tricking me. If I need courage for that I need courage for . . . for . . ."

"Of course I'm tricking you." Annie leaned across the table, getting chocolate on her sleeve. "But I'm tricking you for your own good."

"All right, all right." Long, long pause. "I hate Karl."

"Your mom has said things aren't good between you. She thought that maybe it was because you thought his being there meant that she'd never get back with her last boyfriend."

"Werner. I wish she'd married Werner, that's true, but he found another woman who fits him better than *Mutti*. I guess you can have two nice people but that doesn't make a good match."

Another long pause, which Annie found hard to let ride. When she couldn't stand the silence any longer, she said, "This is true. And your mother and Karl?"

"*Mutti* is wonderful. I know girls aren't supposed to get along with their mothers, and maybe we did because Papa died and it was just the two of us."

"It does change the dynamic, but it also could make you less happy when it's three."

Greta shook her head. "I want *Mutti* to be happy and she is. But Karl has done things to me he shouldn't do."

Annie got up and led Greta to the couch and engulfed the girl in her arms and let her sob. When she was reduced to hiccupping, she let go and went for a glass of water. "Block your ears. I'll feed you the water."

It worked. The girl stopped hiccupping. "I'll let you stay here, but you have to let your mom know where you are."

Greta shook her head.

"I'll call her if you don't want to talk to her." She searched for her phone then called Renate.

"Your daughter is with me, and we're going to have a sleepover."

Annie heard a muffled "Karl, she's with Annie, she's okay" and guessed that Renate had put her hand over the mouthpiece.

"We'll come get her immediately."

"Renate, I really think it better she stay here tonight. She was really upset and it will cool everything down."

"You're probably right. I'll drop off her school clothes in the morning, and drive you to work."

Greta ran to Annie and hugged her. "Thank you."

Annie busied herself making up the couch into a double bed. "If you don't want to sleep with me, there's an extra *Eiderdown* you can wrap yourself up with."

There was a knock at the door. Greta jumped.

"It's probably my next-door neighbor. He comes by at the strangest times."

It wasn't Gregor.

Karl stepped into the studio without being asked. "Greta, get your things. You're coming home with me."

Greta put on her coat and scarf and walked toward her stepfather who was halfway into the room. She ducked by him and was out the door.

"That goddamned brat," Karl said and ran after her.

CHAPTER 27

Bergedorf, Germany
May 1943

Hilke was enjoying a blissful moment of calm. TOB had taken his bicycle and gone into the village.

That he could still ride should have been something of a miracle, had she not seen him walking without a limp one night. She had gone to bed, but the moon was so bright she wanted to look closer. Outside she saw him walking normally among the vegetables, bending down from time to time as if checking up on her weeding.

Whenever she was around he leaned heavily on his cane, saying that she had to help him because he suffered so from arthritis.

A knock at the door disturbed her peace. No one ever visited, but sometimes people, usually from the city, stopped to buy eggs, asparagus and spinach. TOB once sold sausages he had made to the local butcher, but now the butcher slaughtered the pigs for him. TOB gave him a portion of the sausages he'd made in payment. The old man complained how much the butcher cheated him, but he no longer could do the work himself. He threatened Hilke with the project come fall when the piglets that were occupying the pen next to the barn were grown.

Until she lived in Bergedorf, she had had no connection with her food when it was alive. Although she felt badly doing it, she was now able to take an old chicken whose egg-laying had stopped and sever its neck with a single blow of the small axe. She may have hated killing it, and she would curse the chicken for getting even by making its feathers so hard to remove. When the smell of boiling chicken made her stomach growl, she looked forward to every bite she would eat, adding just one more dichotomy to her already turned-upside-down life.

She went to the door. It was the farmer's wife. Her hair was in a long single braid down her back. She did not have on the scarf that she'd worn last time. Her dress was freshly washed and ironed. "Please come with me. Herr Suchland's nephew called. The great-grandnephew, Kurt. He'll be calling you back in about half an hour."

Hilke wondered if she should lock the door or leave a message. If she'd known where TOB had gone and why, she would have had a better idea about what to do. To hell with him. She had her own life to consider.

"I'll be right with you." She washed her hands in the leftover dish-washing water and joined the woman.

"My name is Joanna," the woman told her as they walked down the road and passed a field where an unknown crop was pushing up its first green sprouts. That Joanna had used her Christian name rather than the Frau Family Name took Hilke back. During the months she'd been in Bergedorf, she had had so little chance to talk to anyone that any hope of friendship was an unlit match tucked away in its cardboard box.

"I grew up here. Sometimes when Kurt would come out with his father to visit the old man, we would play together. They didn't come all that often." Joanna opened her unlocked front door.

Joanna's house, although furnished with furniture as old as TOB's, was bright. Clean curtains, although mended, hung on the windows. Someone had stenciled red and yellow flowers of no known species around the top of the wall where it touched the ceiling.

Joanna saw her looking. "I did those when my in-laws died. I wanted to make the house mine. I just baked a cake. Would you like a piece and maybe a cup of coffee? Real coffee? It was a gift at Christmas. I save it for guests."

Hilke hesitated—taking the woman's real coffee—that implied?—she wasn't sure what it implied. Her world had turned so upside down that nothing that had worked in her old life applied anymore.

"*Bitte.*"

"City folks I know are more formal, but come into the kitchen. I always think the kitchen is the soul of the house, don't you?"

Hilke nodded even though her mother's kitchen had been small. Käthe had considered the kitchen her territory and anyone entering was only there on a mission such as chopping onions, transferring food to the dining area or washing the dishes. Maybe someday she would have a kitchen that could become the soul of the house. After the war . . . after Dieter was home and working as a doctor.

The kitchen had been whitewashed recently and pans hung from a thick wooden beam that had darkened with age until the type of wood was impossible to tell. The dark contrasted to the whitewashed ceiling. A bunch of lettuce had been washed and was drying on a rack. The soapstone sink had an indoor pump.

Joanna measured the coffee into a pot, added water and threw in another log. The fire broke into flame and within minutes the smell of coffee permeated the room.

How long had it been since Hilke had smelled coffee. She remembered a Tex Avery cartoon she'd seen at the *Kino* with her husband. A cloud representing the smell of fish attracts the cat hero and he follows the smell half floating, half dancing to the source.

"Milk? I only have honey, no sugar."

"Black, no, honey is perfect."

The woman took down two thick cups and looked at them, started to put them back but then changed her mind and poured the coffee into them.

She cut two slices from the frostingless cake. "It's only a honey cake made from a spice cake recipe. One has to be really good with substitutions these days, but I had the flour, honey, eggs, milk and butter, but not cinnamon, nutmeg or ginger."

"And you just changed the name."

The woman smiled.

Hilke realized that this was one of the first normal conversations she had had in months. She didn't count the egg transaction the week before with Joanna.

The first bite of cake made Hilke want to stand up and sing. The first sip of coffee could have been accompanied by a chorus of angels and she wouldn't have been surprised. Such simple treats were now so out of her ordinary reach that the experience was priceless.

What was her mother doing? Hilke felt a wave of guilt at being so caught up in her own situation that she sometimes went several days without thinking about her mother. Maybe she had been released when the SS saw how little Jewish blood her mother had. Maybe that was what Kurt Suchland wanted to talk to her about. Then she could go home. She was sure she would no longer have a job, but she had little doubt that Herr Walter Suchland would help her find a new one. Maybe Else would let her stay with her and help her with the baby. As for her father, she was still too angry to even consider ever being under his roof.

The phone rang.

Joanna lifted the receiver. "Kurt, she's here."

When Hilke took the phone, she realized her hand was shaking: her first contact with her old life.

"Wie gehts?" In the last few months she and Kurt had worked together they'd fallen into the informal, but she could never imagine using informal anything with his father.

"As well as can be expected, *danke.*"

"I suppose you're wondering why I've called."

Stupid question. She said nothing.

Kurt's voice continued wending his way from the place she'd spent day after day working and taking it for granted. She promised herself she would never take anything for granted ever again. Nothing: not a violet, not a soft-boiled egg, not a smile.

Assuming her assent he said, "Your in-laws were here. They thought I might represent you in an annulment."

"Annulment?"

Joanna brought a chair to where Hilke was standing with the phone. Gripping the phone so hard her knuckles were white, she sat, unaware she'd done so.

"Annulment or divorce. Your husband wants an annulment on the grounds he didn't know you had Jewish blood. There is doubt that the marriage was legal, but your father-in-law seems hell-bent on making sure that all connections are severed. If the annulment isn't approved, they will go for a divorce."

Hilke didn't know what to say. The word *they* bothered her. Not Dieter. *They.*

"Are you all right?" Kurt asked.

"I'm not sure," Hilke said.

"Of course, we'll represent you at no charge, my father says. And we'll say your whereabouts are unknown." He made that little half laugh she'd heard so often in the office. "It's not a total lie. We don't know which room you're in at my uncle's house or if you're in the fields."

Hilke nodded as she searched for her voice, which had disappeared.

"What happens next?"

"It will probably take a few weeks, and I'll contact you when it's over. Calling to find out about my uncle shouldn't raise any suspicions."

From his tone and their earlier conversations, Hilke knew the Suchlands were not pro-Nazi, but they thought that Germans should always support their government, good or bad. Herr Walter Suchland bemoaned more than once that anything became legal if a government voted it, but legal and right were not necessarily the same thing. However, once it was legal it was his job to follow whatever had been decreed.

"We miss you. Fraulein Schmidt is not as efficient as you were, and certainly not as pleasant."

A *hmm* was the most Hilke could manage.

"Oh, and before I ring off, your mother-in-law wasn't totally in agreement with this."

"What do you mean?"

"She deliberately left her handkerchief and came back alone. She said to give you a message."

"Message?"

"She said to tell you how sorry she was."

CHAPTER 28

Kirchdorf, Insel Poel, Germany
"1614–1618 Duke Johann Albrecht II of Mecklenburg builds a fortress near the church. In 1629, during the Thirty Years War Duke Johann Albrecht II surrounded the castle with a Catholic coalition."

The History of Insel Poel by Manfred Dederich

Annie was awake a good part of the night trying to think what to do. Karl, as a stepfather, did have the right to retrieve his stepdaughter, especially if he had Renate's permission, but Annie wasn't sure that Renate was in agreement. She half expected Greta to come back. Maybe she'd gone to a friend's house.

At two thirty she decided to call her mother and ask her advice. Susan Young was the wisest woman that Annie had ever met. An artist, ex-hippie, Susan grabbed life as no one else Annie had ever met. Her mother could make a celebration about an egg that hadn't broken when Annie's father wanted his eggs served sunny-side up.

For a moment she debated about the hour, but this was not a problem about Roger and her having a fight. A young girl was in danger.

Dave Young answered the phone. As soon as he heard Annie's voice his tone went from sleep-laden to alert. "What's wrong, Kitten?"

"I'm okay, but I really need Mom's advice for something that has nothing to do with me or anyone she knows, but it's serious."

Susan's voice was alert. Her first words were "Your dad says you've a problem, but it isn't with you."

Susan listened as Annie told her about the evening.

"Do you know what agencies are around for abused children?" Susan asked.

"Not a clue. I suppose I could ask at the hotel desk."

"Certainly not the usual question they might get," Susan said.

"Mom, should I tell Renate?"

"You can't *not* tell her. From what you've said, she certainly loves her daughter."

"If you found out Dad was abusing me what would you do?"

"After I cut his balls off, I'm not sure."

Annie was not surprised at the answer. Her parents had the type of marriage that didn't seem real. She guessed it was all the moves, when they only had each other until they settled in that brought them close. Or maybe it was Dave's support of Susan's art when she couldn't ever build her own career with the frequent moves.

"Greta is in danger. Sexual abuse can affect her whole sexual life."

Annie knew her mother was right. "I'm not hesitant because I might lose this assignment, although I might."

"I know that, Sweetie. But what are you scared of?"

"That Renate will side with Karl. They haven't been married very long and she adores him."

"Which would hurt Greta, but not as much as what Karl can do to her. Talk to Renate first thing. Then if she doesn't respond in a way that will protect Greta, find out what agencies can help. Or help Greta file a formal complaint. Maybe even check with a lawyer on the island about the case."

"I wish you were here, Mom."

"Me too. I could take the poor girl in."

Annie had no doubt her mother meant it. More than once her parents had sheltered some young person when life had been too complicated for them in their own home. However, as much as she would like to, she couldn't send Greta out of the country to her mother without getting involved in an international kidnapping.

"Can I go back to sleep?" Susan asked. "Or at least try. I'll be worrying about that child and you. You will keep me posted."

"It's the least I can do after waking you up in the middle of the night."

Annie was surprised to find she did sleep after talking with her mother. Rising early, she showered and dressed, even though it was much too early to go to the museum. Some people eat when things make them nervous. Annie was the opposite. She had joked more than once, that if she wanted to lose weight all she had to do was have a crisis, although she doubted *The Crisis Diet* would ever make a salable how-to book.

She opened the drapes then pushed the button to raise the automatic *Rolladen*. Outside the sky looked as if it were on fire over the harbor. Feeling a bit shallow that she should even consider taking a photograph after last night and what lay ahead of her with Renate, she still grabbed her camera and rushed to the docks where she could get the best shots. It wasn't that often the sky was so spectacular, she told herself, adding that she couldn't do anything until the museum opened at nine anyway.

She shot at least ten photos using different settings and angles, with and without including the boats moored in the water. Only when she put her camera away did she notice that the parking area had several luxury cars: two Porsches and one

Lamborghini made the Mercedes and the BMW look plebian. The license plates did not carry the NWM letters to show they were local. One was marked M for Munich. All but one of the remaining cars were from Zurich. The Lamborghini had a right hand drive and an English license plate.

"Quite a parking lot."

She jumped.

"I've seen more expensive cars in the last month here than I have in the last ten years before all together." The voice came from the fisherman she'd spoken to the other day.

"Obviously a bit of wealth around."

"Obviously, but not from the island. Did you ever find the harbormaster?"

"I found my answer on the Internet."

"Computers." He made it sound as if he was talking about offal.

Annie didn't say anything. "Going out early?"

"Yup. Going to look around too." He didn't say for what he was looking.

CHAPTER 29

Lübeck, Germany

"You look like hell and then some," Hans-Peter Leiter said as his partner unwrapped his scarf and shuffled off his down jacket, then slumped in his chair. "Shouldn't you be home?"

"Drives me crazy just being in bed. We don't even have a TV in the bedroom. Wife, she says it would keep her awake if I watched; and she knows I would if it were there."

Hans-Peter wished he were able to sleep in his own bed with or without a TV and that his wife would be there to complain that he wanted a TV. He'd had a TV in the bedroom and it had seriously compromised their sex life as much as his falling into bed exhausted after too many too long days.

"So what's up?"

"Full moon fake bomber struck again."

"Do you think it's some dumb kid getting his jollies?"

Hans-Peter had wondered the same thing. For the last thirteen months at the full moon, a letter had come to the station that there was a bomb at such and such place—a school, a shopping center, a hospital, a deserted building—never the same type of place twice. When the bomb squad arrived they found a plastic grenade that kids playing war would use. With it would be a note with cutout letters from *Der Spiegel* saying "HA! HA! HA!" No fingerprints. The letters were always mailed from different parts of the city.

Fritz hacked into his handkerchief. "We can't ignore it in

case the next one is real."

"We've wondered if it was a decoy, you know, so that attention would be off what he was doing elsewhere, but there are no patterns of other crimes while we are out looking at the fake bomb site."

"Someone just likes to see us spin our wheels. Or wants publicity." Hans-Peter moved back a little. Supposedly the early stages of flu or colds were contagious and he'd not picked up anything from Fritz while they rode together in a car, but he still didn't need to be sick. "We found another body yesterday?"

"Not Asian?"

"This was a bum, frozen to death near the harbor."

"And the two Asian girls?"

Hans-Peter let out a long sigh. "Nothing. No one in Lübeck where they might live knows them."

"Did you send the photos to surrounding cities?"

"Every major one."

"I suppose we could publish the photos in the papers."

Hans-Peter had thought about that, but most papers didn't want to publish gruesome pictures. It annoyed their readers, which in turn annoyed the advertisers. TV stations felt the same way. In special cases they could be persuaded but Hans-Peter didn't want to use up a chit with those he knew in the media. "Nothing."

With no witnesses, no sure national identification, although Claudia leaned toward Thai, not even clothing that wasn't available from a chain that had outlets in almost every country in the world, he knew as soon as the required time had passed, this would be a closed case unless he was very, very lucky. He had not been lucky this year at all.

CHAPTER 30

Bergedorf, Germany
May 1943

Hilke had imagined that her husband might be killed in the war, making her a widow. Never, ever did she imagine that he would ask her for a divorce. The last time they were together, even though it had only been a couple of days, she'd awakened in the middle of the night to find him holding her hand. When he left to go back to the hospital near the Russian front, he caressed her face as if trying to imprint the memory on his hand to take it out and look at it like he would a photo.

The elder Herr Suchland had said that it would be better if she didn't write her husband for his and her own safety. As for his letters to her, she hoped that they would stack up at her father's, out of reach temporarily. At least once a day she imagined that sometime in the unknown future, she would retrieve them and have a treasure trove of his words. Maybe she and Dieter would go over each sentence together, sharing what they had gone through while they were forced apart.

Hilke was becoming good at burying her dreams. She had not mastered dissipating her anger when her dreams were destroyed by factors outside her control.

At what point had Dieter thought she'd deserted him? What had her father-in-law said to him, to make him go for an annulment? If only she could reach him.

She stumbled as she walked on the dirt path between her

neighbor's farm and where she'd been existing. A cow walked up to the wire barrier between the path and passage and looked at her, its mouth going back and forth. Had Hilke reached out to grab the wire, she might have saved herself a fall, but then she could have cut her hand.

"*Scheiβ!*" She landed on her knees and two hands without breaking the skin, but the fall still stung. Maybe after the war was over, she would see Dieter: he would realize he still loved her. More likely he would have met someone else, and besides even after the war, when Germany had won, her mother would still have Jewish great-grandparents.

She'd never understood the problem with Jews. A couple of her friends at school had been Jewish as had some of her father's colleagues. They had come to the house for dinners and the Fülmers had gone to their houses as well. There was the nice Jew who ran the jewelry store where she'd bought a ring for her mother's fortieth birthday with money saved from her allowance. When he realized she didn't have enough money he reduced the price and suggested she work off the rest by watching the store for a few afternoons when his wife had their first baby. When the family had disappeared, she'd not thought much of it.

Sitting in the dirt did no good. She needed to get back to the house. The hens needed to be fed and she was behind in the weeding, not to mention the fact that the laundry she'd hung on the line would be dry and that supper needed to be cooked.

When she turned into the path leading to the house she saw that Herr Suchland's bicycle was at the gate. He would complain about how much riding it hurt him, but he rode it anyway. Then she noticed to the side of the house was a car, an official car.

When she opened the kitchen door, hoping not to be noticed, two *Polizei* grabbed her, one on each side. Her first impulse was to struggle but realized that she could not fight one of them, much less two. Instead she went limp. Not expecting it, they loosened their grip and she broke free and ran out the door. The door had an automatic lock when shut, buying her a few seconds.

Not sure where to go, she grabbed Herr Suchland's bicycle and took off down the path, knowing she couldn't outrun a car, but that it would take them time to start their engine, open the gate and come after her.

Get off the path. Hide in the woods. If the *Polizei* were clever they would follow the tracks, but there was a stream just off the path in the trees that she remembered from when her family had picnicked there. She turned her bike into the shallow water that bubbled and gurgled over grass and pebbles. She never would have guessed peddling in water would be so hard but the mud and rocks made it almost impossible. After a few yards she left the water with the bike.

The woods on each side of the stream grew a little denser. She hoped that the *Polizei* did not consider her important enough to chase. There was no reason for them to come for her. She had new papers that the Suchlands had arranged for her. They had only helped her as they had helped others. Not enough time had gone by in between her talking to Kurt Suchland and her returning to the house for an arrest order to have been issued.

It couldn't have been the TOB. He would be losing his only help, but then again, he had never wanted her there.

There was a copse of trees to one side. She scrambled out of the stream and pulled the bike deeper into where it was darker. There were enough fallen branches from winter storms to hide the bike, but barely. She stopped and listened.

Birdsong.

No thrashing about, no voices. But if she was listening for

them, maybe they were listening for her. The best thing would be to sit still. Looking around she saw a few large rocks, but they were not big enough to hide her. The woods were not deep enough for them not to be able to search them thoroughly.

She heard voices.

"Where the hell could she have gone?"

"She probably cut through to the other road."

"Go back and get the car, I'll meet you on the other side."

The one *Polizei* who was not much older than Hilke walked within feet of her. She had no idea where the other one was.

Hilke wanted to sneeze. Moving her hand she pinched her nostrils as the man tramped within thirty feet of her.

What now, she thought, when he was gone. Only he wasn't gone. He grabbed her.

CHAPTER 31

Kirchdorf, Insel Poel, Germany
"*The Ice Fishermen* was the best known work by Karl Christian Klasen, who died in 1945. The painting has been lost for some time, but we have preliminary sketches done by the artist." (A handwritten margin note reports, "The painting was located in Switzerland after this book was published and the owner allowed us to exhibit it anonymously.")

The History of Insel Poel by Manfred Dederich

Annie had been working on translations about the painter Karl Christian Klasen, who had lived and worked in Kirchdorf. Most of what he did reflected the bleak landscapes, but he also had a number of portraits so vivid, even though done only in pen and ink, that Annie felt she could walk down the street and see the people. Too bad he'd died so young before he'd had a chance to do his best work.

She was working on a description for *The Ice Fishermen:* one young, one old. The men stared out of the left of the canvas, their faces serious. Annie wondered if they ever spoke to one another, for it didn't look like it. Maybe they didn't need to. She'd seen other sketches of the men in the *Gasthaus* where she'd eaten with Gregor. Both must be dead by now, if they were painted in the thirties.

This was not the first time Annie had been called on to translate words about art. It was all she could do each time not

159

to create imaginary scenarios. What were the people saying? Why had they chosen the clothes they were wearing? That sort of thing. With *The Ice Fishermen* there was no doubt: they were each lost in their own thoughts. She wondered if their coats would have been warm enough and did they wear them because they had no others.

Despite her interest in the painting, she kept her ear out for Renate's arrival. Only Karine had been there when she arrived before the opening of the museum and had unlocked the door to let her in. She had not heard anyone come in, Renate or visitors, but then December was one of the slowest times for the museum. No tourists; and Kirchdorf was too busy getting ready for the holidays. A class visit from the local school was scheduled for later in the week, the teacher saying her pupils had trouble concentrating so close to the Christmas break so she might as well take them out and about.

Annie glanced at her watch. Coffee time, or in her case, tea. She left the gallery. "No Renate?" she asked Karine who was sitting at the desk.

"She called and said she wouldn't be in today. Do you mind making the coffee?"

Annie went into the staff room and ran the water into the pot.

Rather than go home to lunch, Annie walked to Renate's. Karl answered the doorbell. She could see Renate standing behind him. Her face was blotched and her eyes were red. "Haven't you done enough already?" he asked.

"I came to see how Greta was."

"How should we know? We can't find her."

"May I come in?"

"No. You probably gave her ideas about running away." He started to shut the door.

Annie put her hand up to stop it, knowing full well he had more strength that she did. Her movement must have surprised him because he did not force it. "I was having her stay with me, where I knew she would be safe."

She wanted to add, and if you hadn't wanted to drag her out of there, she would have been with me all night. It was a dynamic that she did not want to tackle at the moment.

Over Karl's shoulder she could see Renate mouth something that she thought was *"Ich telefoniere später."* She was fairly sure that Renate would call her later. She hoped the woman wasn't as angry as her husband. In the short time they'd known each other, she felt that they could be good friends, one of those instincts women have when they meet.

Realistically she knew geography would make an ongoing, drop-in-for-coffee, let's-go-to-a-movie type of friendship impossible, but more than once she'd found a friend on an assignment and they did see each other from time to time, e-mailed and communicated on a level deeper than Facebook would allow because there were some things one did *not* want to put out for all the world to see.

Annie took her hand away from the door, turned and walked down the walk, picking her way over the icy patches on the bricks.

CHAPTER 32

Kirchdorf, Insel Poel, Germany
"Fishing had been a major part of the island's activities but by 1939 it was down to 70 fishing boats and that was further reduced to 55 fishing boats in 1947."

The History of Insel Poel by Manfred Dederich

Annie inserted the key into the lock of her studio just as Gregor came through his front door and nodded to her. Instead of being his usually chatty self, he rushed down the hall to the exit. Once outside he ran to a car where a driver was waiting with a passenger. The car took off, leaving gravel flying in the air.

Strange man, she thought. Inside she took a hot shower, made up some soup from a packet, threw together a salad, and sat down to eat in front of the television. The room was equipped with a satellite giving her over 300 channels. By the time she would work her way through, the evening would be over. She decided on news but even then she had the choice between CNN, MSNBC, BBC, Al Jazeera, France 24, DW, RT, a Chinese station on three channels, one broadcasting in English, one in French and one in Chinese. She flipped back and forth as always, looking for different slants. As always, she found them.

The doorbell rang just as she spooned the last mouthful of split pea soup into her mouth. Her first thought was it might be Greta, but then she was afraid the girl blamed her for calling

Renate, which had brought Karl to her door. Wherever the girl was, she hoped she was okay. She could be hiding out at a friend's, but then again maybe she'd headed to the city, where she was much too young to be on her own.

"May I in come?" Renate shivered. Her nose and eyes were red.

"Of course. Have you found your daughter?"

Renate shook her head no. "Karl is out looking. He doesn't know I'm here. He'd be furious. He says it's your fault."

"And what do you think?" Annie helped Renate off with her Loden coat. The green boiled wool was cold to her touch.

"I don't know you all that well, but I saw how you were with Greta. I can't believe you'd do anything that wasn't in her best interest."

Annie led Renate to the couch. If Renate believed that Annie's heart was in the right place, she might have a chance to talk about the problem Greta was having with Karl.

"Tell me about Greta. She doesn't seem all that difficult and you two seemed to have a nice relationship."

A smile flashed across Renate's face so fast and disappeared that Annie wasn't sure she hadn't imagined it. "Maybe because it was just the two of us for so long, we were closer than most mothers and daughters."

"I know I was closer to my parents because we moved around so much, that sometimes we were all we had—each other." Annie wasn't sure how much to share or if sharing would bring forth enough information so that she could proceed. Damn it, in books these conversations always went smoothly, perhaps because the writer controlled who asked the questions and what the respondents answered. Here she had no control, just instinct.

"Something like that."

"When did you notice the change?"

Renate looked at her hands. "Usually when I dated, I didn't

163

really let the men, not that there were that many, get to know Greta. The one before Karl because he was local, she knew and really liked. Told me it would be all right if we got married."

"But you didn't."

"And she was disappointed."

"How did she feel about Karl in the beginning?"

"She admitted she wanted me to get back with the former one, but Karl and she seemed to get along. He took interest in the things that interested her. She'd never been a discipline problem, other than not picking up her clothes, or forgetting to empty the dishwasher."

"Compared to drug use and some of the things teens do, not serious."

"Not serious at all." Renate got up and began to pace. "Sometimes Karl made a big thing about it, but since he was away so much, Greta told me that she would humor him. Those were her words, 'humor him.' "

"I don't know her all that well, but it sounds like the little I do know about her."

Renate came back and sat on the coffee table in front of the couch where Annie was.

Annie searched for her words carefully. God, how she hated these delicate situations. "Was there ever a black-and-white change?"

Renate shook her head. Then she was silent. She frowned. Annie resisted jumping in. Then Renate cocked her head and said, "Wait a minute, maybe."

"Maybe?"

"I was at a regional museum director's conference. It was especially for those in charge of small museums for towns and villages. There were a few theme museum directors there too, one for stamps, another for a cheese maker, that type."

Annie nodded.

"Usually when I go away, Greta stays with my neighbors, although one time I let her stay alone and the neighbors checked on her. That was one of those times. While I was gone Karl came back . . . I think he'd been traveling somewhere in Thailand or the Philippines. I can't remember where he goes when."

"And?"

"And when I came back, Greta would leave the room whenever he came into it. I figured they had had a fight over something. Greta refused to talk about it. Karl accused her of being a teenager. He also said it was my fault because I'd been too lenient with her. In fact Greta was about the only thing we ever disagreed on. And Karl was the only thing she and I disagreed on. I hadn't put it together before you asked."

"You must feel torn."

"It gives new meaning to being in the middle."

Annie reached out and put her hand on Renate's knee. "I understand. Roger and I fight over Gaëlle, although I'm usually on her side. There's nothing stricter than a policeman father." If this were truly a conversation of women sharing about their problems, she'd have told Renate about all the other things they fought over, but this was not the time.

"Well, I was often on Greta's side, too. She gets top grades, has nice friends, and as far as I know, she never did drugs. She comes home before curfew. What Karl would take as being rude or sassy is how we've always joked with each other."

"She absolutely refused to be alone with him since September. Won't even run errands with him when he asked if she would like to go. See, he was trying to build a relationship, but she would have no part of it."

Annie put her head in her hands. When she looked up, Renate was watching her closely.

"I don't know how to tell you this Renate, when Greta came

here last night, she wanted my help. She implied that Karl was abusing her."

"He was tough on her."

"I don't mean that way."

Renate's facial expression went through many changes. "I don't believe it."

"I do know that kids seldom lie about things like that. Although . . ."

Renate said nothing more. She stood, put on her coat and left, ignoring Annie's call of "Please come back."

CHAPTER 33

Bergedorf, Germany
May 1943

Hilke gave the *Polizei* a fight, landing blow after blow. The two had to work together to throw her on the ground. Because she was face down in pine needles she couldn't see which one wrenched her shoulder as they forced her hands behind her back and tied them with a rope that cut into her skin. The older one turned her over. She kicked out.

"Get more rope," the older one said. While the younger one went to the car, the older one turned Hilke back onto her stomach and sat on her.

With the new rope they tied her legs and then fastened the rope around her to keep her from kicking out. The two of them carried her through the trees until they came to the car.

"We'll take her to Neuengamme," the older man said.

The drive lasted less than ten minutes by Hilke's estimation, although she couldn't be sure. She could not see anything except the sky and clouds moving through the window from the rear seat where they had laid her prone on her back.

When the car stopped, the man behind the wheel leaned out the open car window. "Hey, Friedrich, we've a robber for you! Stole some money from a farmer, then his bicycle."

Hilke heard footsteps and a man in uniform stuck his head into the driver's side. The back of the seat blocked her from seeing anything but his bulk.

167

"Jewish?"

"*Nein.* Here are her papers. She was working for old man Suchland."

"Take her to Processing."

The car moved again for two minutes and stopped. The police carried her into a building and dropped her on the floor in front of a desk.

"Hildegard, we've got a new one for you."

A woman in an SS uniform, maybe in her early thirties, maybe younger, looked at Hilke and then took the papers that the older man had thrust at her.

Hilke wondered what her rank was.

"Why is she tied?"

"She put up a fight."

The SS woman cocked her head. "From the scratches on your face, looks like she equals two of you."

"Caught us off guard."

The SS woman pulled a gun from her desk drawer. "Untie her." She looked at Hilke. "If you so much as lift a finger, I'll shoot you. There's no way out of this concentration camp, so your best bet is to go along with everything. *Verstehen Sie?*"

"I understand," Hilke whispered. She had heard rumors about concentration camps. Herr Suchland had given them credence, but felt he could do nothing. He had said that he thought her mother had been taken to one. Had her mother gone through this? Hilke made a decision to become a model prisoner until she could escape. "I'll do whatever you want."

The rope had left welts on her wrists. She wanted to rub them, but that would show them they had hurt her. Being docile didn't have to mean giving them satisfaction.

"She's all yours," the older man said and tipped his cap.

Hildegard stared at Hilke. She wrote something in a book. "Your number will begin with a zero, which shows you were brought in by the police. Most of our zero prisoners have come from other camps." Hildegard opened a closet and took out blue and gray striped trousers and shirt. Opening a drawer, she rummaged through a number of armbands marked with colored triangles. She found a yellow one that didn't have a Star of David and threw it at Hilke. "Change."

Hilke debated asking for privacy, but decided against it. Trying to ignore the pain in her shoulder, she stripped and dressed as fast as she could. The outfit had been partially mended, but the cuffs were frayed and there was a tear on the arm.

Hildegard watched her. "You're in Block Thirteen. I'll get someone to take you over there."

CHAPTER 34

Kirchdorf, Insel Poel, Germany
"In 1631 Gustav Adolf II of Sweden helped the dukes of Mecklenburg regain their power, and when Johann Albrecht II returned to Poel he found his castle almost destroyed."
The History of Insel Poel by Manfred Dederich

Annie sloughed off her coat and headed for the telephone. After Renate had left she had tried to find her. The woman's house was dark. She drove around the island, hoping to spot her car, thinking that her friend was trying to locate her daughter.

Renate had struck her as the type of person incapable of doing nothing even if doing something might be useless. What Annie, herself, was doing was probably equally useless. Even if she saw Renate's car, what would be the next step? Chase it?

Dumb, dumb, dumb.

Her parents' phone in Geneva rang and she heard her mother's warm, soft voice: "Hi, Kitten."

"What are you doing? Have you time to talk?" Silly question. Her mother always found time to talk to her. Susan Young had always listened for hours when Annie was upset when she was first in school in Holland and couldn't understand what anyone was saying, then when she cried her eyes out over Jean-Claude who broke up with her, and yet again about the perfect dress she'd found on Longemalle. Her mother listened to complaints about papers that Annie needed to write and celebrated when she got good grades.

"What's up?"

"Where are you?"

"In bed. The *bise* is blowing, the house is cold, and the lure of the electric under-sheet and a book far outweighed sitting in the living room, fire or no fire, watching a football game with your father."

Annie pictured her mother in the bedroom with one chocolate-colored wall and the others painted a soft beige. The thickly puffed *duvet* would be tucked up to her armpits. The chocolate-colored drapes would be drawn, hiding the view of the lake and the Jura Mountains.

In a way she was glad that her mother was in bed. In that room they had had so many conversations, everything from what to have for dinner to why Annie didn't want to go back to university in the States but transfer to the University of Geneva.

"It's the girl. Greta, you said her name was, didn't you?"

"That and her mother." Annie told her mother about the conversation. "Maybe I shouldn't have told her."

"What else could you have done?"

"Aha, the old ask-the-questions trick until I come to the answer you want me to."

Susan's laugh tinkled through the telephone line. "What would you have done if you knew Karl—that's his name isn't it . . ."

"Hm hmm."

". . . if you knew Karl was just cheating on Renate? Say with another woman? An adult?"

"I wouldn't say anything. But Greta is a child."

Again Susan laughed. "*Voilà.* Question answered, you did the right thing." Her voice changed. "Now this is important. Have you any idea where Greta might be?"

"No, but I could try and find out."

CHAPTER 35

Lübeck, Germany

"Telephone, Hans-Peter." The policewoman on reception duty that day called across the room to where the detective was sitting. He and Fritz were reviewing files to map out their day's efforts. "Someone from Kirchdorf."

Hans-Peter put his head in his hands as his partner Fritz Gärtner voiced what he felt. "I hope that redhead hasn't found another dead body."

Fritz listened as his partner answered the call, but he said nothing that would give away what the speaker was saying. He watched Hans-Peter reach for a pencil and paper and jot down notes.

"We'll be there as soon as we can. Don't touch anything and stay away from it. Yes, I know you know." He disconnected the phone, and punched in a number. "Claudia, we've another death in Kirchdorf. No, not a girl this time. An arm, a man's arm by the description: hairy and with a tattoo."

The snow where it had been pushed at the end of the parking lot near the Kirchdorf beach had melted then refrozen, trapping dirt and turning it almost a shiny brown.

Hans-Peter and Fritz sat in the cruiser with the engine running trying to decide if they wanted to go into the small shop that sold both souvenirs and coffee while waiting for Claudia.

"This is boring," Fritz said. "The third time we've been here in little over a week."

Walking down the wooden-slatted planks that ran from the parking lot over the sand to the water was the old policeman that they had met on both of their earlier trips to look at the bodies of the girls.

The old policeman opened the back door and got in. "Hadn't expected to see you again so soon."

"Likewise," Hans-Peter said. "What's with Kirchdorf these days? No murders for decades . . . then three?"

"Not sure this is a murder. It's just an arm."

"Not a normal way to die," Fritz mumbled under his breath. The old cop appeared not to hear. Hans-Peter flashed Fritz a *shut-up* look.

The medical examiner's car pulled up next to them, and Claudia hopped out wearing ordinary clothes. She quickly pulled out the white covering she wore over her clothes when examining crime scenes.

She's really cute, which does not match her competency at all, Hans-Peter thought. He shouldn't be thinking like that, but he knew his chances for getting back with his wife were minimal and he didn't like being without a woman . . . and not just for sexual reasons.

Claudia, unlike his wife, would not stay home and make sure his shirts were ironed; that he could guarantee. He wanted company, something he had missed in his marriage for a long time despite the well-ironed shirts. Shirts could be sent to the laundry. A cleaning woman could be hired. Dinners are served in restaurants.

"We have to stop meeting like this." She pulled her equipment from the backseat. "Where's the redhead?"

"She didn't find this one," the local policeman said.

"Who did?" Claudia looked at the local policeman.

"A mother who was gathering shells for some kind of

173

Christmas decoration while her kids were in school. She called me. Because she had to pick up her kids, she left, but I've got her contacts," the old cop said.

For a moment Hans-Peter pictured a Christmas wreath with the arm in the center, a bit like the circle and diagonal strip marking no parking signs.

The Lübeck threesome followed the local policeman. The arm was caught up in dune grass not that far from where the first body had been found. Last night there'd been a high tide, made worse by winds.

Claudia snapped photos. "This is so much easier since I got a viewfinder." The other three looked at her. "I couldn't see what I was shooting before until I could find a shady spot because of the sun." She zoomed in on the arm. "Unfortunately dune grass doesn't show much about the location. Dune grass on one beach is like another." She made some notes, a sketch and then brought out a folded up body bag from her pack and put the arm in.

"Did anyone look for other body parts?" Fritz asked. He was standing as far away from the scene as he could and still be in it.

"No."

"We should, while Claudia is still here," Hans-Peter said.

"If I don't have to make another trip out here again, it will be more than fine. In the summer for a picnic with the kids, that's okay."

Hans-Peter wondered if his boys would like her girls. He motioned for Fritz to walk with him. Rough-edged planks were also strewn along the beach. They were painted a faded blue. "Was there a bad storm last night?" he called to the policeman, not thinking that the weather wouldn't have been all that different in Lübeck.

"We've had no snow, some wind, nothing abnormal for this

type of moon, it being December and all. Thought there would be. Heard some thunder as I was going home last night but it was only two claps back-to-back."

Hans-Peter thanked him and told him he could go home if he wanted.

"*Danke.* I've only one more day on the job and then I'm retired."

"We may need to contact you," Fritz said.

"The wife and I are going to the Costa Brava for the Christmas holidays, but I'll leave a phone number with the station." He got into his Panda, but before he drove off, he lowered his window and added, "I don't have any problem leaving unfinished business for others." He raised the window and disappeared.

"Hell of a way to end a career," Claudia said. "Can we get some coffee before we head back?" She'd placed the arm in the trunk of her car. "It'll keep in this cold."

The coffee shop was empty except for the waitress who brought them demitasses of steaming black liquid. It mixed with the smell of the cold coming off their woolen coats.

"Do you think there's any connection?" Fritz asked. "Three bodies or two-point-two bodies in just about a week."

"Except this was clearly a man. Older I would guess. His hands were well-used. And it looked as if his arm had been ripped away from the rest of the body."

The three were provoked into silence by the image.

"Think all that wood is connected in any way?" Fritz asked.

"Damn it. We should probably go back and pack up what we can find."

The temperature seemed to have dropped as they left the coffee shop although the sun wouldn't be setting for at least another hour.

As they walked across the dunes, another lot of attached

boards bounced on the incoming waves. Whitecaps that had been there when they were there a half hour before were now regular waves making their way to shore.

"Have you noticed," Hans-Peter said, "that most of the wood is either varnished or this blue color?"

"I am now. If the stuff is drifting in, do we have to stay here until more arrives?" Fritz had his arms loaded. "*Scheiß!* I can't believe there's grease on one of them. I just had this damned coat cleaned."

"I don't think the wood has been in the water that long. I would need to run some tests, but then again it could have been waterproofed," Claudia said. "I wonder if we'll get any more body parts."

As she spoke, Fritz with his arms holding a stack of recovered planks and standing at the water's edge looked down. He jumped. "A foot! In a boot!"

"We need to call local police and make sure that they rope off this area," Hans-Peter said. "We could stay here all night and wait to see what else the sea gives up, but I for one, prefer to go home to my own bed, even if I have to come back."

Fritz dialed the Kirchdorf station. "No answer."

"Try Wismar, the Kirchdorf station in winter is only a satellite to Wismar."

When Fritz hung up, he said, "They're sending someone now. I guess the old man hadn't briefed them on this latest development."

"Oh, goody," Hans-Peter said. "Claudia?"

"Let me call my babysitter and tell her I'll be back later than planned." She shoved her hands into her pocket. "She's used to it."

"Let's get some coffee, where it's warmer," Fritz said.

When the coffee shop closed, the threesome from Lübeck went to sit in the car. Fritz gave Claudia the passenger seat and he climbed into the back. "Killing the environment, letting the engine run," he muttered.

"Better than having us freeze to death or ending up in the *Krankenhaus* with pneumonia," Claudia said. "And I'm hungry. Fritz, the grocery store should still be open. Would you consider going and getting us something? A sausage? Some *Brötchen*? An apple?"

Fritz got out of the car. "Better than being bored here."

Claudia handed him some money. "My treat. Coffee or an *Apfelsaft* would be fine."

"Alone at last," Hans-Peter said, only half joking.

"Nothing as romantic as an idling car in the middle of December with body parts in the trunk."

"Actually, they are in your car." He was wondering if he should make a move. If he failed, it could ruin an excellent working relationship. "Are you dating anyone?"

"With two small girls and a job where I seem to be on call 24/7? Who would put up with that?"

"Maybe someone who is in the same field." He then changed the subject. It was a start.

Chapter 36

Bergedorf, Germany
May 1943

Hilke could hear the other women breathing or snoring. By her estimate the night before, she guessed that there were close to 300 of them. She turned on her bunk—just a thin straw mattress with no sheet—that was barely wider than her body when she lay on her side. The hard wood pressed against the bruises inflicted by the men who'd arrested her. Hers was the bottom of three bunks.

The sky, which she could see through the unshuttered windows, had gone from black to dark gray. A bird sung out a single melody, then stopped.

"You're awake?" Ute was in the bunk across the narrow aisle. Her voice was a whisper.

"Ja."

"They'll be getting us up soon. Stay close to me." The woman turned her back.

Ute was right. The door to the wooden hut opened so hard that it slammed against the wall.

Two women guards came in and started pulling those prisoners who had not jumped up off their bunks onto the floor.

There was a rush to the latrines in the middle of the hut. Hilke noticed that no one showed any modesty as they squatted, their legs and thighs thin between the top of their shirts and where they had dropped their pants.

The smells were of urine and unwashed bodies, although there were ten taps and basins in the room. Hilke thought of the deep bathtub back in Hamburg, which she would fill with hot water from the gas water heater suspended above the tub and then lie back until the water cooled. Back then she'd been impatient for the water to heat.

"*Schnell, schnell,*" one of the guards yelled.

"We can only pee so fast," Ute muttered, so softly that Hilke wasn't sure she'd heard.

One of the guards was looking at the mattress in the bunk over where Ute had slept. "Who moved it?" she yelled. "Whose is it?"

An old woman, or maybe she had aged from being in the camp, came forward.

"Fix it," the guard said.

The woman got out of the line for the latrine and headed for her bunk. The guard pushed her. At the bunk she moved the mattress a slight degree to the left. The guard had lost interest and was looking at the other bunks.

CHAPTER 37

Kirchdorf, Insel Poel, Germany

"Some of the first known inhabitants were from what is now Poland. Place names such as the village of Gollwitz ending in 'witz' and Malchow ending in 'ow' show the influence of these Slavic settlers."

The History of Insel Poel by Manfred Dederich

Renate wasn't at the museum when Annie arrived; but when she came downstairs for a coffee break, Renate had arrived. Her eyes had dark circles under them and her hair did not have its usual sleekness. Mothers with missing children and husbands accused of sexual offenses do not think about their looks. She said almost nothing to Annie.

Annie wondered if she would have trouble and not be allowed to finish the project or worse would she have trouble being paid? Renate did not seem vindictive. Nor was she the sole voice in the museum. Annie wondered if she would be better to stay away or approach Renate again.

Renate solved the problem. She went into her office and shut her door before Annie could say anything other than *Guten Morgen,* which was answered with the same and nothing more.

Karine, whom Renate had been growling at when Annie entered the room, shrugged. "Do you know what's up?"

Not feeling she had any right to comment Annie shook her head. "I better get back to work." Upstairs, she tried to concentrate on the paintings. She'd done enough work on art and antiques for auction catalogs to understand more than the subject matter, and although it wasn't in the contract, she enlarged on the original technical information given to her in German.

Manfred in his history of the Insel Poel had spent two chapters on the artist Klasen and had included information on who the people were or where the landscapes were, giving more meaning than just looking at an old woman or a wind bending trees. He had a second chapter on the biography of the artist.

Annie's hands flew over the keyboard. Only when she looked out the window and saw that the setting sun had turned the sky fire-red did she realize that it was five and the museum would be closing.

She packed up her mini-laptop, the one she used when she traveled because of its weight and ease.

"I was going to get you," Karine said as Annie entered the reception area. "Otherwise you'd be locked in until morning. You really *do* get caught up in your work."

"If you only knew how much more fun this is in comparison to explaining how to operate software."

"I can imagine," Karine said. "Renate has already gone."

Annie was both relieved and sorry. She wished she could find the words to make sure that the woman understood . . . understood what? Understood that Annie only meant to help? That Greta was in danger? That the man she loved wasn't worthy of her love?

Gaëlle flashed through Annie's mind. What if she'd discovered Roger had been abusing his daughter? That would be a thousand times worse—incest *and* pedophilia. Roger was incapable of any such act, but wasn't that exactly what Renate had thought about Karl? No woman wants to admit the man she loves is unfaithful . . . no, the word unfaithful was not strong enough . . . no woman wants to admit that the man she loves is a child molester, especially of a child under her protection. In some cases it is worse when the woman is totally dependent on the man financially. At least that wasn't the case here. Or maybe it was. The couple had taken on a larger house than the flat where Renate and Greta had lived before the marriage.

Compared to Greta's safety, the money issue was minor.

Annie pulled her cap over her ears and shoved her hands into her mittens for the short walk to her rented studio. The temperature was milder, not mild. Another week and she'd be in Geneva for Christmas. Gaëlle and Roger would be there with her parents for one of her mother's let's-pull-out-all-stops Christmases that matched the soppiest Christmas movie, only with Susan Young the sincerity was a thousand percent.

In one house, a gray-haired man was lowering his *Rolladen* but not before Annie caught a glimpse of the heavy red-leather living room suite and the wall that was totally lined with books. She was tempted to wave, but didn't. Her wave could have meant your little scene has given me pleasure. The man might mistake such a gesture, more that she was being nosy and intrusive into his world.

Outside the entrance to her building, Annie noticed a car with its engine running. As she walked by, Renate opened the window. "May I talk with you, *bitte?*"

"Do you want to come in or should we talk out here? Inside is more comfortable."

Renate rolled up the window and shut off the engine. As they walked by her neighbor's door, two angry male voices drifted out into the hall, but not clearly enough to understand.

Inside, Annie took Renate's coat and directed her to the couch. "Would you like tea, coffee, hot chocolate, *Glühwein?*"

"*Nein, danke.* I didn't come for a beverage. I really came to apologize."

Annie sat on the coffee table in front of Renate and took both of the woman's hands between her own. They were cold, and she rubbed them. "No need for any apology. I don't think there's an etiquette book in the world that would cover this situation."

The smile that played on Renate's lips could only be described as rueful. "I need to tell you what has happened."

"Only if you want to."

"I need to. You were being a friend to me. And to Greta. It had to be hard for you."

Not easy, Annie thought, but she knew silence was better.

"When Karl was out I went through his computer. As smart as he is, he hadn't password protected anything. It was filled with pornography of young girls. I also found a video of Greta in the shower through our clear glass door."

Annie remembered seeing it when she passed the bathroom to use the toilet room. Still she said nothing.

"He hadn't edited it. At first she didn't know he was there. Then she saw him and came screaming out. She reached for a towel, and he must have used one hand to hold the camera and another to grab the towel. It went black." Renate started to cry.

Annie got up and went to the bathroom and tore off some toilet paper. "I'm afraid I don't have any tissues."

"I threw him out. I've no idea where he is, and I only care because I want him to be miserable." More sobs. "How could I not have believed my own daughter?"

"Because you wanted Karl to be real."

"What do I do now?"

"Have you talked to her friends?"

"All of them claim not to know anything."

"Do you believe them?"

Renate was silent. "Maybe . . . some of them . . . maybe one of them she told where she was . . . or maybe one is hiding her."

"I think what we need to do is go to them all and ask them if they know where she is, to get in contact with her and to tell them that Karl is gone. Are you friendly with their parents?"

"I went to school with most of them. The island is a tiny place."

"Do you want me to go with you?"

As they put on their coats, Annie realized that she hadn't asked Renate if she'd made a formal complaint, nor if she'd secured Karl's computer—a step at a time.

Annie waited by the open door for Renate to get more toilet paper from the bathroom. Finding the girl was the top priority. "Let's start by visiting her best friends."

"I telephoned already," Renate said.

"Maybe if we show up in person, it might help."

CHAPTER 38

Kirchdorf, Insel Poel, Germany
"In the 11th and 12th centuries Kirchdorf produced ceramics."
The History of Insel Poel by Manfred Dederich

Kristin tried not to look at her twin, Elke. She worried that their mother might pick up on their thoughts. Gisela Rosher had long ago learned to know when the twins were up to something, although she'd never mastered knowing what it was, thank goodness. Kristin hoped by not looking at Elke she might not sound another alarm. "I don't know, I told you I don't know."

Gisela got up and put another log on the embers in the fireplace. The room would have been drafty with or without the fire, which did nothing to dispel the cold even as the wood caught and flamed.

The twins were on the couch. Renate and Annie sat on the edge of two overstuffed chairs, which faced the couch. The fire was on their left. Gisela had brought a chair from the dining room for herself, which she placed on the same side as Annie and Renate—adults one side, kids another.

In between was a large square coffee table covered with the girls' schoolbooks and papers. They preferred to do their homework in the living room because their bedrooms were kept at as low a temperature as possible without allowing the pipes running between the rooms and the bathroom to freeze.

They're making a wall. Not good, Kristin thought. They are older and want to appear united, but we will always be stronger.

Gisela offered Renate and the other woman coffee. Kristin took her mother's lack of attention on her to glance at her sister, who widened her eyes just enough for Kristin to think that they had to keep their secret.

The twins were both dressed in jeans but their boots and sweaters were different. The difference in clothing was how people told them apart, especially on days they wore their long blonde hair identically. They never told anyone that midway through a school day, they might switch outfits and the one who had the ponytail would let it down while the one with the hair hanging down her back would swoop it into a ponytail.

All this year they had switched off on taking tests, when their classes were different, earning both of them better grades. Kristin was always better in anything that didn't involve numbers, where Elke excelled. They were quick to point out their differences academically whenever their mother worried that she hadn't done enough to make them individuals. Gisela, they thought, had taken a contract on a perpetual guilt trip from the day they were born. Her hovering sometimes drove them a bit crazy. When necessary they would take turns "diverting *Mutti*" by going off with their mother alone and reassuring her she was being a good mother. Overall she was, they agreed, just too interfering.

Why their mother worried so, they never quite understood. Their grades were good and would have been even if they didn't switch off. Their friends were also good kids with the same strict limits that Gisela put on them. They didn't drink or do drugs. Kristin wanted to be a lawyer and Elke a doctor.

As for their father, he had remarried and had moved to Berlin. They visited him at Easter break, three weeks in the summer and some weekends individually during the fall term.

The trips were neither horrible nor wonderful. Their stepmother hadn't read the *Ugly Stepmother Manual,* but she didn't coddle them either. She was too busy with her two children, the twins' half brother and half sister, born three months and three years after their parents separated.

The girls debated holding their little brother responsible for the breakup of their home, considering the timing of his birth and the rushed divorce but decided he was innocent. Their father just couldn't keep his pants zippered, and it had hurt them all. Both twins had decided to never marry. Men were not to be trusted. Women were to be protected wherever possible.

The girls talked about their father favoring his only son over his three daughters, something they couldn't understand for Luke was a spoiled brat at best who knew enough screaming brought him anything he wanted. Luke, they could do without.

Kristin turned her attention to Greta's mother and the woman with the long curly red hair and the funny accent, which she guessed was English or American—she wasn't sure because it was so slight. All she knew it wasn't any of the regional accents although it had traces of *Schwäbisch.* "May I ask where you're from?" Kristin looked at Annie.

Gisela put down the bellows she'd been using. "Kristin, that's not important, now."

Annie smiled. "It's all right Frau Rosher. I've lived in many countries, which has messed up my accent. I learned my German in Stuttgart."

I was right, *Schwäbisch,* Kristin thought. "How do you know Greta?"

"Kristin! Enough! They need you to give them information, not the other way around."

Renate rubbed her hand over her forehead as if she were rubbing away a headache. "It's fine. This is a conversation, not an interrogation."

"What we really need to know is if you have any idea, any hints, any insights into where Greta might have gone," Annie said.

"Why wouldn't we tell you, if we did?" Elke took over.

"Some strange sense of loyalty, perhaps," Gisela said.

"Can you ask around at school tomorrow, *bitte*?" Renate asked. "And do you have any idea of one of her friends who might know . . . someone she would have run to for help?"

"I thought you and Greta got along fine. Maybe she's been kidnapped," Elke said. Kristin appreciated her twin keeping the heat off of her.

"Elke!"

Elke threw herself back onto the couch where she was seated next to her sister. "Anything is possible."

Kristin felt Annie staring at her in the same way her mother did when she knew something wasn't what it seemed. She held the look as long as she could and then tilted her head before looking away so it didn't look like she was giving in. At least that was the message she hoped she conveyed.

"Can you do one thing for us . . . well, two really?" Kristin felt Annie's eyes boring into her. She would have to be so careful of what she said. Fooling her own mother or even Greta's wasn't that hard, but this American was an unknown.

"Probably. I don't like to say yes until I know what it is. I mean you could be asking me to do something I don't know how to do, like drive a car," Kristin said.

Gisela went over to Kristin and put both hands on the girl's shoulders. "Kristin, this isn't a game. Greta is missing. She could be in danger. Cooperate or you'll be grounded until your wedding and maybe even during and after your wedding."

Kristin knew that when her mother joked like that, it wasn't joking. Strange how different families communicated. Greta had been close to her mother, but not close enough to make her mother believe what her stepfather was doing to her. Kristin had believed her. Elke had believed her. Why would Greta make up something like that?

"What do you want us to do?"

Renate leaned forward in her seat. "Ask all her friends if they know where she is and ask them to get in touch with her and tell her it is safe to come home. Karl is moving out."

"And the second, if you know, contact her and give her the same message," Annie said. As the women got up to leave, Kristin was sure that Annie, at least, knew they had been lying.

CHAPTER 39

Colerne, Wiltshire, England
May 1943

Gordon Tibbitts sat in the third pew on the left where he had the best view of Martha, who sang in the choir. She'd told him she sang softly, so that all the notes she missed were drowned out by the other singers.

God, how he loved her. He smiled inwardly because he used the word "God" to emphasize his feelings, when he doubted there was a god or gods at all. If there were a god, and he let this war happen, then Gordon didn't want anything to do with him. If there were divine spiritual beings, they probably were playing a giant chess-like game with paltry humans.

Vicar Willson droned on and on and on. Gordon had been to other Anglican churches where the sermons were at least interesting or gave realistic guidance. He had never cottoned to all the biblical writings, which he thought of as scratchings from tribesmen long ago. Still, there was some wisdom in the Bible, which the vicar seemed to miss so intent he was on the negative.

Martha still had not told her father that she was seeing a "fly-boy," the pit of society in terms of daughters having any type of relations with them, although Vicar Willson always concluded his sermons with a prayer for "the brave men who are defending our island from the heathen Germans." Maybe the vicar thought them heathens because Germans were probably

Lutheran or—maybe worse—Catholic in his hierarchy of what was acceptable in his God's eyes.

Gordon tuned out the rest of the sermon, instead watching the dust flicker through a ray of sun coming through the narrow church window. The church smelled of age and dust. Only the rustle of people standing and walking over him brought him back to the present.

Martha had told him to be patient. His patience was at an end.

The parishioners filed into the hall where tea and biscuits had been set up for all. Martha was seated at the table pouring milk then tea into the cups and handing them out. He walked over to where she was sitting and whispered, "I love you," into her ear.

A bit of tea slurped over the rim of the cup. She put it down. "This is mine, Mrs. White. I'll make you a clean one."

"I'll take this one," Gordon said. "It'll be cold by the time you get to drink it."

He moved over to where Vicar Willson was talking with a man that Gordon now knew was on the church board and seemed to have even less humor than the vicar, if that were possible. He waited until the board member moved on.

Gordon deliberately had worn civilian clothes. When he'd started going to the church, he'd dressed in his uniform until Martha had shared with him what her father thought of the character of the RAF men: they were all right to defend England, but represented a danger to the virginity of local girls. Gordon did grant the vicar a certain amount of rightness in his opinion. In a small village like Colerne, there had been more than one quick marriage, as well as the few girls who suddenly had gone off to live with relatives.

He and Martha had kissed, held hands, but as much as he wanted to, he had not even put his hands under her blouse, much less under her skirt.

This could not go on. He waited until the board member moved away. "Vicar Willson, could I speak to you in private, please? After people leave, of course."

Vicar Willson scanned the room. "Martha does have lunch ready."

Gordon knew that the lunch was a cold plate. "It won't take five minutes. I'm sure your daughter won't mind. You can set your watch."

The vicar was being approached by two members of the flower committee. "No, let's do it now." He turned to the women. "Excuse me ladies, but this brave pilot needs a few minutes of guidance."

The women nodded and headed back to where Martha was sitting. She looked up at him and tilted her head as if asking what he was doing talking to her father. He smiled and nodded back at her. He could see her eyes opening further.

Gordon followed the vicar up the stairs to the man's study. It was a small room, overpowered by a big oak desk covered with papers. Bookcases on each side of the casement window were filled with leather-bound texts with gold-leaf titles too small to read from Gordon's point of view. Two Bibles, one closed, one opened, were on the desk amid piles of paper. In the corner next to the door was a typewriter. Gordon knew that was where Martha typed up her father's sermons, letters and various church announcements.

The vicar had a big leather chair with a carved back of leaves and vines that could have been likened to a throne. Two visitors' chairs, both with green, cracked leather, were on the other side of the clerical barrier.

"Sit, sit, sit." The vicar waved his hand once for each "sit" toward the chairs. He seated himself in his chair, took out his pocket watch and placed it in front of him. "Five minutes, son."

Gordon resisted saying, "I'm not your son, but I'd love to be your son-in-law." It was far too early for that. "You may not know much about me other than seeing me in church when I'm not on a mission."

"We don't get a lot of boys from the base." Vicar Willson fiddled with his pocket watch.

"I grew up in Bath. My father was killed last April in the third air raid."

"My deepest sympathies. I'll pray for his soul."

"That's very kind of you." He wanted to say his father was good and his soul didn't need many prayers.

"My mother has rented a cottage here in Colerne to be closer to me. Our house and garden were totally destroyed. Perhaps my mother would like to be on your flower committee." Get to the point he thought. But he needed to establish himself as a decent man. "When the war is over, she'll go with me to Glasgow. I was a lecturer there at the university. In economics."

"That is a subject I never understood," Vicar Willson said.

"One of my goals is to make it more understandable, but that's not why I'm here."

"You need spiritual guidance?"

"No, I want to see your daughter."

Vicar Willson stood and picked up his pocket watch. "Out of the question. Martha has much too much to do around the vicarage."

"Sir, if you please, it is very normal for a young woman of Martha's age to see a man who is interested in her and her in him."

Vicar Willson held the door open for Gordon, who had not yet stood. "I'm sure she has no interest in you."

"That's where you're wrong, Father," Martha said as the door opened to reveal her about to knock. "I've every interest in seeing him."

"You've been going behind my back, young lady. There will be consequences."

"Father, I'm twenty-three and have a right to see a person I'm learning to care about."

"Well, I forbid it."

"You cannot forbid me, Father. You do not have to like it, but it would be much better if you accepted it. The congregation might not understand if I moved out and in with Ruth and had nothing more to do with the church."

Gordon had read about people spluttering, but he had never witnessed it until that moment.

"I want my lunch," Vicar Willson said and stalked out of the office.

Martha went to Gordon and put her arms around his neck. She only came up to his shoulders. "I wish you'd warned me what you were going to do."

"I didn't know myself. I just knew we needed to get to the next step. I love you."

She stepped back, her mouth opened. "I hoped you did. I would hate to be the only one who loved in this."

He kissed her open mouth.

When they broke apart, she said, "I'd better get Father's lunch. I'll see you later at Ruth's. The atmosphere around here this afternoon will probably be glacial at its warmest."

As Gordon left the church to go home to where his mother had lunch ready for him, he wondered if he even should try to talk her into joining the Ladies Flower Committee. She had a much closer relationship to flowers than she did to any god.

CHAPTER 40

Kirchdorf, Insel Poel, Germany

Elisabeth Schwartz opened her eyes. The morning light was filtering through the slats of the *Rolladen*. The clock on the night table read 08:07. She shut her eyes again for a final snuggle under the thick feather *Eiderdown*, still good since her aunt had given it to her and Edvard for their marriage.

The linen of the *Eiderdown* cover and pillow slip were soft after years of washing and whitening. It was smooth because she ironed the covers in the special large press. She could have bought new covers that never needed ironing, but her aunt had died shortly after their wedding and it was her way of preserving the old woman's memory.

And even if it weren't for her aunt, Elisabeth believed in quality which lasted. She could never bring herself to throw out anything that still had use. The only reason she'd agreed to the plasma screen, when the old television worked, was the transfer to digital, whatever that was, although she had to admit the flat screen was beautiful.

Besides, she considered herself a specialist in domestic arts, taking care of Edvard and her son and daughter, although her children had moved many years ago: one lived in Berlin and the other in New York.

She did not expect Edvard to be beside her. He was out and down to his boat early and told her that he would leave coffee for her. She'd packed his lunch for him the night before, although when she had done so, he still wasn't home from the sea. Not that this was unusual. If he had a good run, he might stay out late or even pull into one of the bays and sleep on the boat so he could get an early start.

He and the boat had provided a satisfactory life for them all. They were by no means rich, but with careful planning they had enough, far more than her parents and grandparents had had. Life for them between the war and the Communists had been terribly difficult. Her mother, until she died, would mention at least twice a year how wonderful it was to have electricity on the island, where it had been installed somewhere in the early 1950s. Even a week before she died, her mother would turn on a lamp and stand back and smile at it.

Better him than her. She hated being on the water and the small cabin, which Edvard thought of as his home away from home, was cramped to the point of creating claustrophobia.

The alarm, set for 08:15, went off. She sat up slowly. Her knees and back let the arthritis announce that today would not be a good day. She found the pain so frustrating, forcing her to admit she was aging in body faster than in mind. Well, she wasn't going to let that stop her from starting her Christmas baking.

She glanced behind her as she sat on the edge of the bed. The other side was as freshly made up as when she went to sleep. She hoped Edvard had not been too cold overnight.

Elisabeth tied her apron around her waist and opened the small box that had her favorite recipes. Some were in her handwriting, some in her mother's. A few had been cut from magazines and glued onto the cards. Not one of the cards had ever *not* been used and some had been used hundreds of times over her lifetime and her mother's. The gingerbread cookie card was covered with stains from spilled molasses and butter.

She read off the ingredients and as she did she checked to make sure she had them.

3 cups flour—she had plenty
1 teaspoon baking soda—check
1/2 teaspoon baking powder—check
3/4 cup soft butter—it would be soft once she let it sit outside the fridge
1/2 cup brown sugar—just enough
2 teaspoons ginger—a new jar bought last week
1.5 teaspoons cinnamon—she was at the end of the jar
1/4 teaspoon ground cloves—she was out
2 eggs—just one left
3/4 cup molasses—she had to rummage to find the bottle, but she located it behind her other spices

That meant a trip to the store. She might as well take her caddy and pick up a few other things. Her man would be grumpy having spent the night on the boat and wouldn't want to drive her anywhere, preferring to take a nap by the television instead. Because of her cataracts, driving made her uncomfortable and even if her knees and hips ached from walking, the exercise in the fresh air would do her good. Also, it was only a couple of blocks.

The alternative was to make the cookies another day, but they really should go into the mail to Berlin and New York. She knew her children would roll their eyes, but she also knew that the one year she hasn't shipped the cookies thinking they were too old, they both called and asked if she were all right . . . did the cookies get lost in the mail . . . was she tired of tradition . . . think of what their *Oma,* the creator of the tradition would have said if she were alive and knew . . . and on and on.

Among the regular gingerbread men and women, she always made one special one. Her son's had skis, for he was an avid skier, just missing the Olympic team by a hair, but a hair was enough to create major disappointment, from which he recovered with only a faint trace of bitterness. Her daughter loved flowers and her gingerbread woman carried a bouquet of flowers decorated with multicolor icing and light-yellow frosting hair. The cookies were a work of art.

Whenever she made the cookies, she was transported back to childhood, standing next to her mother as she baked watching every step. Her *Mutti* . . . the woman who cheated death and had lived in a frenzy as if not to miss a single moment. A spring daffodil would send her into spasms of joy . . . and a sad advertisement on the television would make her sob all out of proportion to the content. The mood swings were exhausting for Elisabeth and her father. Her mother had died, a very old woman, five years before . . . a simple death for what had started out as a very complicated life . . . she just forgot to get up in the morning.

Enough reverie, she thought as she bundled up. The brick sidewalk was slippery and she shuffled along, hating that she looked like an old lady before her time. Well, almost before her time. There were women her age who didn't have arthritis. At least she still was thin and had minimal wrinkles. Her hairdresser had hidden the gray with highlights, a luxury, but her man never argued about it. He used to boast that his *Frau* could make one *Mark* into three and now he said the same thing about the Euro so he let her have her rare luxuries.

Once in the supermarket, she added lamb chops, which were on sale, apples and oranges. Her man loved fresh squeezed orange juice, which was his treat with Sunday morning breakfast before they went to church.

"Elisabeth."

She turned to see Anka, one of her neighbors, not one of her favorite people. The woman spent too much time delving into other people's lives and sharing her discoveries. And not only that—she had the indecency to look ten years younger than Elisabeth even if they were the same age. "Jealousy does not become me," Elisabeth murmured under her breath as she greeted Anka.

"Did you hear what washed up on the beach?" Anka's body closed off the area between them as if she were to convey a secret that could affect world peace or more likely war.

"Those two poor girls?" Elisabeth would admit only to herself that she liked to know what Anka knew, but the difference was her ears had a brick wall between them and her mouth. If Anka had hoped to spread the word, whatever word it might be, it wouldn't be via Elisabeth.

"No, this time it was a man . . . well, not a whole man . . . just an arm."

Elisabeth shuddered. "Horrible." How much better it would be to concentrate on Christmas cookies and welcoming home her man.

CHAPTER 41

Kirchdorf, Insel Poel, Germany

"The first written trace of the island comes from a document written by Heinrich de Löwe in 1163. He wanted to Christianize the island."

The History of Insel Poel by Manfred Dederich

Annie ran over what she'd say to Roger several times before she called him. She'd settled on the couch in her sweats, a cup of tea on the coffee table but not so close to her laptop that there was danger of spilling it onto the machine. Their conversation started off with all the normal chit chat until he said, "So . . . you're basically done there."

"As far as being at the museum, yes. There's a couple of things I need to polish, but I'll hand in the translations at the end of the week." She took a deep breath and barged into it. "I was thinking of staying for a few days extra."

Roger's intake of breath told Annie the rest of the conversation might not go as smoothly. "I'm still planning to meet you for Christmas at my folks."

Silence.

"It'll give me time to do most of the translation of the history book so I'll be free for the holidays. You know I work better when I don't have any distractions and in Geneva there'll be my folks, you, Gaëlle, Hannibal to walk, seeing some of my friends . . ."

Silence.

"And the island is adorable. It might be a great place for our honeymoon." The mention of marriage would calm him . . . or so she hoped. Hope is like a feather, it can fly away with the slightest breeze. It sounded so Emily Dickinsonish. Roger wouldn't know the poet.

"You are not, I repeat NOT going to work on the murder of those girls if you have any sense at all."

"Did I tell you a man's arm washed up in about the same place?"

"You discovered that too? If I knew you wouldn't explode, I'd tell you I forbid you to have anything to do with the murders, but it wouldn't do any good."

Annie laughed. "I didn't find the arm. In fact, I've not been near the beach since the girls were found, and I only found the first two bodies anyway. Someone else found the arm."

She reached for her tea and took a sip. Whatever problems she and Roger had, lying was not one of them. They both preferred to fight out whatever was bothering them rather than covering it up.

This did not stop her from lying by omission from time to time, however. She really would have liked to scope out possibilities on the murder, because she had a theory. No need to mention that. She would tell him a different truth. "I would really like to concentrate on the history, but I'd like also to help Renate look for her daughter. If it were Gaëlle . . ."

"If it were Gaëlle, I'd have already killed whoever tried to abuse her."

Annie knew Roger had killed in the line of duty, a kill-or-be-killed situation, and how it still bothered him to take a life. He was one of the least violent people she knew. He had not killed the people who had killed his wife. He hadn't even wished that France had the death penalty. The fact they were behind bars

201

was enough for him along with his fervent prayers they were miserable. The man was not a saint.

"We were at the house of twins, girls and friends of Greta. I'm convinced that they know where she is. Not that they said anything, just a feeling."

"If they know, I suppose there's a greater chance she's safe. Not a young girl at the mercy of any pimp."

"She might end up in a *Bordell.* Although prostitution is legal here, she's still a minor."

"*Bordell,* a whorehouse?"

Good, she had diverted him. "Still I suspect those twins have her stashed someplace. I want to see them and convince them that her stepfather won't bother her anymore. I do feel sorry for Renate though. What she thought was *Herr* Right, turned out to be *Herr* Awful."

Roger let out a long sigh.

I've got him, Annie thought.

"I can understand you wanting to help. *When* do you *think* you might be back in Geneva?"

"At least by the twentieth when you and Gaëlle are due to arrive. That means I need to leave here by the eighteenth. It's too long a drive to do in one day, especially if there's snow."

"*Je t'aime. Bisous.*"

"*Ich Liebe dich. Küsse.*" See, I love you and can send you kisses in many languages." And that was one of the biggest truths she had ever told him. She did love him for—unlike anyone else she had ever dated—what he added to her life was not just by sharing his daughter and dog, but by making her think in ways she hadn't thought before. If his protectiveness sometimes drove her a bit crazy, she understood because of the loss of his wife.

His desire for her to not go roaming the world, leaving him behind for weeks at a time, was normal. It is always easier to be the leaver than the leavee for the leaver has new places to investigate while the leavee has only the space left empty by the leaver.

Annie threw on her coat and walked across the parking lot to the main building. The reception area opened onto a large room with a table where the guests had their *Frühstück*. At night however, the breakfast table was empty. Two locals in the alcove to the left were watching a football match, steins of beer in front of them. One roared when Hamburg scored.

The receptionist was setting up tables for the morning. When she saw Annie she came over and exchanged pleasantries.

"Is it possible to stay for five more days?" Annie asked.

The woman went behind the desk and opened the guest book. "Hmmm. We did rent the place for the fourth and fifth days, but we don't have one of the houses rented. I suspect they wouldn't mind an upgrade. And it's better for us not to have the houses empty."

"Is Christmas time slow for you?"

"*Ja und nien*. Sometimes when families come home to see parents there isn't room and they rent one of our places. We aren't a winter tourist destination. Summer, yes."

A groan went up from the men watching the television. Mutters about missing a goal followed by another groan as another block came from the Stuttgart team. "*Schwabs*." Annie knew it was not a good time to tell them she'd spent two years in Stuttgart and she liked the *Schwabs*. If they didn't pick up the *Schwäbisch* twang in her German accent it was okay.

"I'll call the people and see if it is okay and let you know *Morgen* when you come in for *Frühstück*.

If it hadn't been so cold Annie would have loved to take a walk: instead, she scuttled back into the comfort of her place. This time her neighbor's place was quiet. No angry men, no crying women.

Something Roger said jumped to the front of her mind—prostitution. Not for Greta but perhaps the two women were prostitutes.

After making a cup of tea, rather than doing the final proofing of the museum materials so she could really buckle down with the history book, she went online to learn about German prostitution.

St. Augustine considered it a necessary evil . . . smart man, she thought. Some 1,500 prostitutes had been provided for the Council of Constance in the early four hundreds. That council was designed to end the papal schism.

Right up to the Third Reich it seemed prostitution was more a matter of regulation than condemnation. Maybe, Annie thought, I'm not going in the right direction.

German prostitutes currently could have work contracts not unlike her contract with the museum. Regular health checks were required. Hookers even had unemployment benefits.

Maybe the Asian girls weren't prostitutes. She didn't know if there was a *Bordell* on the island. If so, why would they be washed up on the beach? The phone book didn't list any brothels, but she found several on the Internet in Hamburg and Lübeck, including a listing of how health cards were available for potential clients to see.

Still, Asian-origin women didn't seem to fit. Maybe the girls had been trafficked. Her tea was cold and she decided to make herself a nice *tisane* with mint. As she waited for the kettle to boil, she wondered if some entrepreneur was offering something a bit different from the local trade. After all, men traveled to Thailand and other Asian countries to participate in sexual activities. Why not bring Thailand and Asia to them? Service the men too busy to travel.

The kettle boiled. Annie went back to the Internet and checked out sex trafficking to find that it was increasing in

Germany with several hundred cases handled each year. What the real number was couldn't be determined, because there was no reporting of those off the radar. But most of the prostitutes were from former Eastern Block countries. The girls had to work somewhere, and the island, although not out of the way, was not a major business center that would attract customers.

It could be that the girls were prostitutes.

Tomorrow she would call the grouchy policeman in Lübeck.

CHAPTER 42

Bergedorf, Germany
July 1943

Hilke fantasized being able to take a nice long bath rather than the once-a-week dribble of a shower that each of the women were allowed. Afterward she felt neither clean nor refreshed. With the stink of the other women, who were equally dirty and smelly from perspiration brought on by the July heat, lack of clean clothing and their menstrual periods, for those that still had them, she had gone from almost holding her breath to barely noticing.

If her soul railed against accepting the conditions under which she was living in the camp, her head told her that it was better to follow orders as they were given. Anything else prompted a beating and/or the withholding of the meager meals. Three objectors who'd spoken out disappeared for several days. Later, they watched two of them hung. They never found out what happened to the third.

On the other hand she felt grateful that she was working on weaving cloth in the basement of one of the buildings rather than in the heat of the brick factory. At least the basement was cooler despite the bodies of the prisoners being packed against each other on stools.

Hilke's back ached, but she knew better than to slow down.

The noon whistle signaled the prisoners to stand and march to lunch. The meals were always the same bread, water, a little soup that was usually more water than anything else.

Hilke wondered where the vegetables went from the garden that she could see from the parade ground where they stood for roll call each morning. In the center of the garden was a small weeping willow tree. The people hoeing and raking were the political prisoners, those that were suspected of being Communists or trade unionists. She could tell by their red armbands.

No sooner had she picked up her spoon to begin her meal, than one of the SS women, the one called Hildegard, who had done her intake, marched into the room and announced a special roll call. "Women only," she barked.

Hilke picked up her bowl and gulped down the contents before following the other women out to the middle of the camp. As usual everyone lined up on the concrete.

Were the sun capable of being malicious, Hilke imagined that it had set out to cook them. They all stood there as the time went by.

Ten minutes.

One of the older women fainted. The women in front and in back of her tried to move slightly so it would not be obvious that one of them was on the ground. However, trying to help her would only bring negative attention to the Samaritan.

Twenty minutes.

Hilke's clothes were drenched with her own sweat. Her hair was plastered to her skull. The small amount of saliva that her mouth oozed did nothing to quell her thirst. She tried to imagine herself in a pool stroking her way from one end to the other. During a swimming practice, when she had first started on her school's swim team, she hated when the water of the pool was icy. Now she tricked her mind into thinking that wonderfully icy-cold water was cooling her skin.

Twenty-eight minutes.

How long? How long?

Thirty-two minutes.

Finally Hildegard came onto the parade ground with an SS officer. He was blue-eyed and under his cap his hair was light brown.

He walked up and down the rows of women. When he came to the woman lying on the ground he prodded her with his toe. "Take her to her bunk." He prodded the woman standing next to the one who had fainted.

"Does anyone type?" His voice was three rows behind Hilke.

Some of the women prisoners worked for the SS officers or in their mess hall as waitresses.

A general feeling of *never volunteer* pervaded all the prisoners, but Hilke was willing to risk that her life might be better if she spoke up. "I do."

The officer swung around. "Who said that?"

"I did."

"Idiot," Ute, who'd been standing next to Hilke, whispered. "Stay quiet."

The officer pushed through the rows between him and Hilke until he stood in front of her. He was at least six inches taller.

"How fast?"

"I have been timed at ninety-five words per minute, but I may be rusty. I also take dictation."

The officer turned toward the SS woman. "Get these women back to work." To Hilke, he ordered, "You, you come with me."

Hilke followed him to the side of the camp where the officers worked and lived. He held the door for her.

Inside a fan blew cool air.

"My name is *Sturmführer* Hans Grüber. You stink," he said.

Hilke didn't have to be told his rank. It was obvious by the black patches with three dots of silver on his collar. "It is impossible to smell good after sweating in the sun. Plus I haven't had a real chance to wash except for a bit of water since May and if that happened to you, you'd smell too."

His eyes widened. He started to say something then stopped.

During his silence Hilke had a chance to look around the room. Two desks, one large and one small were to one side. The smaller desk, closer to the door, had a typewriter on it. The wall on the opposite side of the room was chocked full of filing cabinets, each six drawers high.

"I want to test your skills, but I can barely breathe for the stink of you."

It was Hilke's turn to be silent. She was afraid she had already gone too far with her earlier outburst.

Officer Hildegard came into the room. Before she could speak, the *Sturmführer* said, "Make sure she gets a proper shower and clean clothes. Then bring her back so I can test her dictation and typing."

CHAPTER 43

Colerne, Wiltshire, England
July 1943

RAF Flight Lieutenant Gordon Tibbitts lay on his bed at the base that housed Squadron 184. Because it was Saturday night, the barracks were quiet. Those not out on mission were out doing whatever.

He should have been on mission himself at that very moment except for the stupid accident. Despite the pain in his wrist and foot, he had to smile. What was a smart accident?

He shifted in his narrow bed. The cast up to his knee slowed his movements. He winced as he moved his sprained right hand, despite the bandage. He had never realized how much he did with his right hand until he couldn't.

He felt he had no right to whinge. Robert was in the hospital with shrapnel wounds. Tommy had survived his crash but would never see again.

How much longer would the damn war go on? They were dropping somewhere around twenty-seven thousand tons of bombs each month. He was missing *Operation Gomorrah*. His buddies came back talking of all the fires they saw as they flew over Hamburg dropping their bombs. Their glee made him sad. There must be something wrong with him that he didn't want to kill anymore. At least, he didn't want to kill anonymously. Had he found the pilot that dropped the bomb on his house, killing his father, he would have happily strangled him. Perhaps the pilot was dead anyway.

But the people in the houses below were wives, sisters, aunts and mothers, little boys who would never grow up. Only once had he expressed his hatred of dropping bombs on civilians, but it was Alan who had reminded him that the adults probably had voted Hitler into office.

Alan was someone who could understand the desperation of the people because of the economy prior to Hitler's ascent. Had their country not been forced into financial destitution after World War I, he was sure that Hitler would still be painting or working in some factory somewhere, not swaggering around Germany. However, Alan wasn't an economist like himself.

Thus, Gordon never broached the topic. People were like sheep, they believed what they were told and the more they were told something the more they believed it.

Gordon only had on his undershirt and shorts and still he was sweating. He was sure he didn't have a fever. Outside his window, a bird sang his or her heart out. He knew little about birds other than crows, blue jays and pigeons. The rest were birds.

If only he had heard the car that had forced him off his bicycle as he was riding back from Alan's and Ruth's house. He must have hit his head as he rolled into a ditch. When he came to, he couldn't stand on his right foot. He had to crawl up the embankment and lay on the side of the road until someone passed by. Not many people did, what with petrol being so tightly rationed. The first car must have thought him drunk, because they continued.

The third car did stop.

His unit had thought him AWOL, until they knew what happened to him. That was only two nights ago. He leaned over to take the pain pills from the infirmary.

He must have fallen asleep and slept through the night. Birds were still singing, but the barracks were full of footsteps and hushed voices. He reached for his crutch. It was hard using it with his left hand and even harder because it was his right foot in the cast. Still he made it to the corridor, which by that time was empty.

He headed for the dayroom. When he entered he saw his mates sitting around. Jack had his head in his hands. Bruce was sitting cross-legged on the floor. The atmosphere was heavy. "What's up?"

Jack looked up. His eyes were wet. "Alan. He didn't come back."

CHAPTER 44

Lübeck, Germany

Hans-Peter Leiter was rummaging through his desk for a pen that wasn't out of ink. He was forever buying good pens, the kind with a soft felt tip that helped him write so he could read what he had written afterwards . . . and then leaving them someplace. Someone had told him when you loan a pen keep the top. That might work when a pen was shared: it didn't work when he put it down and forgot to pick it up again.

The station was quiet, at least relatively quiet. Most of the men were out working different cases. Fritz had gone out to pick up something for lunch, *Würst,* a salad. What he would have loved was a beer, not that he was a heavy drinker.

Last night had been his night to keep his boys, but neither had wanted to come. The older had had a birthday party he'd gone to earlier in the day and had come home tired and fussy. The younger didn't want to go without his older brother. More and more the younger was treating him as a stranger.

Claudia burst through the doors. She seldom merely *entered* a room, just as she never did anything but stride without losing what Hans-Peter thought of as her femininity, although she had none of that helpless, eye-batting female coquetry. Her coat was open, the scarf around her neck fastened by folding it in half and creating a loop and pulling the ends through it. He never remembered her wearing a hat.

She was holding a folder, which she dropped on his desk

before pulling up a chair. "I've the drug results on the girls. Both had small amounts of cocaine in their system but not any other drugs. Both were HIV Positive, which considering that their vaginas looked well used for their age, was not surprising."

Well-used vaginas, now that was an interesting term, he thought, but before he could make a comment, his cell phone rang. Hearing Annie Young's voice he threw his head back. "How can I help you Frau Young?"

"Maybe I can help you. Have you thought the two girls might be involved in sex trafficking?"

He had. He'd checked all *Bordell* in the area. Most of them would cooperate with the police in fear of losing their license if they did not. "I appreciate the idea, Frau Young, I really do, but we have looked at that." He didn't say that it might be a pimp that was working outside the system. And it didn't explain how the women got in the water.

"They must have been out on a boat and then murdered and dumped."

He rolled his eyes at Claudia. "Deliver me from people who want to play detective," he wrote, borrowing a pencil from Fritz's desk. He hated writing with a pencil. Not only did it smudge, it was so light that it could be hard to read. He shoved the notepad toward her earning a smile.

"They obviously had to be on a boat at some period. They couldn't have washed up on the shore otherwise." A swimming accident was impossible both because of the time of year and the length of time the bodies had been in the water. "I appreciate your calling. *Aufwiederhören.*" Without waiting for her to answer, he disconnected and snapped his phone shut.

"I don't think Annie Young is a stupid woman. She might have some ideas," Claudia said. "You didn't have to brush her off."

Hans-Peter didn't want to annoy Claudia, but this woman-solidarity thing could be annoying. Better to ignore it. "Anything else you have?"

"The arm and the foot belong to the same person."

"Not much to go on."

"When we cleaned and dried the arm off I could see he had a perpetual tan line like from a T-shirt worn in the sun. The skin below that line was definitely weatherworn. At one time he'd broken his radius and there was arthritis, albeit slight in the elbow. I would say the man was in his sixties."

"Not a lot to go on for identification: asking around for a man who spent some of the summer outside with a T-shirt on, who had once broken his arm and who had arthritis and might be around sixty. I wonder how many people that would be between here and Hamburg?"

Claudia opened the second folder marked "Arm, foot male, unknown." She looked at Hans-Peter. "Well, there's one thing that might make it easier to identify him."

Hans-Peter cocked his head.

"The tattoo on his upper arm was a small European Sprat. Remember how we hardly saw it until I pulled the seaweed off? It wasn't very large."

"How and hell did you know what kind of fish?" For Hans-Peter fish came on a plate either covered in bread crumbs and fried or with sauce over it.

"I looked at pictures of fish in the Baltic until I saw one that looked like that tattoo." She took out a photo of the mystery man's arm with the tattoo and a photo she must have pulled off the Net because it was printed on regular A4 paper.

"I don't suppose you're suggesting that a school of European Sprat killed him in revenge for all those caught and eaten."

She gave a half smile, and Hans-Peter reminded himself that he had never been a very funny person. He could never tell jokes properly and usually what he thought was a quip would only bring stares. This was no way to impress her.

CHAPTER 45

Kirchdorf, Insel Poel, Germany

Elisabeth Schwartz looked up from where she was rolling out the last of the gingerbread cookie dough. Almost time to bring down the *Rolladen*. She switched on a second light. No word from her man. This wasn't normal. He never stayed out so long in the winter.

How long she stood with the rolling pin in her hand, she wasn't sure. Then she went to the phone and called the restaurant at the dock. It was too early for dinner customers, but sometimes the fishermen would stop for a cup of coffee or a beer before they made their way home. In the old days, she'd have jumped on her bike and ridden over. Her bike riding days were over and she missed them.

Marianne answered. The woman had worked there since the Wall had come down. She and Edvard had watched her go from a young bride to a mother trying to juggle work and kids. The last time Elisabeth and her man ate there, she'd noticed gray strands. Marianne had mentioned it to them and said she was naming the gray strands after her son and daughter who caused them.

"Would you mind terribly glancing out to the parking lot and seeing if Edvard's truck is still there and if his boat has come in?"

"Hold on." A few minutes passed. "*Nein* on the boat. I walked around back as well to see if he might be anchored out in the bay. The truck is where he always parks it."

After thanking her, Elisabeth hung up and walked to the kitchen table, which was covered with baked cookies, oven-ready cookies and half-rolled-out dough. Now she was worried the same way she had been as a young woman when a storm had hit while the men were out fishing. There was more than one fishing widow in Kirchdorf. But last night had been calm.

As much as she hated to do it, she called the *Hafenmeister.* Joachim Lenk was new at the job, having replaced his father who had retired the year before. Elisabeth remembered when Joachim had been born, watched him toddle around the docks and grow into a man that loved the sea. "Our family doesn't have blood, we have seawater," Lenk the Elder would say.

The same could be said for her man. Even in the hardest years, he could have imagined no other life. Sitting in an office would have killed him.

The words *killed him* bounced into her consciousness. Maybe the sea finally had killed him. No, she wouldn't let herself think that way yet. Maybe the boat had become disabled and he was floating somewhere out of sight of land. He couldn't be too far out because he hadn't planned to spend more than a few hours. All this she told the young Joachim, who replied, "Don't worry, we'll send a boat out to look for him."

"I am worried."

"That's normal."

As soon as Joachim Lenk hung up he called the Lübeck police. He'd hoped he was wrong, but the police had been by to see if any fishermen were missing. They'd taken him to the beach and he was sure that all the wood that had washed up on the beach was from a boat, but there wasn't enough to identify which one. "Hans-Peter Leiter, *bitte.*"

"He's out of the office."

"I have his cell." Joachim realized that he wasn't sure where he had put the card that Hans-Peter had left with him. His desk was at best disorganized, something that had never been the case when his father was *Hafenmeister.*

Maybe he should call the *Wasserschutzpolizei* first. They could start looking for a stranded boat. At one point he had wanted to go to the *Wasserschutzpolizei* school in Hamburg. He hadn't passed the physical. He was well aware that he would never have taken over from his father without connections. Still no one had any complaints about the job he was doing. Most days were deadly dull.

He pondered which way to go. Then he noticed the policeman's card sticking out from under his desk calendar, which doubled as his blotter. The phone rang so long he disconnected and was debating sending a message when his phone rang.

"Hans-Peter Leiter. You called me?"

"Joachim Lenk, here. Insel Poel *Hafenmeister.* You are investigating where the last three bodies or two bodies and an arm showed up?"

"*Ja?*"

"We have a missing fisherman named Edvard Schwartz. An older man. Went out yesterday morning for half a day and hasn't come back. His wife is worried. He's never done that before."

"I would think his wife might be worried," Hans-Peter said. "Do you know the man personally?"

"Everyone knows everyone here personally. Yes."

"Does he have a tattoo?"

Joachim thought about it. When he was little his family and Edvard's family would go on picnics together in the park behind the church. After eating, the men would stretch out and take a nap. He'd been fascinated by Onkel Edvard's tattoo of a silver fish.

His father would tease Edvard saying he better be careful in the sun or the fish would be smoked and end up on someone's dinner table.

"A fish. A European Sprat. I remember because he and my father would make me tell them all the names of the different fish found in the Baltic. I'd get a *Pfennig* for each one I got right and my mother would complain that I would spend the money on candy."

"I think we might know something. I'll come out and talk to the wife," Hans-Peter said.

Joachim knew that tone of voice. "I'd like to go with you. She'll need someone to comfort her."

CHAPTER 46

Colerne, Wiltshire, England
July 1943

"I don't care what the official way is, I want to tell her myself." Gordon spoke to his commanding officer. "She's my friend. I'll go get my girlfriend, who is Ruth's best friend, and we'll tell her together."

John Rath, who had been an officer even before the war, sat behind his desk and twirled a pencil in his hand. "Then I suggest you go put on some clothes, and I'll have a car ready for us."

Gordon remembered Rath having danced with Ruth at a base get-together on Guy Fawkes Day. There had been no bonfire, just in case the Jerries had thought the lights would be guides for their targets. They did set up a tent and built a miniature fire inside, one that wasn't even as large as one in a family fireplace. After it went out they had moved the party inside for it was too cold to stay in the tent outside the officers' mess.

The RAF car pulled up in front of the vicarage. Gordon had not seen Martha since the night of his accident. Since he had been scheduled for missions, they had not planned to meet until tomorrow. He had not had anyone tell her of his accident either. No need to worry her before it was necessary. As he hobbled out of the car, he realized how stupid that was. She worried more when he was on mission. Him, lying in a hospital bed because of his stupid bike accident, would be nothing in comparison.

The uneven brick path leading to the vicarage was almost his undoing. His commanding officer grabbed him as he almost toppled into the pink rose bushes lining the walkway. Pain shot up his leg.

"Careful," his commander said.

The bell on the vicarage was not a pretty tinkle, more like a clang. Martha answered the door wearing a flour-dusted apron. Her hands flew to her mouth. "Oh my goodness." She grabbed onto one of Gordon's arms. His commanding officer held the other and helped Gordon into the salon where Martha guided him onto the sofa and moved a hassock in front of him where he could rest his leg. "Your plane?"

"Not mine. Alan's."

"Noooo. No, no!" Then she seemed to realize that Lieutenant Commander John Rath was with Gordon. "I'm sorry, John."

Rath waved his hand. "Nothing to be sorry about. It must have been a shock to see Gordon in a half-leg plaster and bandages."

Martha took in his words with a nod of head. "Alan? Is there any hope?"

"No hope. His plane went down in total flames. No report of a parachute before, during or after," Rath said.

"Does Ruth know yet?"

"We're going to tell her now, but I thought you might like to be there to help her," Gordon said. He was trying to ignore the pain in his ankle, his wrist and his soul. Had he not had the accident it would have been him. Alan had been in the plane that he was scheduled to fly. Then again, he might have been in a different position and the antiaircraft shot would have missed him . . . or got him sooner. Mourning for his friend mixed with guilt that it wasn't him or rather guilt that he was glad that it wasn't him.

Vicar Willson opened the front door. In the past year it was not possible to say he had melted toward Gordon. Martha described her father's attitude as butter taken out of a freezer and left on a countertop just long enough to be able to hack at it, but not soft enough to spread on anything. His mumbles about her reputation and church duties were less frequent, more like every week or so rather than daily. He felt duty-bound to criticize something she typed or a person he thought she should have visited, along with, "If you didn't spend so much time with that Tibbitts boy, you would have had time to . . ."

Gordon's mother had tried to help, but it was an uphill battle. She had joined the flower committee and attended services every Sunday, having whispered to Martha that she was doing it for their relationship as a couple, more than because of any suddenly found religious fervor. Her talent at flower arranging had given strength to Janet Masters's ideas and Mabel Lafferty had left the committee in a sulk after her failed coup, much to the relief to all the other members who viewed the committee as a chance to help the church—not build a tiny, tiny kingdom. Even Vicar Willson seemed relieved that he no longer had to listen to complaints on something so unrelated to spiritual matters.

"What is going on?" Vicar Willson asked. "Martha, why are you crying?"

"It's Alan. He was shot down over Hamburg last night," Gordon said.

The vicar took the first chair closest to him. "How old was he?"

"Twenty-six. I'm Lieutenant Commander John Rath. We were picking up your daughter to go and tell Ruth."

"I'll go with you."

"Perhaps, Father, it would be better to wait. She'll have me and Gordon. Then when she's ready she'll need you for things like the funeral preparation."

Gordon felt a wave of love for Martha. What she didn't say to her father was that Ruth couldn't stand him and his presence would only make things worse. He had thoroughly annoyed Ruth during Ruth's mother's funeral when his remarks bore little resemblance to the woman that Eleanor had been. And the difficulties he had created for Gordon and Martha did nothing to endear the vicar to Ruth, who was savagely a friend to Martha and, by extension, to Gordon.

Vicar Willson started to say something, but Martha interrupted him quickly. "Besides, Father, you haven't finished your report for the diocese, and I'll need time to type it." She got up from the chair. "Let me change and shut off the oven."

For the first time since his arrival Gordon noticed that Martha had on the ratty trousers that she wore for cleaning and gardening.

As usual when Martha was not with them, the silence between the vicar and Gordon was uneasy. Rath broke the discomfort. "This war has gone on too long, but I think we are beginning to see a turnabout."

"I pray to God we do soon."

At least that's something we agree on, Gordon thought. He started to use both hands to propel himself out of the couch. The pain from his swollen ankle as he pressed it into the sofa made him almost want to vomit.

They found Ruth behind the house that had once belonged to her mother and was now hers. Her son was in his pushchair. He only wore a diaper. Both of them were sweating. Ruth had on an old dress that bore dirt stains and something that looked like mashed carrots.

She looked up to see Martha, who had come ahead of the

two men. "I wish weeds were good to eat; they are so much easier to grow. You didn't say you were coming over today. Your prison guard let you out of work?"

"I wasn't planning to come, and I'm not alone." She looked over her shoulder to see Gordon and John Rath making their way slowly to them.

Ruth jumped up. "My God, Gordon. What happened?"

"Bike accident." No need to say more.

Than Ruth saw John Rath and her look became guarded. "John?"

Before Gordon could say anything, Martha took over. "It's Alan. He was shot down. I'm so sorry, Ruth. There is no way that he could have survived."

Ruth stood, holding a trowel. Her eyes went from one to the other to the other as if she hoped one would say it was a joke. Then she threw the trowel as far as she could and stalked into the house.

Martha looked at the two men. "Watch the baby." She followed Ruth into the house.

CHAPTER 47

Kirchdorf, Insel Poel, Germany
"In 1170 the Mecklenburg Princedom was under Kaiser Fredrich I."

The History of Insel Poel by Manfred Dederich

Annie drove over to the school at closing time. As in any school, the kids seemed to burst through the doors in a mob, an almost single entity, shattering the quiet. Once free of the building, the girls huddled in several bunches talking among themselves as if sharing great secrets. The boys pushed each other back and forth. The decibels were only partly defused in the air.

Annie searched for Kristin and Elke among the sea of teenagers with jeans and long blonde hair. Because she had only seen the girls once, she found herself wondering if she would recognize them.

The problem solved itself when she heard a voice, "Frau Young?"

Annie turned to see either Elke or Kristin. The only reason she'd been able to tell them apart the other night was that they were seated in the same place when she'd been introduced to them.

"Yes."

"What are you doing here?" The tone was more curious than impudent.

"I wanted to talk to you and your sister when your mother

226

and Renate weren't around."

"Kristin will be out in a few minutes. She had to see a prof about something."

Not sure what to do next, Annie said nothing. Slowly the area in front of the school emptied. Then Elke's double emerged from the building. Elke waved her over.

"She wants to talk to both of us. Without *Mutti* or Greta's mother around," Elke explained.

Annie noted that Elke wore a teal-blue, down-filled jacket. Kristin's was red. Elke, blue, Kristin, red. At least I can tell them apart for a little while.

"Is there somewhere we can go, maybe for a hot chocolate? My treat."

The girls exchanged a look. "We do have to be home soon."

"It won't take long. If you want, I can call your mother."

Another look exchanged. Elke glanced at her watch then back at her sister.

"Twenty minutes. I can drive you home afterwards."

"There's a coffee shop about a block from here." Elke ignored her sister's frown.

The shop was small, only four round tables and a barrier behind which a middle-aged woman emerged carrying a book. She held her place with her middle finger. It looked as if it were the living room of a private home, which is exactly what it turned out to be. A home that was a bed-and-breakfast that also served coffee to anyone who came by.

"May I help you?"

"Three hot chocolates, I think."

The twins nodded.

"Do you have a *Torte* or other pastries?"

The woman pointed to a case that Annie hadn't noticed. The twins got up and chose pieces of pastry with apples arranged on top of them. "Sometimes her pastries are stale," Kristin whispered when the woman disappeared to get their hot chocolates. "But these look okay."

Annie decided to try a piece.

Once their hot chocolate had arrived, Annie began. "I think you know where Greta is."

The twins both folded their arms across their chest. Annie mimicked the body language and said nothing. When they moved she moved in the same way. The silence was not comfortable.

Elke broke that. "She's not safe at home."

"Shut up, Elke," Kristin said.

"Renate has thrown Karl out."

"He should be in jail." This came from Kristin.

"How do we know that Renate won't take him back?"

"Very pragmatic question," Annie said. "Renate raised Greta alone for years. That's a stronger bond than any husband."

"He raped her," Kristin said. "Will Renate press charges?"

Although Annie wanted to cut Karl's balls off, or at least damage them, she hadn't discussed with Renate what she wanted to do legally. "I think that would be something Renate and Greta would have to discuss. It might be hard for Greta to go through a court trial."

Elke gulped her hot chocolate then almost slammed her cup down. She looked at her watch. "We need to get home."

"Another minute," Annie said, noticing that Kristin hadn't finished either her *Torte* or her chocolate. "Could you take me to Greta?"

"Why should we trust you?" Elke had not stood up, giving Annie hope that she could get more information. "Assuming, that is, we knew where she was."

"I think you do know, and I don't mean that . . ." How did she mean it? "I think you are doing a wonderful thing protecting your friend. I've only known Greta briefly, but I like her.

She reminds me of my future stepdaughter . . ." Maybe that was the wrong thing to say. Stepmothers got a bad rap from all the children's stories. "And she's a wonderful girl that I love to pieces. My fiancé says if we were to break up, Gaëlle, that's her name, would probably go with me, not him." I'm talking too much but at least Elke hasn't looked as if she were about to go away, Annie thought.

"We can't take her to you," Elke said. "She's too far away."

"Shut up," Kristin said.

Progress, Annie thought. They know where she is. "What if I call her?"

"She won't answer her cell. She's afraid of a trace," Elke said.

"Stop it!" Kristin's voice was so loud that the owner came from the kitchen.

"Is everything all right?" she asked.

"Teenagers," Annie said. The woman went back behind the door. "Sorry girls, but you don't want her overhearing this conversation and blaming your age . . . well you know how it is."

They nodded in unison.

"Look, I'm worried. A girl of Greta's age is ripe for trouble. A pimp searching a train station, for example, will always be looking for fresh meat."

"Like Greta's stepfather?" Kristin asked.

"Yes, like her stepfather."

Both girls seemed to register surprise that Annie agreed with them. Annie picked up on it. "I don't condone abuse of anyone, anytime, anywhere. Full stop. I can't prosecute Karl because I have no proof. I just want to make sure that Greta is safe. Her mother is frantic with worry." She reached for her pocketbook and took out the necessary Euros to pay the bill. "I wish you'd contact Greta and get her to contact her mother, so Renate can stop worrying." She resisted grabbing and shaking the girls until they did. Many years from now, when they were adults, they would understand Renate far more than they did today. Before getting to know Gaëlle she wasn't sure she would have had the same degree of empathy.

Elke and Kristin put on their jackets. "I see you've switched coats, but I still know which one of you is which."

They drove back in silence. Annie was afraid she would only make matters worse if she kept harping on calling Greta.

As they pulled up to the house, Kristin, wearing Elke's jacket, or maybe they had switched in school, said, "Are you going to talk to our mother?"

"I'd like to. But if you promise me that you'll contact Greta, I'll say nothing to her and nothing to Renate."

Elke, who had opened the backseat car door, leaned forward and touched Kristin on the shoulder. The streetlamp, although providing light in the car, still left the girls' faces in shadow. "What do you think? Should we trust her?"

Annie again said nothing. Never a patient person, she wished she'd never made that promise. If she made the wrong call, Greta could be in danger, if not now, then later whenever the haven she was currently in disappeared. A fourteen-year-old girl could not survive on her own indefinitely, not in any good way. "I will add to my promise. I'll see that Karl never comes near her again."

"You can't do that." The girls spoke in unison.

"Yes, I can. I have no standing in court, but I do have standing with Renate. I can make sure she'll protect her daughter. And what he has done is criminal, and he should be put away." Of course, the courts don't always do the right thing, Annie thought. And she wasn't sure that Renate would press charges, and even if she did, would Greta be able to stand up for herself in court?

Silence.

"*Bitte, bitte, bitte* . . . tell Greta she's safe now. Give her my phone number and have her call me collect if she has to. Have her call from a phone booth or the post if she doesn't want to use her phone, but *bitte*, for Greta's sake." She wanted to add, this situation has got to come to a close, but when a girl is raped by her stepfather, closure is more than just going back home.

"If you promise, we promise," Elke said.

"Speak for yourself, Elke, I'm not so sure," Kristin said.

Annie could see their mother looking out the window. Then she closed the *Rolladen*.

"Kristin, I know you want to protect Greta, but by not giving her the option of calling me, and perhaps making it possible for her to come home safely, you are making a decision for her that only she has a right to make."

Kristin drew in a deep breath. "I never thought of it that way."

"I know you didn't, because you want to be the best friend possible to Greta. And Greta may decide *not* to call me. But, it will be her decision about her life." Let it sink in, let it sink in, Annie thought as she waited for Kristin to mull it over.

"Frau Young is right," Elke said. "If you were in Greta's position, you'd want to know that maybe it would be safe to come home. She must be so scared and lonely right now."

"Maybe . . . you two are right," Kristin said. "She doesn't have to call you. That'll be up to her." She reached for the door handle. "I promise."

After the girls entered their home, Annie sat in the car until she stopped shaking. She wasn't sure that she had handled the situation properly. She wasn't sure she shouldn't go to Gisela or Renate. Then she decided if she didn't hear from Greta, rather than break her promise, she would go back to the girls and ask for a release from it.

CHAPTER 48

Lübeck, Germany

Hans-Peter sat at the table directly across from Claudia. She was sipping a glass of Reisling while waiting for their fish to arrive. He considered himself lucky that he got her to go on this half date, which is what she called it, because they were discussing the various cases on which he was working.

His cell phone rang. Damn it. He should have shut it off. He looked at the number. A three area code. Double damn. From past experience he knew whom it was from. It was the nosy redheaded American. She'd called several times leaving messages saying he should call her, that she had an idea.

As he started to put it away, Claudia said, "It's all right to take it. If it's personal, I can always go to the WC."

He shook his head and motioned for her to stay as he mouthed, "Probably work." He pushed the button. "Leiter *hier*. Can I help you, Frau Young?"

"I'm surprised I caught you. You must be very busy," Annie's voice was so gentle he wasn't sure if she was upset, being nasty, or sympathetic.

"It has been hectic."

The waiter appeared with their fish and put the dishes down. Hans-Peter stewed. He had finally gotten Claudia alone: he was off duty and work was intruding. He felt he had a right to a few hours when he wasn't giving a thousand percent to solving crimes and this was one of those times.

"I'm off duty. Can this wait until tomorrow?"

"I won't keep you long. I'm even more sure that the murdered girls were prostitutes."

The woman must be operating on instinct, because she couldn't have seen the autopsy reports or talked to anyone. "We are handling it."

"I think you should check the Kirchdorf dock. I suspect that wealthy men are being taken out on a boat to . . . to . . ."

Mein Gott. Was she being delicate? "And why do you think that, Frau Young?"

"Because I've seen very expensive cars on the dock frequently. I mean expensive. Not just Mercedes but Ferraris and even a Maserati."

He motioned for Claudia to start eating. She cocked her head, but picked up her fork and cut into the fish.

Was that all she had? "Wealthy people do come to the island, Frau Young." He heard her sigh. What right did she have to be exasperated? He was the one who had a half date interrupted. "*Danke* for the information. *Aufwiederhören.*" He clicked his phone shut.

"The redhead?"

He took a bite of his fish and nodded.

"What did she have to say?"

He told her. "Overactive imagination." He sipped his wine. He did not want to talk business, but he told Claudia anyway.

"Her theory does make sense," Claudia said.

He did not want to hear it.

"So you will check it out?" she asked.

"Probably, but definitely not tonight."

CHAPTER 49

Colerne, Wiltshire, England
July 1943

"It isn't right." Vicar Willson stood in front of the door leading outside, his arms folded across his chest. What hair remained on his head was standing up. "I forbid it."

Martha thought her father looked a bit demonic. "It doesn't matter, Father. I'm going to Ruth's to babysit while she goes to her mother-in-law's for Alan's funeral."

"People will talk."

Martha clutched the small brown faux-alligator suitcase with leather straps containing her nightdress, two changes of clothes, her hairbrush and her toothbrush along with a few basic toiletries. "Probably. You know what they'll say?"

"That you're an immoral woman."

"They'll say, wasn't I kind to look after a sick baby, a half orphan, for a poor widow whose husband was killed trying to save us from the Germans."

"It will be a chance for that Tibbitts boy to see you without a chaperone."

"That Tibbitts boy is probably somewhere over Germany right now." She wished that his injured ankle hadn't been cleared and he was safe in the barracks.

"But he might be back before you come home."

Martha hoped both that "that Tibbitts boy," her man, not only would come home from his mission but that he would come to her at Ruth's and chaperone be damned. Her father believed that all young women should have chaperones whenever they were in the company of any male, all of whom were just waiting to pounce on innocent virgins. He was a Victorian relic. Her own sense of religion made her chant, "honor thy father and mother" more than once to herself. With each passing day, she had more belief in God, but less and less in the way her father expressed his beliefs. Despite his collar, she did not think of her father as Christian, but someone who warped all the wonderful things that Christ taught.

Instead of pushing through the front door, she turned and walked toward the kitchen, which was in the back of the house, and fled out the back door.

Outside the sun after the dark vicarage almost blinded her. She pushed her bicycle, which had been resting against the front gate, until she was out of sight of the vicarage. Then she balanced her case on the back of the bike, fastening it with rope. The suitcase had been part of a set that had belonged to her mother since her honeymoon and had been seldom used. Her mother had rarely accompanied her husband when he had to attend church events in some other area. The family did not take holidays because Vicar Willson thought that since God was never off duty that he should not be either.

Within minutes of pedaling toward Ruth's house, Martha was sweating.

As she arrived, Ruth stepped out of the house. She was dressed in what she called her traveling clothes, although she, like Martha's mother, had never traveled much. The suit was navy blue with a jacket over the skirt. A belt showed off Ruth's slim figure. If anything the news of Alan's death had caused her already too skinny body to lose even more pounds.

"Some people eat when they are upset. I can't swallow anything," she'd said to Martha, who had spent as much time with her friend as possible the first few days after they had learned of Alan's death, playing with the baby, making meals that went untouched and just listening.

A suitcase much like Martha's only bigger and with smooth brown leather was on the doorstep. "I hate leaving baby Walter. He still has a fever."

"And the doctor says that's because he's teething."

"Maybe I should take him with me."

"Do you really want the train ride to Lancaster with a fussy baby? Is it really good for Walter when he can be in his own cot in the cool of his own room?"

"I just got him to sleep. He's been unhappy all day."

"My point. Exactly!"

Ruth looked at her watch. "My mother-in-law will be so disappointed. She wants to see him."

Martha understood. Ruth's mother-in-law had come to the wedding and whispered she was delighted she was going to be a grandmother. She'd said that she hoped Ruth would help her son grow up. Martha realized that the woman who was in her mid-fifties was doing everything possible to re-create a family for her daughter-in-law and grandson. Ruth was lucky.

Gordon's mother had embraced Martha from their first meeting. "I always knew I'd accept anyone my son was interested in, but you make it so easy," she'd said one day when Martha had stopped in to deliver a pint of strawberries from the vicarage garden.

Not that she and Gordon had ever discussed marriage, but she was sure that was the way they were heading. Until now, he had been very respectful of her, kissing her good night, but lately the kisses had grown longer, he had held her tighter and she could feel his desire.

She wanted everything her father had taught her was sinful. Her mother had given her the whole "birds and bees" stories, adding that even after marriage a man who respected his wife would make minimal demands on her.

However, the feelings that she had when Gordon kissed her, when he held her tight, made her wonder if her mother had perhaps left something out or was not telling her the whole truth.

"Ruth, Luv, you and your mother-in-law need each other right now. You need to find a way to say good-bye to Alan. The memorial service will help do that."

"But . . ."

"No buts. Go. You'll get a chance to meet Alan's friends, see where he grew up, learn things you can tell Walter."

"But . . ."

"Unless you don't think I can take care of Walter?"

Ruth hugged Martha. "Of course you can take care of him. His face lights up every time you come near him."

Martha picked up Ruth's case and handed it to her. "Go."

Ruth started down the walkway then turned. "I've written out everything you need to know."

"Go."

Martha went into the cottage. It was an old-fashioned cottage with tiny windows and a living room with a big fireplace, which once had been used for cooking family meals. Its darkness protected it from the July heat.

Martha went into the kitchen. The sink had an old-fashioned pump, which she used to wet down her face and arms. On the kitchen table a small notebook was open. As she read the instructions she laughed. Ruth had written down every possible detail . . . including not only in which drawer she could find Walter's little shirts, but where in the drawer: right or left.

There were descriptions on how long to cook his carrots before mashing them, how he liked a bit of honey in his porridge.

A plaintive cry wafted its way down the stairs. Martha headed for the baby's room. Ruth had drawn pictures of teddy bears and pasted them to the whitewashed walls between the half-timbers. Some teddy bears were having a picnic: another group picked flowers. Her friend was really talented, Martha thought.

Walter was on his stomach, his head raised, screaming.

"Fine, fine, little fellow. It is you and me for the next few days."

The first thing she did was to change his nappy. The poor baby was red all around his genitals. She looked at the notebook, where Ruth wrote when Walter cut a tooth, he got nappy rash. "Cream is in the basket next to the changing table." Martha found it and applied it liberally. "Better, young man?"

He stopped whimpering, although tears encrusted his face. Because the cottage was cooler inside than out, Walter did not seem to need anything more than his nappy and shirt.

Downstairs again, Ruth put him in his high chair and handed him his stuffed rabbit, which he threw on the floor. She picked it up. He threw it on the floor. This time she left it: he screamed.

"You've a choice, rabbit or dinner?"

He looked at her.

Martha danced and sang as she prepared his meal. Walter seemed to find it amusing enough to not scream. Once the first spoonful of food went into his mouth, he seemed to forget that he had ever been unhappy.

Someday, she thought, maybe, if I'm lucky, I'll have my own baby. She hoped it would be Gordon's.

CHAPTER 50

Kirchdorf, Insel Poel, Germany
"After 1210, the village names took on a Germanic flavor when a Slavic ruler, Henrich Borwin I, imported Germanic settlers from Dithmarschen and Holstein to build the church that still stands today on what was once swampy land."
The History of Insel Poel by Manfred Dederich

Annie woke early. She debated reading a bit in bed before getting up because she didn't plan to go into the museum at all. Her work was finished. However, she was hungry and the *Frühstück* across the road was calling. It didn't take her long to shower.

As soon as she entered the dining room, she saw Karl sitting at the table. She wanted to go up and hit him but resisted.

She headed to the buffet table laden with sausages, eggs, fruit, cold cuts and cheeses. Being in the same room with Karl almost made her lose her appetite: almost, but not quite, because she had not eaten dinner the night before.

Her back was to the tables as she put a *Brötchen* on her plate. Her mobile croaked. It was a sound that was less disruptive. The area code was thirty-three for France but it was not an Argelès code. Out of habit she jotted down the number, which was a landline, as she answered it. She had to repeat hello several times.

"Annie?" It was a young girl's voice.

"Yes."

"Greta. The twins said I could talk to you."

"You can, but I need to walk about twenty meters so it can be private. Please, please don't hang up."

She picked up her coat and headed for the door. She did not want to be talking to Greta while Karl was in the same room. "I'm not through with breakfast," she said to the woman at the reception desk.

Outside she shifted the phone so she could put the coat on. "I'm so glad you called. I was worried about you. Your mother was worried about you."

"I'm sorry she was worried, but I didn't know what else to do."

"Where are you?"

"I'm not sure I can tell you. You might tell my mother and she would tell Karl."

"Your mother has left Karl."

"Can you guarantee she won't take him back?"

She saw Karl leaving the hotel and heading toward the dock. Annie went back inside. "I can't guarantee the sun will come up ever again, even if I'm pretty certain of it. Your mother wants you back. She'll leave it up to you if you want to prosecute . . . Karl." She had started to say stepfather but thought better of it. "Do you have enough money? You're not out on the street?"

"*Nein und ja.* I'm in a private home, but I only have five Euros left. Don't tell my mother where I am."

"I can't. You haven't told me, but I wish you would. Then we can figure out what to do next."

There was a long silence. Annie was afraid Greta would hang up, but she also was afraid to say anything.

"I'm in Sète."

Glory hallelujah, Annie thought. Not that far from Argelès. "Honey, listen. That's not that far from where I live. I can get my fiancé to come get you and bring you home. He is a police-man! And he'll come with his daughter Gaëlle, who is about your age. Give me your address."

"I don't know."

"Think about it and call me back in an hour. I can get Gaëlle to call you, so you know I'm not kidding about you having a chaperone with my fiancé. I can understand that you might not want to be alone with a man right now, even if he is a police chief."

There was no answer. Greta had disconnected. She hoped she had heard what she said.

She sat back at the table. Her hot egg was now cold. Her tea was cold. It didn't matter as she dialed Roger.

As soon as she explained what happened, he said, "Of course I'll pick her up and I'll take Gaëlle with me. She'll be delighted to miss the last few days of school before the Christmas break." Both of them knew that the teenager's grades were high enough that she could afford to miss a few days of school and that an adventure like picking up a runaway and driving her to Germany would be preferable to sitting in a classroom. "Or maybe we should fly."

"You can decide that after you get her."

Annie gave Roger the number of the landline so he could trace the address in case Greta didn't call back. "But don't call her until I give the okay. I don't want her spooked."

Back inside as she got up to get herself another cup of tea, she debated whether or not she should tell Renate. The mother would like to know that Greta was safe, but she hoped the woman wouldn't do anything foolish that might scare the child off.

CHAPTER 51

Kirchdorf, Insel Poel, Germany
"In the 13th century Henrich de Lowe II, the ruler of the island at that period, had so many debts that he sold much of the island to Wismar. Kaiser Karl IV from Prague reinstated his rights to part of Poel in 1348 mainly for hunting rights."
The History of Insel Poel by Manfred Dederich.

"I didn't know you were coming in today." Karine's bright red sweater set off her white hair. Annie wished she would look as good in her sixties.

"I was planning to work on the history in the studio, but I need to see Renate."

At the mention of her name, Renate appeared from the office behind the reception desk. The area under her eyes had dark circles, she wore no makeup, but her hair was neatly done. Pretending things were all right, Annie guessed.

Inside the office, Annie poured them each demitasses of coffee. "I've heard from Greta. She's okay."

Renate jumped up. "Where is she? Is she on the island? When can I see her?"

"I don't know where she is exactly." This was true. She knew the town, but not the street or house. Her phone rang. It had a thirty-three country code. "Excuse me, it's private." Rather than have Renate leave her office, Annie grabbed her coat and went outside.

"Hi Greta. I was just with your mother, but I didn't tell her where you are." Maybe it wasn't wise to let that on. "And my fiancé and his daughter are more than happy to come get you and bring you home."

"Why did you tell my mother anything?"

"Because she looks like hell: she's so worried. I know you love her."

"But she married that bastard."

"Greta, Karl is a first-class phony. He fooled your mother, who saw a chance to have love while making a better life for both of you. Although I know it's hard can you see that at all?"

"I suppose so."

"She misjudged. But the second she found out the truth, Karl was out of the house."

"It's his house."

Shit, Annie thought. Renate had a long way to go to extricate her daughter and herself from that marriage. "Listen, can we make a deal?"

"Depends."

"Come back with Roger and Gaëlle. See your mother. Stay with me."

"But you're going back to wherever."

"And you can come with me, if you don't feel safe here." Please, please let her feel safe, Annie thought. She really didn't want to deal with another teenager, no matter how lovely.

"Here's my address."

After they hung up, Annie rushed into the museum and took a pencil and paper from reception and wrote the address down. Then she went back outside to call Roger to give him the information.

"I'll pick her up and we'll fly up to Hamburg. Can you meet us?"

"Give me the flight information when you have it."

243

CHAPTER 52

Colerne, Wiltshire, England
July 1943

Gordon taxied to a stop. He switched off the engine of his Hawker Typhoon, took off his helmet and ran his hand through his hair. He sat there trying not to cry. He could see Thomas's, William's and Jeffrey's planes to his left. The cockpits were empty, but he knew they'd arrived back safely.

On his right Peter, Harry and Jack were pulling up. Everyone was back. No losses. *This time.* On the ground where they'd dropped their loads, there were new widows, new orphans. He knew he could never express sympathy for the German families, although there had to be those here in England that hated the war as much as he did.

He was sure that his friends would say to hell with all Germans . . . they'd put Hitler into power. Would England have done the same if they had found the rate of inflation escalating to the point where the price of a loaf of bread increased from morning to night of the same day?

Destruction was always bad, he decided. Killing could be dressed up in patriotic clothes, but it was still killing. Did he feel any gratitude to those that had died in the Hundred Years War? The American Revolution? In any war from the years before he was born? Would children born 200 years in the future even know about what they were doing now?

He wanted to cry. He wanted to sleep. He wanted to be with

Martha where he couldn't smell the oil of his plane.

"Hey Tibbitts! You planning on spending the whole day in there?" Thomas, his helmet under his arm, was standing outside Gordon's plane.

"Just thinking."

"Come on, let's get a beer. We've time before the debriefing."

"I'm going to take a shower."

Gordon didn't want a beer. He didn't want to be debriefed. He would pretend to be excited about his kills because anything else would hurt the morale of his squadron. But he just wanted to see Martha, although he would do his duty until the whole fucking war was over.

Walter had just fallen asleep when Martha heard a soft knock. The first thing she thought when she saw Gordon standing in the doorway was that he was a menacing shadow against the bright outside.

She glanced into the sunlight behind him. No one was on the street and Mrs. Summers next door had departed to the shops, her wicker basket over her arm. Mr. Paulson, the neighbor on the other side, was probably out walking his dog as he did every day at that hour. No one had seen her and Gordon together.

Not that it mattered. Whatever she did, word always got back to her father. Even the time she had the highest grades in her class, the word reached him before she got home to tell him herself. Being a vicar's daughter in a small village had more notoriety, at least locally, than being a Hollywood star.

Once Gordon limped inside, she saw that he was sobbing, without tears and without noise. Just his body shook. She led him into the salon with its comfortable sofa and large fireplace, the flame extinguished in the summer heat. He put his head on her chest. His sobs were no longer silent, but came out in great galloping sounds.

She stroked his hair, which was just beginning to wave as it grew out from the normal RAF cuts. She thought that he needed a haircut before one of his commanding officers called on him. Strange, a war was on, and they worried about hair length.

"I'm sorry, I'm sorry, I'm sorry."

About what was he sorry? she wondered. But rather than ask, she kept saying "it's all right, it's all right," even if she wasn't sure it was all right at all.

The ticking of a grandfather clock, its wooden case dented and pitted from years of use, replaced the sound of Gordon's crying.

He kept his head on her chest. She kept stroking his hair. Then his hand went to her breast.

She let him. He continued to stroke her breast until she reached for it, not to stop him but to put it under her blouse.

As if in slow motion, movement by movement, he progressed until they were both naked and he was moving back and forth within her.

At no point did she try to stop him or even want to stop him. She had only felt like this in the privacy of her own bedroom when her hand had brought her great pleasure, the same pleasure that her mother had said would destroy her ability to pee until her bladder burst. Martha knew how wrong her mother had been.

Gordon collapsed on top of her, although she still wanted more and more. "I'm sorry. I'm sorry."

Although she felt abandoned, she said, "There's nothing to be sorry about."

"I should have used something. What if you get pregnant?"

At that moment, pregnancy was the furthest thing from her mind. Comforting him had given way to her own desire for a release from the delight she was feeling except for that one second when he first thrust himself into her.

Upstairs Walter let out the wail that proclaimed he wanted attention, and he wanted it that very second.

Martha didn't want to abandon Gordon, but Walter had been left in her care. "I'll be back."

She slipped on her skirt and blouse without any underwear, which she carried and tossed onto the bed in the room where she was sleeping, then went on her way to the baby.

He was standing up in his cot, holding the bars. The second she walked in, he slowed his cries, as if waiting to see what she had on offer.

She scooped him up. "You're drenched. Let's get you changed."

Once dry, she put him back into his cot along with several of his favorite toys. "I'll be back."

Walter did not seem to mind her leaving.

Downstairs, there was no sign of Gordon. The front door was open.

Martha went out, just as Mrs. Summers walked by with her shopping basket. "Hello, Martha, dear. If you want to get anything from the store, they are running low on almost everything."

Martha didn't want anything from the store. She wanted to know what was wrong with Gordon, and now that she'd given him her maidenhead, would he ever want the rest of her.

Chapter 53

Kirchdorf, Insel Poel, Germany

"A series of fortress walls shaped like a five-point star protected the island from outside attack. A plan was drawn by Gerhart Pilooth in 1612. Inside the villagers were superstitious. The last witch was burned on Insel Poel in 1699."

The History of Insel Poel by Manfred Dederich

Although Roger had made Annie promise not to get involved in the murders, she resented that the stupid detective didn't seem interested in all the expensive cars at the dock and if there was any connection to the bodies. Then again, he probably knew the area.

She saw two men in a Jag turn into the road leading to the boatyard and for a moment was tempted to check them out. Roger was right when he said that she sometimes put her imagination in overdrive. Instead, she went back into the museum, to report to Renate that her daughter would be home shortly.

"Thank God, thank God." But when Annie also told her about their deal, Renate's first reaction was, "You can't take my daughter."

"I don't want to take her, and I don't see any need because you'll do what is needed. Only Greta still has doubts, and she needed to know she has an alternative."

Renate sat back in her chair. "I barely know you, but you've proven yourself to be a good friend. And I'm so sorry you got involved. Probably not what you expected on your assignment."

"Where else could I be underpaid, come across two corpses, see a family break up and get snowed on most of the time?"

"I hope nowhere."

Annie walked around to Renate and took both of the woman's hands in hers as she squatted in front of her. "Some things in life are just too important to ignore. Now what have you done about Karl?"

"I've talked to a lawyer. As soon as Greta is back, we'll decide whether to press charges or not. I mean, putting her through that could be worse and naturally, I'll be starting divorce proceedings. I've a psychologist lined up as well to help us both through it."

"Renate, I'd love to stay and talk, but I can't. Why don't we have dinner tonight? My treat."

"I'd like that."

Annie buttoned her coat against the cold and headed for the boatyard. She hoped she would see something that made sense to her.

CHAPTER 54

Kirchdorf, Insel Poel, Germany
"In autumn 1845 there were 34 widows living on Poel. The island also had four goldsmiths, four wheel makers, eleven weavers and eleven woodcutters. The statistics from the period show that 174 residents were either day workers or eel fishermen."

The History of Insel Poel by Manfred Dederich

Annie did not want to seem suspicious as she headed to the boatyard. She wasn't sure whether she would call more attention to herself if she walked or drove, then decided to walk. What was more normal than strolling into the restaurant for a late afternoon cup of tea?

For a nanosecond Roger's disapproval of what she was doing flashed through her head, but she pushed it aside. Although the sun was setting, she kept on her dark glasses so when she stared, the men, if they were still there, wouldn't see her observing them.

The wind had picked up as she navigated the short distance. She shoved her hands into her pockets, bent her head and made a beeline for the restaurant, never tilting her head. Still she could see two well-dressed men on the dock. If Annie's awareness of brand names in women's clothing was nonexistent, her knowledge of men's was even less if possible. However, she could recognize expensive and the two strangers fell into the expensive category.

As soon as she entered the restaurant, she chose a seat by the window, but with her back to it. She picked up a menu so if they were by chance curious, and glanced her way, they wouldn't think she was watching them. Hopefully, they would forget that a mirror looked out over the dock.

The waitress came over. "Back again?"

"I need a cup of green tea."

A boat was pulling into the dock. Annie knew not much more about boats than she did about clothing labels. She guessed this one was expensive by its size. It looked fresh scrubbed. As it docked, Gregor looked down from the deck where the captain would be in charge.

My God, her neighbor picked up the two men. Maybe the girl she had heard crying when she was first in the apartment was one of the murdered girls.

Inside one of the portholes, she thought, but she couldn't guarantee, that there was a young woman with an Asian face. She was sure enough to call Hans-Peter, The Doubter, or That Stupid Policeman as she'd christened the Lübeck policeman. She wasn't sure he'd give her any credence. She wondered if maybe the medical examiner might listen to her, but she knew neither her name nor how to contact her.

She pulled out her mobile and dialed. The sigh she heard as soon as he realized it was her made her very annoyed, but she couldn't give into it.

"Men on a boat in a boatyard, now that's suspicious," he said.

Annie held the phone under her chin and reached for her notebook and a pen. She tried to jot down identification of the boat, which was backwards in the mirror. "With two Asian faces in the portholes, don't you think that's a little strange?"

"Where are you?"

Annie told him. "I'll get the license plates of the cars the men came in."

"You do that." Hans-Peter hung up.

CHAPTER 55

Martha had returned with Gordon from the nearby forest where he had cut down pines to decorate the church for Christmas services. Several times when they planned to do it, it had not worked out. Either a cold drizzle had kept them inside, or Gordon had yet another mission. However, now he was on a two-day leave.

"If it weren't so cold, I'd make love to you right here." Gordon pointed to the wheelbarrow that was almost filled with pine branches and cones.

"And think how sticky our buns would be from the pitch, not to mention all the branches scratching us."

Finding a place to make love was always a great difficulty. Ruth's mother-in-law had moved down to be with her daughter-in-law and grandson in January. There had been talk of Ruth and baby Walter moving to London, but everyone felt that if Jerry decided to launch another major attack, they would all be better off in Colerne despite the base being a potential target. Alan's mother had fit in nicely, and had become good friends with Gordon's mother.

Together they had joined the church and done everything possible to convince the vicar that Gordon was all right for his daughter—although never addressing the issue directly, of course. They might have a conversation as they were arranging flowers, knowing full well that the vicar could hear them talking, and mention one of Gordon's good points, such as his potential future as a university professor, his promotion to squadron leader.

At no point did either woman, or Gordon for that matter, ever mention that they had limited faith. Nor did any of the three ever mention their campaign to either Ruth or Martha.

However, with Ruth's mother-in-law living in the cottage, it was ruled out as a place for the young couple to make love.

After the first time, they never made love unprotected.

"I did bring something, just in case we had a chance," Gordon whispered to Martha.

"What tree do you think will overhear and tell my father?" She put down the basket that was almost full of pinecones and put her arms around his neck.

"You never know." He wanted to say so much more to her, but until the war was over, or at least closer to being over, he didn't dare. He did not want her to end up like Ruth with a baby and his mother. If he had a son, or a daughter, he wanted to be around to help raise them.

The Americans had marched into Rome. D-Day had come and gone with some two million men and untold equipment lost. Paris was liberated. His countrymen had liberated Brussels. Greece was free. Still in September the Jerries had attacked London, validating Ruth's decision to stay in Colerne.

He shivered. Despite all his flights, he still felt like a coward because he killed from the air. He never had to look any German in the eye and watch the light of life go out. And that his chances of survival were greater in an airplane than in a trench meant that the lights in his eyes would stay on—or so he hoped. Too much fighting, too much bombing and both were still part of his near future, when all that he wanted was to have a nice little house in Scotland and his heading for the university each day, leaving Martha and his children at home.

In his daydreams, his father-in-law would remain far away in Colerne, and Martha would be the dutiful daughter with weekly letters.

His mother had encouraged him to say something to Martha about his long-range plans, but he refused. He wanted to know he would survive before he proposed.

"I think we have everything we need," Martha said. "Let's go back. I need to start my father's tea."

They walked back through the wood, stopping here and there to exchange kisses.

When they reached the church and began to unload the pine boughs and cones, Vicar Willson stormed out of his office. "You're late."

Most times, Gordon would apologize to the vicar, but he was tired of groveling. "We did what we set out to do. No one told us what time to be back."

"Martha should know," Vicar Willson said.

"I'm sorry, Father."

Gordon held up his hand. "Sir, your daughter does as much as she possibly can for you. Perhaps a thank-you for her efforts, rather than constant harping on what still remains, would not be out of order."

"Gordon, please!" Martha looked from her lover to her father.

"No, 'please.' I'm tired of seeing you treated this way. If you weren't here, your father would have to hire a secretary, a housekeeper and probably a diplomat to handle all the divergent forces in this church." Gordon knew all too well how much Martha did to keep the board, choir and committees happy. More than one volunteer had complained about how the vicar got up his or her nose.

"Young man! That is enough! I will not, I repeat *will not*, have you telling me what rules I make for my daughter."

Martha sat down in one of the pews.

"Don't be sitting there. I'm hungry. I think beans on toast for tonight's tea. Now go."

She stood up. Gordon pushed her down. "Martha, we were invited to eat with Ruth tonight."

"She has too much to do," Vicar Willson said.

Before Gordon could reply, the church door opened and Thomas came in. "I thought I might find you here." He winked. "Everyone is ordered back to the base. There's something big happening in Belgium, and we need to be on standby."

"What's happening?"

"Not sure. Can't do anything but wait. Our targets are fogged in, but if they clear we have to be ready to take off."

Vicar Willson stepped toward Gordon. "One more outburst like today, and I'll forbid my daughter to ever see you again."

"I think that is a decision you will regret." He pulled Martha by the hand out of the church. The temperature was dropping as night descended. He took her in his arms. "Nothing will stop me from seeing you."

"And my father won't stop me."

He kissed her deeply, hoping the vicar wouldn't burst through the door. In case he didn't come back, which was always his fear every time he climbed into the cockpit, he wanted her to remember the feel of his lips on hers, his tongue in her mouth.

"I love you," they whispered at the same time.

As he headed to the RAF vehicle that Thomas was using he noticed Robert and Andrew were in the backseat.

"Nice kiss," Andrew said as Gordon climbed into the front seat.

CHAPTER 56

Lübeck, Germany

Hans-Peter Leiter let out a long sigh as he hung up the phone. The main room was full of empty desks. Most of the other policemen were out doing their whatevers. He was waiting for an autopsy report on the wife of a wine importer found dead in her car in a garage. It had run out of gas and the muffler was blocked. No suicide note had been found, and the husband was seeing arm candy. Their children blamed their father, whether it was murder or him driving his wife, their mother, to suicide.

"What was that all about?" his partner Fritz Gärtner asked.

"That redhead. She thinks she saw men and a boat. Well, she did see men get on a nice boat in Kirchdorf. She was at the Kirchdorf dock. Nothing unusual in that."

"That's all?"

"She imagined that she saw Asian women on the boat."

"Maybe it's worth checking out."

Hans-Peter jumped at the feminine voice. He turned around. Claudia Niemann stood behind him. She was wearing a heavy winter coat over her scrubs. Snow melted off her boots and puddled on the linoleum floor of the station. She carried a briefcase. He jumped up. "Coffee?"

"*Ja*, but I don't have much time. Just brought over that autopsy report. On Frau Hausmann." She handed it to him. "I can't tell if it is suicide or not. There was a little bruising on her arm and a slight bump on her head. There were tranquilizers, many more than normal, but she could have taken them herself to make her death easier."

As Hans-Peter thumbed through the report, Fritz said, "So you think we should check out Kirchdorf?"

"With the number of Asian women washed up on the Kirchdorf beach and perhaps some in a boat at their dock, are you really asking?"

"We don't have the manpower to hang around a dock waiting for a boat to come in." Hans-Peter did not want Claudia to think anything other than the best of him.

She frowned. "And why did you ignore 'that redhead'?" She seemed pretty bright to me, or are you just being a macho sexist?"

Hans-Peter read her tone as disapproving. "We'll take a ride out when we get a chance." He had no intention of finding the time to do so.

CHAPTER 57

Hamburg, Germany
"In the 14th century four villages formed the Heiligeist Hospital. These four villages became more socially developed. Farms in the Swedish part of the island were given to people who already were running them after the Thirty Year War, which ended in 1648."

The History of Insel Poel by Manfred Dederich

Annie stood under the domed ceiling of Terminal 1 at Flughafen Hamburg-Fuhlsbüttel airport waiting for the Air France Toulouse flight to land. She was early: the flight was on time, the arrivals board said.

Roger was normally easy to spot not just because he was handsome, but because he was slightly taller than many Frenchmen. However, the average German man was taller than the above-average Frenchman, so she couldn't see very far ahead into the crowd of passengers tugging their suitcases.

Then she spied him. His slightly graying hair curled over his collar. He wore his tan sheepskin winter jacket and had his carry-on slung over his shoulder.

Gaëlle was next to him. She'd given up rainbow hair colors once Annie had convinced her father to compliment her on them rather than ground her. Now she wore it shoulder length in dark waves. She would be a beauty as an adult once she passed through the gangly stage where she was merely pretty. As soon as she saw Annie she waved.

Annie chose to hug Greta first. "Thank you for being brave enough to come back."

"She kept changing her mind," Gaëlle said. "I told her she could live with us if it didn't work out."

Roger nodded as he swept Annie into his arms. "My daughter is turning into a younger version of your mother. Adopt everything and everyone." He whispered into her ear, "Another great gift you brought me is your family." Annie knew that his former in-laws were cold, ignoring him and Gaëlle after their daughter had been murdered. Annie could understand that they might be angry at Roger for bringing a criminal element into their daughter's life that ultimately destroyed it, but she could never understand the rejection of Gaëlle—maybe because she resembled her father. However, she'd met his in-laws and most of her tiny amount of generosity toward them had vanished, thinking them cold, selfish. The revenge was that they missed out on this wonderful woman-to-be.

"She's scared," Gaëlle said.

"Of course you are." Annie and Roger said it together, but then Annie went on alone. "Your mother will be waiting for you at her house. We'll be with you every step of the way."

Roger drove through Hamburg in the Youngs' car, listening to the GPS rather than relying on Annie's directions. They both knew that too many times, they'd been lost when she'd said take a right or left only to discover how wrong she could be. He never wanted to stop to investigate whatever surprise might turn up before they found the correct route. He was strictly a go from point A to point B kind of person, unlike Annie who hated to pass up anything interesting.

This night, the goal was to get Greta home as fast as possible, before the girl changed her mind. The backseat doors were locked in case she bolted. Neither Annie nor Roger had discussed doing this: he locked them, looked at her, she nodded. Greta wouldn't be able to bolt if they stopped at a traffic light. Thank goodness for child safety standards, which as a single woman without small children had never really entered her mind until now.

They stayed silent until they were on the Autobahn. That late in the evening, there was almost no traffic. Roger kept his pedal foot down hard.

"In three hundred meters take the next left," the GPS said.

Everyone jumped then laughed.

"I guess we're all lost in our own thoughts," Annie said.

"Do you think my mother is mad at me?" Greta asked.

"I think she's mad at herself for not protecting you, for believing in Karl. I think she's worried how the two of you are going to rebuild that good relationship you had." Oops, not a good thing to say, Annie thought. "Which you can build again. Sometimes a crisis can make a relationship stronger."

Roger glanced over at her quickly. He wasn't one of those drivers that looked at his passengers as he talked to them. "Hmmm."

"That's true with them," Gaëlle said pointing to Roger and Annie in the front seat. "They really had their bad times, but now they've worked it all out. They'll be married in June."

"Greta, not every man is like your soon-to-be former stepfather. Karl is sick," Roger said.

Greta didn't answer nor did she say much until they turned the corner of the street where her house was. All the other houses were in the dark, but the *Rolladen* were still up at Renate's. Single bulb candles were alight in each window.

As Roger drew up in front of the house, Renate burst through the front door and down to the car. She tugged on the locked door, which Roger released. Renate pulled Greta from the car. For a moment Annie was afraid that Renate would hit the girl, but she hugged her, saying over and over, "Thank God, thank God," intermixed with "I'm sorry, I'm so, so sorry."

Renate was crying. Greta was crying. Gaëlle was crying. Annie felt tears on her face.

Roger blew his nose. "I think it's okay for us to leave them alone. Are you okay, Greta?"

She nodded. Her mother led her into the house and Annie, Roger and Gaëlle headed to the hotel. This time he trusted Annie's directions. As he said, "The place is tiny enough that even you couldn't get lost."

Once inside the studio, Annie made hot chocolate for everyone. "They can give us a house, instead of just a foldout bed for Gaëlle, if we want more room."

"I thought we'd get on the road tomorrow," he said. "It'll give us a little more time with your parents than we originally planned."

Annie was grateful that not once did Roger mention the cost of flights.

"Is the house as cute as the studio?" Gaëlle asked.

"I don't know," Annie said. "I was hoping to spend a few more days here."

"But you've handed in your work."

"All except the history book translations."

"You can do that at your parents', can't you?"

Annie was stuck. Of course she could, but she hated leaving until she knew who had killed those two girls. "Wouldn't you like a day to look around?"

Gaëlle was sliding around the heated floors in her stocking feet. "I would. Can we? Papa, s'il te plait. These floors are really cool . . . and I really want to see the beach where you found the bodies." When her father frowned she said, "What? I really would. It's not like they are still there."

"This might be a nice place for a holiday, sometime," Roger

said, "even if I can't get away in summer. I imagine late September or after Easter and before the summer crowd arrives in Argelès we might be able . . ."

He couldn't finish his sentence because Gaëlle grabbed him. "*Merci, merci,* Papa, I can practice my German. Greta and I spoke English most of the time. She's really good."

She took the cup of hot chocolate from Annie. "I was really good with her. I asked her open-ended questions, just like you taught me. I didn't rush her. Maybe I should be a social worker when I get out of school."

Roger and Annie exchanged looks. Gaëlle's future career plans changed weekly. That she planned on a career was enough to make them both content.

"I'm going to get undressed." The teenager took her suitcase into the bathroom.

It took about thirty minutes for everyone to get settled under the *Eiderdown*s with the lights out. Roger reached for Annie's hand.

"I'm glad you listened to me about not getting involved in the murders," he whispered when Gaëlle's breathing became regular. They were like two spoons, her back to his front. She felt his erection grow, but they would not act on it with Gaëlle in the room.

"I have some theories that we can talk about tomorrow."

"This is not our problem, not our country, not anything we need to get involved in. Do you hear me, Annie?"

"Annie?" Gaëlle mumbled.

"Yes, *chérie?*"

"Annie, when you and Papa get married, will you adopt me?"

Annie and Roger sat up in bed. There was enough light from outside through the *Rolladen* which had not been rolled all the way down for her to see his face.

"If you want to," he mouthed.

"I would consider it an honor. *Bonne nuit.*" She let Roger's comments about the murders go unanswered . . . for now.

CHAPTER 58

Bergedorf, Germany
November 1944

Hilke was busy typing up the work orders for the satellite camps where men and women were making armaments. Others were being sent out to clear rubble from where bombs had fallen in cities around the area. The system was complicated, but she was able to get the reports out on time.

Unlike the hut where Hilke slept at night, the office was kept warm with a ceramic wood-burning stove not unlike the one her parents owned. Looking at it first made her homesick followed by anger at her father for what he'd done to her mother directly and her indirectly. Had he left things well enough alone, they might never have arrested her mother. She, herself, would still be married, maybe even pregnant, had Dieter come home on leave at the right time.

During the days, she was almost too warm, while at night she nearly froze under the one blanket allowed each bunk. Her hut now held almost double the number of women as when she arrived. They slept two to a bunk, which at least let them share their body heat, such as it was. Ute, the woman who had befriended her in the beginning, was her bunk mate.

Although her boss, *Sturmführer* Hans Grüber, gave her many advantages, a real meal at noon was the most helpful. The prisoners who waited on tables at the officers' mess also had real meals and the chance to skim the remains off the plates. At

265

times she was able to smuggle some of it out to Ute. She had to be careful that no one saw her, either smuggling food or sharing it. Many of the other hut occupants refused to even speak to her.

"Spy!" and "Nazi's Bitch!" were the two insults most often hurled at her.

A few women tried to cultivate her friendship. Hilke had learned any kindness was followed by a request for a special favor, which she had no power to give.

Ute was the exception. She offered friendship and asked for nothing. At the same time she accepted the little bit of food, a piece of cheese, a carrot, extra bread . . . never minding that it had been carried next to Hilke's skin in her underpants.

What animals we've all become, Hilke thought at least once a day.

She made sure that she was efficient and her work was fault-less for the risk of being sent back to normal work details was far too great, although had they been in normal life, her boss, *Sturmführer* Grüber would be considered a good one in the way he gave directions and expressed appreciation at the quality of her work. If he'd had extra beer at lunch, he would talk with her.

"If you're not Jewish how did you end up here?"

"How did you get to be such a good secretary?"

"Where is your family?"

At times, he would put a hand on her shoulder and rest his head on hers as he stood behind her to check what she was typing. Those times his hand might slip to her breast, but he never went further.

Hilke wished she could use her position to help others. Two days ago, a prisoner, a good worker in the brick factory, had been caught with stuffing in his clothing—a discarded news-paper he'd found and used for extra warmth. He'd been taken aside and beaten to death on the parade ground.

Many of the prisoners were dying of malnutrition and dysentery. The smoke from the new crematorium was a reminder. To be able to work was to live. To not work was to become ash or to have one's remains shipped off to the medical school in Hamburg when the school called for more cadavers for their students to use in dissection classes.

Part of Hilke's job was to transfer the names of those that died from the handwritten books into the reports that were sent to Berlin.

Conditions were getting worse. The striped uniforms were no longer all the same. Some prisoners wore regular clothing taken from earlier arrivals. Food was getting scarcer, only two meals, bread in the morning; a watery soup at lunch.

Hilke, because of *Sturmführer* Grüber's gifts of sausage, onions, eggs and sometimes beets, was not as skeletal as the others. But even those donations were smaller and smaller.

Dr. Rudolf Metzer opened the door letting in the cold air.

He was one of the handsomest men Hilke had ever seen: everything an Aryan should be. His body was muscular. His eyes looked as if the sky on the brightest summer day had been pasted under his lids. His smile would entice even the coldest woman.

Hilke hated him.

He put a piece of paper on her desk. "Three women and two men died last night," he said.

"*Ja.*"

"*Danke.*"

As the doctor walked out the door he almost bumped into Grüber. "Any more news from Aachen?"

Grüber shook his head.

Hilke pretended to be studying a list on her desk. She put a piece of paper in the typewriter.

Over the last few months there were rumors that the Allies had taken France. The officers would discuss it, but only when there were two of them. They usually talked outside her window, but with the colder weather now, the window was most often closed.

Maybe, just maybe, the war would end. Was it wrong to wish your own country destroyed by its enemies? What happened when your country was your enemy?

Although Hilke had never been religious, she prayed to end her torment as well as that of the other prisoners. She prayed to lead a normal life again.

"Hilke. Hilke!"

She looked up at Grüber who was standing in front of her.

"I'm sorry. I must have been daydreaming."

CHAPTER 59

Kirchdorf, Insel Poel, Germany
"The tourist industry started in 1860 when people started visiting the island. Local residents would give up their homes or rent out rooms to the island visitors. At that point, coffee houses, restaurants and beer gardens began to appear. In 1871 the lighthouse was built. It included a custom house."

The History of Insel Poel by Manfred Dederich.

Annie woke with a start. The clock's face glowed 05:27 in the room. Roger slept next to her, something that always gave her a start after they'd been separated or if she'd stayed in her nest, which she did sometimes just to maintain a sense of independence. She would tell him she had a major project and it was better for her to just get on with it. Most of the time it was 100 percent true: other times she fudged the truth a bit, not much, nor enough to make her feel guilty. She loved her nest, she loved Roger, but she also loved herself enough to take what she needed.

Roger was a sound sleeper unless he was really worried about something. Gaëlle too slept as if she would never wake, and indeed when she did in the morning, she stumbled around in zombie-imitation mode.

Even though she was with two sound sleepers, Annie was very quiet as she slipped out from under the *Eiderdown*. Gathering her clothes from where she'd dropped them the night before she went into the bathroom to dress.

Then she left the flat, grabbing her bag on the way and shutting the door so that it barely made a click.

She could have hit herself for not thinking of taking photos of the luxury cars before and e-mailing them to that stupid detective.

The morning stars glittered through the crystal clear sky. Maybe if she had found Insel Poel instead of Argelès first, she might have ended up buying something on the island instead, not that she regretted her decision. Slowly she was learning there were many places in the world where one could put down roots, even if the roots might be transplanted. Maybe that meant she was finally growing up or growing into acceptance that she was a Third-Culture Kid, never totally of her parents' culture and never totally of whatever place in which she was living. Instead of hating it, she now reveled in the richness it added to her life.

It was still too early for the people at the hotel to put out the breakfast spread. All the windows in the kitchen and dining room were dark. Across the street, she could smell that the baker was preparing the *Brötchen,* but his was the only light on anywhere between the hotel and the dock, which was equally dark.

The hood of her coat kept her ears warm. Her double-lined mittens saved her hands from being cold as she turned the corner to the path that led to the water.

At that time of the morning, the only sounds should have been water lapping the edge of the shore. Instead she heard a motor engine and saw the boat she'd seen with the Asian faces pull from the dock.

Karl Klausson and the two men who owned the luxury cars were shaking hands.

Ducking behind a parked car, she took off her mittens. Her

pocketbook was big enough and filled with enough bulky things that it took her a minute to find her camera. Don't leave, don't leave, she thought. She wanted to shoot the back of the boat, the men and the cars.

Between her hood and the distance, she couldn't make out what the men were saying but she could guess from their body language that the mood was jovial.

Her first photo was of the boat. Damn, the flash went off. The men were so engrossed in what they were saying, they hadn't seemed to notice. She shut off the flash. The photos would be dark, but maybe she could lighten them enough to show faces.

What she wanted to get was license plate numbers, but she was at the wrong angle. Perhaps if she moved back up the path a bit and was behind the tree, she might get the cars as they pulled away.

The streetlamp was out and the sun still hadn't even thought about rising. Had this been summer, she wouldn't have stood a chance of being hidden, she thought, as she made her way to a better photo position.

One car engine started, then the other. The tires crunched on the road.

Click.

A few seconds.

Click.

A few seconds. Click.

A few seconds.

Click.

She regretted the fact that her camera was so slow between shots, but she thought she had captured the license plates. Now all she had to do was wait for Karl to leave and she could head back to the studio. Roger would not be happy with her, but maybe if he took the photos to the dumb detective, one policeman to another . . .

"Well, if it isn't the little bitch, who helped destroy my marriage."

Annie jumped.

Karl was hovering over her. Her back was to a tree, a bush was to the left. There was really no place she could run.

"Let me see the camera."

"Why."

She saw his fist come toward her face. Then nothing.

CHAPTER 60

Kirchdorf, Insel Poel, Germany

"Papa, Papa. Wake up! Annie's gone!"

Roger opened his eyes, tried to remember where he was. He had slept long and hard, showing that at forty-five, travel and emotional events took their toll in a way they hadn't when he was younger. What was his daughter talking about?

"Annie's gone."

"What do you . . . gone where?" He sat up in bed. His daughter usually needed to be pried out of bed in the morning, not firing verbal messages at him.

The place where Annie had been when he'd gone to sleep was empty.

"When I got up to pee at six something, she wasn't here. Now it's almost nine, and she's not back. Her coat is gone."

Roger rubbed his hands over his face. "She may have gone to breakfast."

"I've already checked. She wasn't there. She hadn't been there earlier, either."

Roger realized that his daughter was not only dressed, she had on her coat, scarf and hat. "Maybe they didn't understand you?"

"My German's not great, but we understood each other. They haven't seen her."

"Did you find a note?" The Perret house rule was that you never went anywhere without leaving a note on where you were

273

going and when you expected to be back.

"Let me call her." He threw the *Eiderdown* off and went to his jacket that was hanging on the coatrack at the entrance of the flat. He hit number 1. It rang and rang and rang.

"I already tried her phone. It just rang and rang. No message. It must be off."

Gaëlle began crying. "I'm scared. It's not like her to disappear."

"I'm sure she's okay." He wasn't sure at all and he was even less sure of what to do. No policeman would listen to him this close to a disappearance even if he could communicate with him.

Although he hoped she hadn't done anything about the murders, he feared that she had. All he could think of was if she had and she was okay, he would strangle her for the worry that was seeping through his body.

CHAPTER 61

Swansea, Wales
May 1, 1945

"Close your eyes and hold out your hands, I've a surprise for you . . . We've known each other . . ."

No, no, that won't do, Squadron Leader Gordon Tibbitts said to himself.

"When the war is over . . . We think so much alike."

Well they did, he and Martha, except for religion. He was an atheist or maybe an agnostic. He'd seen too much flying with his RAF squadron during the war to ever believe in a god again. When he was alone in his plane in the sky, he realized the vastness of the universe. Even as a little boy sneaking out of bed at night to look through the telescope his father had given him for Christmas, he wondered at the absolute unknowingness of it. Then he asked why would anyone think that there was a god that cared about his petty sins. As an adult he expanded that to a god not caring with whom someone slept.

If there were some anthropomorphic god who could create such a solar system, he would have had to be playing games with humanity. Or maybe there were two gods on different sides of the war, much like the Greek and Roman gods, who used people as pawns in their own power games. Only miserable gods would allow this mayhem to go on and on for what seemed like forever.

"Will you be my wife?"

No, too direct. That since they met she had learned to love looking at the sky through his telescope, that she knew the name of every star in their constellations, that she drank her tea without milk and sugar, that they laughed at the same things . . . those were only a few of the reasons to marry her.

"I think we should get married." Too wishy washy. Why would she marry someone unsure?

Gordon was dressed in civilian clothes. He had flown in from Germany where the allied forces were making progress. They had taken Hamburg and were on their way to Lübeck when he was given orders to go back to home base with a cargo of papers.

When the war was over, Gordon pictured himself back at university, a full professor someday. "You'll make a wonderful university wife, Martha," he said to his mirror, an antique with worn black spots around the edges.

"Still thinking what to say?"

Gordon whirled around to see his mother in the doorway of the room she had set up for him in this small cottage she now owned. "Oh, I don't expect for you to be with me long," she'd said, "but you need a place to escape to from wherever you are." She'd placed a few of his boyhood treasures, which had survived the bombing, including his telescope, in the room. And he had spent his last night with her rather than on the base.

"I never thought proposing would be so hard."

"Have you bought a ring yet?"

"I was planning to this afternoon."

His mother slipped the sapphire ring off her left hand. "You don't have to use this, but it was my mother-in-law's and her mother-in-law's before her." Her eyes twinkled. "Now, I tend to believe if unhappy people wear jewelry it becomes contaminated, but I had a good marriage, as did my mother-in-law."

He took the ring and looked at it. The sapphires were almost the color of Martha's eyes. "And before that?"

"I don't know, but two generations of good marriages should put happiness into the gold."

He wanted to ask her what she thought of her future daughter-in-law, but was afraid she might disapprove.

"Of course, Vicar Willson is a total jackass. Self-righteous . . . prig . . . no other word for it. No wonder they banished him to that little church. He can't do much damage way out here." His mother would never get over her London-is-the-center-of-the-universe mentality, while still enjoying each day of her life no matter what it handed her. "But Martha, she's a treasure. How she can stand her father is beyond me."

The telephone rang. His mother disappeared. Within minutes she was back. "It was your commanding officer. You need to leave immediately for an assignment in Germany."

He put the ring in the drawer of his night table. A tatted doily was on top and held a night lamp that never quite gave enough light to read by.

"I'll give the ring to her when I get back."

"And maybe by then you'll have figured out how to ask her."

CHAPTER 62

Kirchdorf, Insel Poel, Germany
"She didn't come in for breakfast." The waitress in the hotel dining room put down the basket of hard-boiled eggs between the sliced cheese and cold meats.

"I told you that she hadn't been here, Papa. And you know Annie always needs to eat first thing," Gaëlle said. "Something's happened to her. I know it."

"She could have gotten something out of the *frigo* or gone to the bakery for a roll." Roger didn't want to think Gaëlle might be right. He suspected Annie might have been nosing around the murders more than she let on. It wasn't that she lied to him; she just omitted things that she didn't want him to know.

"Let's eat, then we'll check at the museum."

"Let's go now."

"It doesn't open for a half hour."

Gaëlle emitted one of her teenage sighs, but picked up a plate and started loading it up with the meats, cheeses, breads, honey. "May I have some hot chocolate and my father wants coffee," she told the waitress in German.

"I'm glad your German is up to basic conversation," Roger said.

"I want to be like Annie," Gaëlle said. "I'm really worried. My bones tell me she's in trouble."

"Bones are not necessarily a good predictor of the future." However, Roger ate quickly, because his own bones were insist-

278

ing he get to the museum the moment it opened. Acting casual with Gaëlle was just as important. He didn't want to point out to Gaëlle that Annie couldn't be at the museum if it were closed, but she might arrive at opening.

Renate had the key in the museum door as Roger and Gaëlle approached.

"I want to thank you again for bringing Greta back. We talked for hours last night, and she says she wants to go ahead and prosecute Karl. We'll be meeting with the police later today and my attorney in an hour."

"I'm so glad we could be of service. By the way, have you heard from Annie this morning?"

Renate pushed the door open and flipped on the lights. "Not at all. Was she planning to come in today?"

"She's missing," Gaëlle said.

Renate looked puzzled.

"She was gone when we got up this morning. She didn't take her laptop with her. She didn't eat breakfast either."

"Have you contacted the police?" Renate took off her coat and hung it on the rack. "Silly question, they wouldn't do anything so soon. But you would know that, wouldn't you, as a policeman yourself?"

"If you hear anything, can you call me?" He pulled his notebook and pen from his pocket and wrote his cell phone number.

"Of course."

Outside Gaëlle put on her woolen hat so it covered her ears. "What now?"

"Let's drive about and see if we can see her." He handed her his cell. "Keep trying to reach her."

As they walked back to the hotel, Gaëlle pushed buttons. "Nothing. She probably has her phone off." Then she added,

"As usual." Both knew that Annie's phone was off more than it was on.

CHAPTER 63

Insel Poel, Germany

"In the 19th century the architecture changed. Many of the old houses were torn down. The new buildings had a three-wing configuration. One entered in the middle, which was where the farmers lived, and the right and left wings had stalls for the animals. The farm houses were well built. The farmers were either wealthy or at least self-sufficient."

The History of Insel Poel by Manfred Dederich

Annie felt herself floating to the surface of reality. She tried to open her eyes but she saw nothing. Sleep was drawing her back, but she fought it, lost, and fell back into unconsciousness for a time she couldn't estimate when she came to for a second time.

When she tried to touch her eyes, she realized that her hands were tied. She was lying flat on something hard. She tried to suss out where she was.

Nothing was moving, so she couldn't be on a boat. Why did she think of a boat? Because the last thing she remembered was seeing Karl Klausson at the dock come toward her.

Her mouth felt dry and the phrase "full of cotton" popped into her head. My God! A gag was in her mouth and it bit into her lips. She tried to roll over to see if she could rub her cheek in a way that the gag would move down her face and she could spit it out. That made her realize she couldn't turn at all. Not just her hands were tied; her upper torso was also immobilized.

Her legs were not tied down to whatever she was attached to, probably a bed because it was not as hard as a board would have been. However, they were tied together at the ankles. She moved them from side to side. It was then she realized that someone had covered her with an *Eiderdown*. The air on her face and her exposed leg was cold. She guessed she was still wearing her coat.

On her right, just about six inches away, was a wall but it was curved. On the left another six inches or so, was the end of whatever she was on.

She sniffed the air. It smelled like the sea. Listening, she heard a bird, but since she didn't know one bird from another, perhaps with the exception of a crow, the information was useless.

Outside she heard a car pull up. The engine was shut off. Two doors slammed.

"Are you crazy keeping her here?" She didn't hear the reply, which might have been muffled or might not have existed at all.

Footsteps were above her and then something squeaked and there were more footsteps. She felt the presence of two people and she feigned the heavy breathing of a sleeper.

"She's still out cold." If only she could think clearly.

"Should you give her another shot? Enough to get her out to sea?"

"Probably. We'll have to wait until the middle of the night, in any case."

"And this time we'll dump the body far enough out that it won't wash up here."

"Since we haven't any more parties scheduled until next week, we could go over to Norway."

"Not bad. At least if the body makes it to shore, there'll be no connection with here."

Annie heard more rustling, felt a prick in her arm and then

she could no longer stay awake. Her last thought was regret that she'd given Roger such a hard time about them marrying.

CHAPTER 64

Bergedorf, Germany
March–April 1945

Something was happening in the camp, but no one knew exactly what it was. Hilke, whose life had changed suddenly in the past, felt another change was coming, but she didn't understand what. Her life had become such a routine that foreseeing change was more than she was able to contemplate.

Granted, she thought herself extremely lucky. Her ability to type had given her a work detail that not only saved her from grueling labor, but also gave her the benefit of extra food. At the same time, it had generated resentment with the women who had been crammed into the hut.

Within the last few days she and Ute no longer had to share a bunk. They had their choice of places to sleep as their hut mates disappeared in white buses under the Swedish Red Cross banner. Others were piled into boxcars. In the cool spring night air, they could use the blankets left behind to keep them warm. What both Ute and Hilke found strange was that the guards had done nothing to remove the blankets.

Yesterday, the Jewish children in the doctor's clinic disappeared. One morning they just weren't there. They couldn't all have died in the same night.

The remaining prisoners badgered her.

"Tell us what you know."

"Are we all going to be executed?"

"Are we being sent to other camps?"

"Does this mean Germany is losing the war?"

"I'd tell you if I could, but I don't know anything," was all she could say. They thought she was lying. She wasn't. Although Hilke went to Grüber's office every day, the work was far different. All attempts to keep records had been replaced by a frantic attempt to destroy records.

Hilke spent three entire days pushing paper into the ceramic stove that had kept her warm, records of the satellite camps, outside work done by prisoners, accounting records of products the prisoners had made.

Grüber wafted in and out of the office, barely speaking to her. He would ask for certain papers then disappear with them, reappearing with envelopes that he would tell her to burn. Other officers would come in looking for him, and she would tell them he was in this or that building meeting with this or that person.

Grüber and two of the other officers talked about a prisoner-transport train being bombed in the nearby city of Celle. The word "massacre" was bandied around as if they were talking about a tennis or football match. Two months ago, they would never have spoken so freely in front of her. As she listened, she began to shiver. What was happening? What *was* happening?

With fewer prisoners at mealtime, the prisoners hoped they might be getting more food, but there was even less. The prisoners who had served as cooks had been shipped out. But for Hilke, Grüber deposited full meals with even a small piece of meat on her desk from the officers' mess. "I need you strong."

On April twenty-fifth there was no roll call. Prisoners were told to stay in their huts.

Hilke lay on her bunk. The twelve other women who had not been shipped out either stayed in their bunks or were sitting on them. The silence was loud, because no one dared to speak.

All of them had survived to this point. The dangers had been somewhat known, the rules had been clear. Now nothing was known and the rules seemed to disappear.

Three guards appeared at the door. *"Schnell, schnell."* They prodded the women with their guns to the end of the railway cars where they were shoved in. Prisoners from other huts were already in the car.

"It's like when we came," one whispered.

"Shut up," one the guards said as he closed the door. The last thing Hilke saw of the camp was where the hangings had taken place, but all of the gallows had been taken down.

There was enough room to sit, shoulder to shoulder, but not much more. The car began to move. At first no one talked. Then they began guessing where they were being taken. To another camp was the most common thought.

Hilke had no idea how long the ride was when the train stopped.

New guards opened the door. The sun was overhead. *"Raus! Raus!"* They pulled at the women who did not jump off the car fast enough. Several stumbled. Hilke helped one to her feet and was rewarded with a gun poked into her back, but not enough to really hurt her.

She looked around. They were in a boatyard. A huge ship called the *Cap Arcona* had a gangplank, and the prisoners were being ushered on board. What she wanted to do was to laugh. She had heard of the *Cap Arcona*. It had been a luxury ship before the war. Going from the hell of the camp to a luxury cruise ship? It made even less sense than everything else that had happened to her.

CHAPTER 65

Lübeck, Germany

"Fritz, how's your English or French?" Hans-Peter Leiter held the phone receiver to his chest. "It's some kid about the pain-in-the-ass redhead. She tried speaking German, but I can't understand her."

At the moment the room was half full of officers, all of whom were writing up reports and trying to avoid having to go out. Another storm was just starting up. The weather had reported it would be the worst storm of the season.

Fritz took the phone as Hans-Peter moved out of the way. He reached for a pen as he said things like, "Yes, not usually, too soon, that's possible, I doubt it, were you really?" He started to write a number on the desk blotter that was already filled with numbers and notes. The pen was dry. He flapped his hand and Hans-Peter gave him another.

When he hung up, he said, "That was Frau Young's fiancé's daughter. She disappeared. The girl knew the redhead was messing around with the murders, and she said her father is afraid for her."

Hans-Peter ran his hand through his hair. "Another amateur."

"Except the fiancé was a top detective with the French police in Paris and is a chief of police now. The daughter said to mention the brotherhood and all that."

"*Scheiβ*." Police did stick together and although Hans-Peter would have liked to believe that it didn't count if the cop that needed help was French, he knew that it didn't matter. French or not, Young's fiancé was a cop! He picked up his keys. On the way out, he stopped at the main desk and handed the clerk a phone number. "Call this number, ask for a photo. When you get it, put out an alert." That they had no paperwork didn't really matter.

CHAPTER 66

Kirchdorf, Insel Poel, Germany
"In 1910 there was a health spa. The first cabins were built on the beach for the tourists to change into their bathing costumes. By 1913, the island filled 310 beds. By 1930 the number of tourists grew to occupy 480 beds."

The History of Insel Poel by Manfred Dederich

When Annie woke again, she realized that she had wet herself. Her face was freezing. She could hear the wind howling. Had she not had the *Eiderdown,* her coat and her hat still on, she imagined she'd have frozen to death.

She tugged on her hands but the bindings scratched. They were probably rope, maybe a half-inch thick, and wrapped and rewrapped. She had no idea how her feet were tied because the rope or whatever was over her jeans and boots. All she knew was she couldn't pull her legs apart.

Maybe if she could get her feet out of her boots, then at least her legs would be free. When the two men came back they would know she was conscious, but their threats to kill her didn't matter. Why they hadn't killed her yet, she didn't understand.

By moving her left leg back and forth and tilting her heel she was able to get one boot off. She kicked it out of the way. This left the rope so loose that she could free both legs. Had they tied her legs as they had her upper torso, it would never have worked.

A fat lot of good freeing her feet did. Everything else about her body was so tightly anchored that if she flailed around too much, the only thing she would accomplish would be to cause the *Eiderdown* to fall off.

I won't cry, I won't cry, she thought. Roger and Gaëlle would notice she was missing, but what good would that do. Even if Roger were a *flic,* he didn't know the island. He didn't know the system; he didn't speak the language. Not that many people she'd run into spoke English and even fewer spoke French.

Gaëlle had had five years of German, but the dialect was different. Poor Gaëlle. Annie wanted to live for herself, but she also really didn't want Gaëlle to lose two mothers before she was fourteen.

CHAPTER 67

Colerne, Wiltshire, England
April 30, 1945

Gordon shut off the engine of his Hawker Typhoon and took off his helmet then ran his hand through the dark stubble that once had been a full head of hair. He knew there was gray in it. Thirty was too young to be going gray. Thirty was too old to be in a war.

Other Hawkers from the raid were landing and pulling next to him: Raymond, Paul, Steve, Dick, Joseph, Sean the crazy Irishman—all present and accounted for. They'd lost no one.

The longer the war went on the more confused he felt. Religious people, like Vicar Willson, loved the death of the enemy, but he was allegedly Christian. Vicar Willson would say man had dominion over all creatures. Well man was making a mess of his dominion.

Gordon knew why he was fighting. He didn't want England to become an extension of Germany. That no foreigner had conquered the Island since 1066 was a source of not just pride, but tradition.

He knew he'd been lucky and taken the easy way out. He wasn't slogging through mud. There was almost no chance he would have to look into the eyes of a man he was killing. It had shocked him to realize that he would be able to kill to protect his own life, and that made him feel a bit more animalistic than he liked to think of himself.

291

But each mission was getting harder and harder for him. As he sat in his plane, he debated taking off and going . . . going where? Deserting was not in his nature, but being a killer . . . and that was how he now thought of himself . . . wasn't in his nature either.

"Tibbitts? You going to stay in that plane till your next flight?"

Sean, the crazy Irishman, was on the ground looking up at the cockpit. "We're going for a beer after the debriefing, which if you don't get your balls in motion, you'll miss."

Gordon didn't want to go to the debriefing. He didn't want a beer. He just wanted to be near Martha and sleep.

When Martha opened the door, the first thing she thought looking at Gordon was how old and tired he looked. She pulled him into the house, relieved that the neighbors were not close enough to see and that no one was biking by. Word would get back to her father so fast. Maybe someday she'd be lucky enough to live a life with a bit of anonymity.

Gordon took Martha in his arms and like that they walked to the sofa and sank into it. Then he put his head on her shoulder and cried.

She wasn't sure how to react. She had never seen a tear in her father's eyes, not even when her mother died. Sometimes when she visited a parishioner's house where the body was laid out in the living area, a man would be seen to be bent over with grief. Although the tears could have been freed by the beer, the man would be thoroughly ashamed of appearing weak to his friends and family.

All she did was hold Gordon and rock him as she might have done for Walter. She stroked his hair with her right hand.

When he had quieted, he whispered into her breast, "You must think I'm a weakling."

She moved him with both hands on his shoulders until he

was facing her. "I think you're strong enough to admit when the pain of circumstances are so far beyond your control they overwhelm you. I think you can see all sides of an issue, and that's a strength, although it causes more difficulty for you than people who can only think of one side. Think of my father?"

He pulled away. "Do I have to?"

She nodded. "At least this time you do. He thinks he's right about everything and shuts out all alternatives, making his world very narrow."

"Sometimes I wish my world were narrow. I wish I never had to fly over a target again. I wish I never had to drop another bomb."

"The war can't go on forever."

Gordon felt like it would. All he wanted was to forget everything that had happened in the last few years—that is, everything but Martha.

Chapter 68

Kirchdorf, Insel Poel, Germany

"The last thing I wanted to be was stuck here in a major blizzard." Hans-Peter paced the dining room in the hotel. Gaëlle, Fritz and Roger were sitting at the same table. The storm outside was roaring. The snow was so thick that they could barely see the building next door, although it was only a few yards.

The hotel had found a room for the two policemen on the floor above where Roger and Gaëlle were staying, but no one was ready to brave the storm. To search for Annie was out of the question in this weather. She could walk by them and no one would see her.

"All we can do is sleep tonight, and get going in the morning," Hans-Peter said. "And damn it, I'm hungry." The hotel did not have a restaurant that served lunch and dinner. Only breakfast. Even if two restaurants were nearby, the storm was too forceful to allow them the trip. Instead, they decided to brave the storm back to where they would be spending the night.

"I know Annie has enough food so that I can do something, if you're not fussy," Gaëlle said.

"I'm not fussy," Fritz said.

The three men sat around the table in Annie's studio. Gaëlle fried bacon and added eggs, potatoes and a can of tomatoes, clearing out all the remaining food in the cupboard. She found no wine or beer, but she'd brewed up a pot of tea.

Hans-Peter stared at the tea as if it were some loathsome concoction. Rather than risk being rude, he drank some. "There's nothing we can do until the storm stops. And even then, there's not much we can do. And we better get back quickly, because I hear there's a follow-up storm coming."

He excused himself and went out into the hall to call his ex-wife to tell her he wouldn't be there to pick up the boys. Not that she would be surprised.

The hallway door opened, and a man covered with snow entered. He brushed the snow off onto the floor before he entered the flat next to Annie's.

"I really didn't expect you," Hans-Peter's ex-wife said. "With the weather and all, it's better we're all inside."

CHAPTER 69

Bay of Lübeck
May 3, 1945

RAF Flight Lieutenant Gordon Tibbitts climbed into the cockpit of his Hawker Typhoon Mark 1 bomber. This was the same Tiffy he had flown regularly. In a way, he thought it must be like the relationship between a jockey and his horse at the races, a team. He knew the feel of the stick, just how much pressure to put to get her to turn exactly how and when he wanted. All the Tiffys he'd flown, he'd liked, but this one was his favorite, and he was glad that he was piloting her today. In fact, every time he flew her he felt he had a greater chance of coming back. Too many of his friends hadn't survived their missions, but this Tiffy had come back from all her missions unscathed.

The sixty-pound projectile bombs were already aboard, just waiting for him to drop them.

Planes from squadrons 184, 263, 197, 198 were part of this mission as well to create more death. He never saw his victims. He was sure some were like his neighbors who didn't survive the Blitz, ordinary people caught up in history. The word enemy had less meaning for him every day the war went on.

At times he wondered if his German counterparts were as tired of the war as he was and only wanted to go home to their mothers, wives, sisters, sweethearts. Were they tired of scanning the skies to see if Fritz, Jürgen, or Heinz had made it back and mourning when they did not?

Did they want to wake up in the morning and dress for an ordinary day at work, be it in an office, a field, hospital, factory or school?

These were questions he could never afford to voice out loud, except to Martha.

Rumors were that Hitler was dead. The Russians and the Allies had taken most of Germany. The war was winding down. More and more his mates were saying, "After the war, I'm going to . . ." believing that they just might survive to do the whatever they would have done had Hitler not come to power with plans to rule the world.

He wanted to go home. He wanted to marry Martha. He wanted to start teaching again. In his imagination, he could see himself preparing classes at night, while Martha did the dishes. Then they would listen to the radio before going to bed. On Sundays, they might eat a joint of meat that his mother had prepared, taking home some of the leftovers. They would go to Brighton for summer holidays or maybe even Snowdonia for a mountain hike.

Scotland. Maybe someday he could resume his teaching post. He had loved being a student there in another lifetime that grew hazier every time it came into his mind.

He tried to stop himself from thinking of Jimmy Fitzpatrick, the redheaded Irishman. They had gone through training together and he had gone down on their first mission. Jimmy's death shocked him into a gut-level feel of what war really meant. Before, it was just a concept.

World War I had ended before he was really aware of war, although his parents talked about it. His father, who had had polio as a baby, had not been able to serve, and because he walked with crutches, he had never been criticized for shirking his duty.

Whenever he started out on a mission he tried not to think of the ever-increasing list of his friends who had not come back. Instead, he tried to remember Simon Taylor. He'd been shot down over France, walked to the coast, and somehow got a fishing boat to cross the channel. He supposed it helped that Simon spoke French like a native and was later parachuted behind the lines anyway and now was missing. But he had held dear to the made-it-back part. If Simon could make it out after being shot down, Gordon hoped he could too if he were to be unlucky enough to be hit.

When your time was up, it was up, the ubiquitous they kept saying, but he didn't want his time to be up. He wanted to stick his tongue out at the "they" who believed in fate.

He wanted his life back. No, that wasn't true. He wanted his life to *begin*. Going almost directly from finishing his doctorate to the Royal Air Force at the start of the war meant he never got a chance to start his life. The short time he'd spent in the classroom at the university counted for nothing.

He thought of the pilots that prayed before taking off. Some came back, some didn't. There was no correlation between prayer and survival. He'd heard talk about foxhole atheists, who when gunfire was passing overhead suddenly found religion. He'd been fired on many times. His plane had been hit. He'd brought back more than one crippled fighter. How much longer would his luck hold up?

The planes were taking off. He waited his turn and pulled up the wheels, savoring the second between being on the ground and being airborne. Their target, the pilots had been told in the pre-mission briefing, was several ships carrying fleeing Nazi officers.

More enemy to destroy. More killing. Don't think of them as humans with human needs, dreams, fears just like he had. The enemy was probably blissfully on the water thinking that they were safe, imagining a new life in Sweden perhaps.

He looked down at the gray water. He'd been told the ships were named the *Cap Arcona, Deutschland* and *Theilbek*. He didn't want to get close enough that he could be fired on, but one of them was impressive, maybe 350 feet long. He was good at guessing sizes. Its three chimneys were producing steam. It looked much more like a luxury cruiser than a warship. Probably it had been taken over during the war.

He let loose of his load. Other planes were doing the same. He could see the fires on board the ships.

People were jumping into the water.

Some were in lifeboats.

Others were swimming.

Some of the planes swooped in and shot at the people below them. Some seemed to be getting further and further from the crippled and sinking ships, but when he looked again, he couldn't be sure if they were people or flotsam from the ships themselves. It didn't matter. If they were people he should shoot at them.

He couldn't.

He turned his plane back to home base.

CHAPTER 70

Lübeck, Germany
May 3, 1945

"This is insane," Hilke thought, just as Ute said the exact same thing. They were among the twelve women shoved into what must have once been a luxury stateroom aboard the *Cap Arcona*.

Somewhere from the depths of her memory, when life was normal, Hilke remembered seeing articles about the ship when it was launched, although she could never have told anyone when. Or maybe her parents had talked about it. The world before the camp was more like a movie she'd seen or a book she'd read.

Although much of the ship had been stripped of its luxury accoutrements, for some reason, the rugs were still in place. And the toilet—the toilet was beautiful. It worked. The shock of releasing bodily fluids without being surrounded by the stink of the waste of other humans accumulating for years was a luxury.

The other women had given up asking Hilke where they were being taken and why. Grüber had not given her any information: she'd typed no transport orders.

"It's moving," one of the women screamed. They all rushed to portholes, blocking Hilke's view of the dock disappearing.

"We're headed toward the open sea."

"Then what?"

"Sweden? Remember the white buses from Swedish Red Cross?"

"Norway?"

"Denmark?"

"I don't care, it's not the camp."

"It could be worse than the camp."

Then silence. The women were on the top level of the ship where first-class passengers must have once sat in deck chairs with blankets covering their laps, or played shuffleboard. They had no idea of how many other prisoners were on the ship, only the knowledge that when they were pushed and shoved up the gangplank they could see only prisoners as far back as possible.

The women sat on the floor and talked more than they had ever talked in the hut. They'd guessed there were very few guards on the ship.

Some fell asleep. All were hungry.

An explosion woke those asleep and then there was another and another and another.

Smoke filled the cabin.

Hilke tried the door. Everyone had assumed it was locked, but it wasn't. All the women rushed onto the deck.

Above were RAF planes dropping bombs.

More explosions.

Hilke jumped into the sea and was shocked by the icy cold Baltic water. Even in summer the Baltic was never warm, but in May winter temperatures had not begun to give way to the longer sunny days.

Swim, she thought. Swim. Where?

She looked in the direction the ships were heading.

Shore must be in the opposite direction.

One RAF plane swooped in and started shooting at the people in the water.

She ducked under the surface until the plane passed.

She swam as if she were at the Olympics. With no idea of how much time had passed, she turned only to see the ship list. Turning back to what she hoped was shore, she swam as she had never swum before.

CHAPTER 71

Kirchdorf, Insel Poel, Germany

Eight-year-old Tomas and nine-year-old Reinhardt had moved the sofa and chairs to the center of the living room and arranged them so that they made a single unit enclosing a section of the rug. To get into the middle the boys had to climb over the top, which they did sideways, and then toppled onto the cushions.

Now the pieces were no longer furniture—they were a pirate ship. Freed from school a second day thanks to impassable roads left by what the television had called the "storm of the century," the boys had concocted an entire sea adventure that owed quite a bit to movies.

Sun streamed in through the sheer curtains. They had a lace pattern of unreal species of flowers that made shadows on the wall, duplicating the pattern. Tomas started to lower the *Rolladen* to create nighttime at sea, when their mother entered the room. "Don't."

Reinhardt was always the challenger. "Why not?"

"Because the sunshine is cheery." She disappeared back into the kitchen, mumbling it was just her luck to have her husband stranded in Frankfurt while she was stuck at home with two boys in a closed space.

Reinhardt followed her and opened the closet and took out the ironing board.

"What's that for?"

"It's a plank, in case Tomas has to walk it, *Mutti*."

"No, it's not."

Reinhardt returned to the living room, making sure the door between it and the kitchen was closed. Too much visibility would lead to limitations they didn't want. "No luck."

"Well, we can have a sword fight." Tomas ran upstairs to the bedroom they shared. The boys each had cardboard swords left over from a school play.

The fight started on the back of the couch then went over to the coffee table. Reinhardt tripped over the lamp, which crashed to the floor.

Mutti stood at the doorway. "That's it. Go out and play." She went to the coatrack to the left of the frosted glass front door and threw their snow jackets and boots at them. "Out! Out!"

The boys dressed as fast as they could and ran out the door.

Outside the glistening snow, where it had drifted, came halfway up to the windows and to Tomas's armpits. The family car was buried under a white heap.

Both boys tried to make a snowball, but the snow was too soft. It fluttered from their mittens to the ground. No hope of making a snow fort.

Reinhardt, who'd just finished a growth spurt, took his brother by the hand and pulled him through the white fluff. It was not that easy going.

"Where are we going?"

"To the old boat."

"We haven't played there for a long time."

The boys lived in a cul-de-sac with two other houses. Both were owned by summer residents. Beyond the cul-de-sac were trees, then, before they reached the beach was an old blue wooden boat surrounded by sea grass. During the summer, the boys would spend hours on it pretending they were pirates or treasure hunters. Sometimes they explored the Arctic as

Eskimos and went on whale hunts. Sometimes the boat was a submarine searching for the enemy.

Because of the snow it took them three times as long to reach it. The snow on the water's side had blown against it making a huge drift. But the forest side was clear.

The boat was about forty feet long. It would never see the ocean again. The boys knew each board. A ladder was attached to the snow-free side and they climbed up to the deck. They knew which planks were rotten and avoided them.

"Let's go below deck."

Reinhardt led the way to the cabin and down the few stairs. There was just one huge room with a galley, table and bunks. The head was closed off.

"It stinks like pee and shit," Reinhardt said.

The snow had blocked the portholes on one side, but a little light slipped in on the other side. Reinhardt went to the galley. "Someone has moved our flashlight."

Tomas turned toward the table. "Here it is. I hope the batteries are still good."

They were.

As the light played around the room, the boys spied a lump under an *Eiderdown*.

"It's a person!"

They both ran for home.

CHAPTER 72

Marienkrankenhaus, Hamburg, Germany

"For 100 years rapeseed crossbred naturally and created new types. The oil from the seeds was first used mainly for oil lamps until the mid-19th century when petroleum replaced it. However, rapeseed was cheaper and was called the poor peoples' oil plant. Rapeseed is also known as the "Olive of the North." Hans Lembke started the programmed crossbreeding of rapeseed in 1897. His plants became world renowned."

The History of Insel Poel by Manfred Dederich

Annie opened her eyes to see Roger asleep in a chair to the right bottom of the bed. She was in a hospital bed. Something was dripping into her arm. She fell back asleep, hoping that she wasn't dreaming that she was safe.

When she awoke later, Roger was still there, and this time Gaëlle was with him.

"Welcome back, *chérie.*" He took her hand.

"Where am I?" Even saying the words took energy.

"The *Marienkrankenhaus* in Hamburg. We had to helicopter you here because the roads were still covered with snow."

Annie wasn't sure what snow he was talking about.

"I was so cold. I peed my pants and I also messed them."

"That's really not important. You'll be all right." He pointed to the bottle with the tube to her arm. "That's glucose and saline which has been warmed. They've shoved the temperature up in this room, and covered you with an electric blanket."

Annie hated it when Roger looked so worried. To try and lighten the mood she said, "Soon I'll be cooked."

"We'll serve you with sauerkraut."

She fell back asleep.

The next time she woke up, Hans-Peter Leiter was by her bedside. He and Roger were talking in low voices.

"Can you answer a few questions?" Hans-Peter asked.

"How did you get onto the boat?"

Annie remembered Karl Klausson hitting her on the dock. "Karl, Renate's husband. He hit me. I woke up in the boat and I heard him talking with Gregor, my neighbor. They have some kind of illegal business." Talking took a lot of energy. That her suspicions included some kind of high-class prostitution seemed too much to get out. "I think it has to do with those Asian girls."

Roger reached for her hand. "You're right. They killed those Asian girls."

"Did . . . ?"

"They were trafficking the girls from Thailand, mostly. They had a sex boat, really beautifully outfitted. High class for high rollers. Probably made the old Queen Elizabeth's ship look like a tugboat in its luxury, albeit, it was a lot, lot smaller," Hans-Peter said. "Only it wasn't your neighbor."

"Gregor and Max Theissen are identical twins. Max was Klausson's partner," Roger said. "Both twins were boat captains, but Gregor runs a legitimate charter service."

"So that explains it." Annie tried to sit up in the bed, but it took too much effort.

"Explains what?" Roger leaned over to push the button that raised the head area.

"Why sometimes Gregor was so friendly and other times he ignored me," she said, then found it too complicated to explain further. "How did you find out?"

"After those two little boys found you, they rushed home."

"I thought I'd dreamed children's voices." Annie fought to keep her eyes open; she wanted to know everything.

"Their mother called the police, but it took a little time for us to reach you," Hans-Peter said. "However, the local police alerted the local ambulance, which arrived first. The woman had already taken an *Eiderdown* to cover you and was rubbing your hands and feet trying to warm you up. The local hospital helicoptered you here."

"The snow?"

"Slowed everyone down. The police finally made it. But, the same roads kept Karl Klausson and Theissen from coming back. Hans-Peter knew they'd come back for you, so he ordered a stakeout and waited," Roger said.

"It took three days, but they showed up and we arrested them," Hans-Peter said. "Theissen and Klausson each rushed to sell the other out."

"Hans-Peter was able to piece together the entire story," Roger said.

"At the end, Max even confessed to blowing up the boat of the old fisherman, Edvard Schwartz. Stupid, because we never thought that was a murder, just an accident," Hans-Peter said.

"And Gregor? Where was he in all this?"

"Classic example of good twin, bad twin," Roger said. "He did admit that he thought his brother might be up to no good, but he preferred not to get involved other than to take in Max's wife whenever they had a blowup."

"We learned Max beat her fairly regularly," Hans-Peter said. "She'd run to Gregor's then forgive Max and go home."

Annie lacked the strength to say any more. She did have enough strength to feel smug that she'd known there was something wrong with those men, even if she hadn't pieced it together completely. If the police had listened to her maybe they would have pieced it together sooner and spared her her ordeal. Anger took more energy than she had, but she did want to know how they caught them.

Annie could no longer hold her eyes open. As she drifted off into sleep, she wished she'd asked Hans-Peter for an apology, but she really didn't expect to get it.

CHAPTER 73

Kirchdorf, Insel Poel, Germany
"Land protection is important. Between 1962 and 1972, 80 hectares (197.7 acres) of forest was planted along the coast to protect it from winds and erosion. The sea grass on the sandy beach also stops erosion. Being hit by waves has given it a chemical composition that prevents rotting and keeps pests from eating it. Until the 1960s the sea grass along the beach was collected and used for pharmaceuticals because of its high iodine content."

The History of Insel Poel by Manfred Dederich

"Put down that suitcase," Roger said to Annie as she started to leave the studio that she'd been renting. Both of them and Gaëlle were bundled up in their coats, hats and scarves and were ready to start back to Geneva for Christmas.

"I'm fine," Annie said, but put down the suitcase. She started to go back to make a final check. She knew her papers and laptop were already in the trunk.

"I've double checked the place. We have everything," Gaëlle said.

Annie smiled. For once she didn't hate not being in control. Despite being out of the hospital for only two days, she still felt tired. Giving her formal statements to the police had exhausted her, although they had come to her rather than make her drive into Lübeck after she'd been released. "Can we stop at the museum? I'd like to say good-bye to them all."

Roger parked as close to the front door as possible. "We've a long drive and I don't want you overtired."

As the threesome walked in, both Karine and Renate rushed up to Annie and hugged her. They insisted that everyone should have coffee. With the snow still piled high they did not expect many if any visitors.

The smell of coffee filled the area. Karine had brought in sweet rolls. Roger nodded that they had time to partake before leaving. When they'd finished, Renate said, "I brought the rolls in, just in case you stopped by, although after all you went through, if you never saw any of us again, we would have understood."

"I don't feel that way at all," Annie said. "I've made friends, and maybe we can come back here on holiday when it's good weather. At least Gaëlle and I could. Summers, Roger can't get away."

"I'd love to spend time on the beach," Gaëlle said.

"And we all know it's so different from the Argelès beaches." Roger ignored his daughter's eyes rolling in response to his sarcasm. He looked at his watch.

"I'll walk you to the car," Renate said. On the way she picked up a thick envelope that was in the out tray.

When Annie was strapped into the front passenger street, Gaëlle in the back and Roger behind the wheel, Renate stood by the open passenger door and handed the envelope to Annie. "This might be the book you want to write."

Annie started to open it, but Renate put her hand out and stopped her. "Wait for when you get home. It's hard to read in a car. It's the unpublished memoir given to the museum by Edvard's wife a while back. It was her grandmother's story of how she spent time in a concentration camp and how she survived the sinking of the *Cap Arcona.*"

"How come I didn't see it before?"

"We didn't have you go into the archives because of time. She was quite a lady, and I'd love others to know about her."

A shiver of fear ran through Annie. "Not your only copy? I couldn't live with myself if I lost it."

"You've the photocopy. I kept the original."

"Thank God. I can't promise publication, but I will guarantee I will write it."

"The handwriting is terrible."

Annie didn't want to say she'd studied medieval handwritings, which helped her decipher even the most difficult modern writing—too much like bragging—and maybe this would be the handwriting that defeated her. "Just keep in touch on how you and Greta are doing."

Renate gave a sigh. "There are no words to thank you."

"You don't have to," Annie said.

"We've got to get on the road." Roger started the engine. Renate shut the passenger door and waved good-bye until they were out of sight.

Annie didn't say anything until they were well onto the mainland.

"You're quiet," Roger said.

"I keep thinking about how cold and scared I was on the boat."

He reached over and took her hand.

"And I had one big regret." Annie covered his hand with her mittened one.

"That was?"

"I hadn't married you."

"You can correct that," Gaëlle said from the backseat.

"Maybe over Christmas?" Annie said.

312

Roger stopped the car and pulled up the hand brake. "Do you mean it?"

Annie nodded, before she could change her mind.

ABOUT THE AUTHOR

D-L Nelson, a Swiss citizen having been raised in the US, is a Third-Culture Kid in adult form, taking parts of both cultures and making a third. She currently lives in Geneva, Switzerland, and Argelès-sur-mer France. Other Five Star books in the series are: *Murder in Caleb's Landing, Murder in Argelès, Murder in Geneva* and *Murder in Paris.* For more on Third-Culture Kids: http://tckid.com. Read her blog at http://theexpatwriter.blogspot.ch and visit her website at www.donnalanenelson.com.